# THE FEAR OF FALLING

## A DI KIDSTON CRIME THRILLER

## JOHN HARKIN

BLOODHOUND
— BOOKS —

www.bloodhoundbooks.com

Print ISBN 978-1-914614-63-7

*For Jacqueline*

*"Farewell to all the feelings that expand the heart! I have been heaven's substitute to recompense the good – now the god of vengeance yields to me his power to punish the wicked!"*
— *Alexandre Dumas,* The Count of Monte Cristo

# 1

## August 1957

It started with the promise of home-made fudge.

The four children, dressed in T-shirts and shorts, were sitting at the edge of the common close, shaded from a sweltering hot afternoon; Florence and Grace swapping paper scraps on the steps, Lucas and Robert were swapping some of their *Batman* and *Superman* comics. Florence had some lovely scraps; bright-coloured, die-cut angel figures in the Victorian style. Grace had some embossed kittens in her neatly maintained scrapbook. The girls were swapping some of their 'doublers'.

'Fresh fudge, children!' their neighbour, Mrs Wilson, shouted from the open bay window of her top-floor tenement flat. The lure of sweets was irresistible and four hungry seven-year-olds gathered up their comics and scrapbooks and hurried up three flights of tenement stairs.

Jeannie Wilson was a long-widowed, retired primary school teacher in her early seventies and one of the long-term residents in the street. She'd been serving up home-made fudge to the local kids for years. In recent months, Mrs Wilson hadn't been seen much in the neighbourhood. Once she'd been a regular sight, with her two-wheeled, tartan shopping trolley; now she struggled with the tenement stairs. There had been recent complaints from the next door and downstairs neighbours about her playing piano in the wee small hours, and some families had warned their kids to stay clear of the eccentric old woman.

She greeted the children warmly. The sweet, enticing smell of freshly made fudge floated towards them through the open door.

'Come in, my little angels, come in.' Mrs Wilson, in a cardigan and housecoat, seemed overdressed for the hot weather. Lucas noticed a film of sweat on her brow.

She ushered them into the living room, past an upright piano, towards a folding dining table that held a large tray of fudge. The large, middle bay sash window was fully raised, a gentle breeze blowing the net curtains back into the room.

'Now, children, God has given us a beautiful, bright summer's day and before you eat this lovely fudge, I want you to see the angels out in the sky.'

'I've got angels in my scrapbook, Mrs Wilson,' said an excited Florence. The cute little blonde-haired girl ran to the window and pressed her nose to the glass, examining the blue skies for traces of the heavenly beings.

'If you stand up on the windowsill and stare out into the glorious, heavenly sky, I promise you'll see the angels.' Mrs Wilson had placed an old footstool at the window. 'I want the little girls first, then the boys.'

She helped tiny Florence up onto the ledge of the closed left-hand bay window; then Grace, then Lucas, and finally Robert. As the ledge became busier, Florence had to shuffle along towards the larger, open middle window. The cool air served as a warning.

'Mrs Wilson, that's dangerous!' Lucas shouted. 'You need to close that window.'

'You cheeky wee devil. You won't see any angels.' Mrs Wilson was ushering the children along to the point where Florence now stood on the ledge of the large open window.

Lucas edged past Grace in an attempt to get to Florence but before he could reach her, Mrs Wilson pushed her out. Robert and Grace froze in terror – too petrified to move. Lucas was horrified but knew he had to act.

'No, no! Get down, Grace!' Lucas snatched at the flapping net curtain. Mrs Wilson lunged, pushing him. He got enough purchase on the curtains with his hands to swing his foot up, making solid contact with Mrs Wilson's mouth, knocking her over. As the curtains came away in his hands, Mrs Wilson's shocked face and her shriek of anguish were the last things he saw and heard – before he fell.

The eerie sensation of no ground beneath his feet. He flailed around, trying to grab something or find a foothold in the merciless, empty air. As he hurtled towards the ground, his eyes, wide open in terror, took in the clear blue sky.

They had been promised angels...

In the nightmares that followed Lucas fell again and again. Each dreamed descent was longer, extending the fall to an interminable duration. He felt the same sickening sensation as the ground rose to meet him, convinced that this time, surely, the fall would kill him as it had killed her. But it never did. As he lay broken in his neighbour's garden, he saw the pretty roses; the same shade as the slick red halo forming on the concrete garden path around Florence's head.

Lucas' broken femur would heal relatively quickly, but it was the psychological scars from the incident that would linger much longer, through his life.

After the event, many families and neighbours chatted about the obvious physical and mental decline in old Jeannie Wilson. All that isolation, the late-night piano playing; someone should have noticed that her mind was going. The confused old woman would live out her remaining years in the mental hospital. The wee boy, Lucas, he was the hero of the piece; saving his two pals from going out the window.

Lucas didn't feel like a hero. His young, troubled soul was tormented by grief and guilt; emotions he couldn't fully comprehend. In his first two years of primary school, Lucas had been a bright, friendly and jovial little boy but in the early months of primary three his teachers saw a dramatic change. Haunted, he withdrew from his classmates and struggled to concentrate on his lessons.

It was Lucas' mother, Maggie, who arranged the intervention that would help her son find a path back towards a normal childhood. The parish priest, Father Owens, suggested that Lucas might benefit from a session with the Sisters of Notre Dame, who operated a child psychology unit in Dowanhill. It was on the other side of the city from the family home in the Gorbals and involved an underground train ride to Hillhead in

Glasgow's douce west end. Working with the nuns would be a long shot, but Maggie was willing to try anything to get her bright, happy boy back.

Six subway stops and a short walk away, Dowanhill was like another world. The leafy west end starkly contrasted with the grim, grey, crumbling tenements of the Gorbals. The nuns of the Notre Dame convent were kindness personified, especially when they heard the story of the young child thrown from a tenement window. One of the senior nuns, Sister Jude, greeted the pair and noted the full background to Lucas' situation. She explained that he would be assessed, and a dedicated educational therapist would help him work on his issues.

Sister Jude introduced Lucas to Sister Marie Therese. She was young with rosy cheeks, a big wide smile and bright blue eyes. It took Lucas a while to get used to her wimple, but Sister Marie Therese put him at ease very quickly with her kind and patient manner. While Lucas played in a sandpit and made plaster cast models, Sister Jude gave Maggie a tour of the expansive Notre Dame complex, including the teacher training college, where the Montessori training methods they used were explained. By the time she returned Lucas was playing happily and he presented his mother with a hand-painted model of Pinocchio.

In the following weeks, over a total of eight half-day sessions, Sister Marie Therese, with a mix of patience, persistence and kindness, won the trust and confidence of Lucas, who looked forward to his weekly appointments. He told her about his nightmares and how he fell again and again in his sleep and woke up crying, haunted by the image of his dead friend.

In week four, they had a breakthrough. Lucas was grieving that he hadn't reached Florence in time to save her, so it was wrong for people to call him a hero. Recognising the acute survivor guilt that the child was experiencing, Sister Marie Therese asked him about his favourite superhero, Superboy. She tasked him with painting a picture of Superboy, and when he was finished, she asked him a question.

'Can Superboy save everybody?'

'He's Superboy.'

'But he can't be everywhere at the same time. So, he can't save everyone. Even God can't save everyone.' The nun spoke softly, slowly and deliberately. 'God couldn't save your friend, Florence, so he took her up to heaven to be with him.'

Lucas began to sob.

She looked into the sweet little boy's handsome face, his pale-green eyes filling with tears. 'Lucas, you saved Grace and Robert.' The nun held his hand. 'You will always be a hero to those two. You did your very, very best and no one can ask any more of you, not me, not you and not God. Now, in your picture, is he falling or flying?'

'He's flying. He's Superboy.' Lucas was certain.

'What if he was falling? What if he had just been exposed to kryptonite and was falling out of the sky?'

'You know about kryptonite, Sister Marie Therese? You're great!'

'Imagine you're Superboy and you're falling out of the sky. When you get far enough away from the kryptonite, you feel your flying superpower kick back in and then – zoom – you're flying.' The nun closed her eyes, clutched the crucifix around her neck with one hand and held Lucas' hand with the other. 'I want you to close your eyes, Lucas. Imagine you're Superboy, and when you're falling too close to the ground, you just zoom off and fly up to the sky again.'

They tried it twice together, then Lucas tried it three times on his own. In his mind's eye he was flying above the ground.

'The next time you dream of falling or even think of falling, I want you to imagine you can fly.' She extended her arms to demonstrate. 'Just like your picture.'

And it worked. On his subsequent visits, Lucas reported that in all of his dreams, he could fly upwards into the sky before he hit the ground. In the years that followed, there was no falling in his dreams; only flying.

## 2

February 1987, Friday evening

'What about those two?' Barry nodded towards the two women making their way up the steep hill on Scott Street. 'They'll not get into the club.'

'Too drunk?' Paul was curious as to how his friend knew so much about the Cotton Club's door policy.

'Nah, the skinny one in double denim won't get past the bouncers,' Barry replied. 'She's a bit underdressed for that club and for this weather.'

Barry had parked the car in Sauchiehall Street with a good view up the hill and the bright lights of the nightclub entrance allowed them to watch the knock-back happen. They saw the two women's animated pleading with the door stewards, but it wasn't happening for them. *Not tonight, girls.*

Glasgow: the city of the last-minute lumber. No need to walk the Boulevard of Broken Dreams on the weekend 'up the town'. Opportunities were everywhere, if you knew where to look.

Even on a freezing cold February night, the icy weather wasn't putting off the punters and partygoers in search of a last-chance lumber. Young women, unsuitably dressed for the low temperatures, moved between the bars, diners and clubs. Well, if you'd spent a serious chunk of your pay packet on a new top from Bus Stop, Chelsea Girl or Selfridges, you wouldn't want to cover it up with an overcoat.

Dear Auld Glasgow Toon.

The two forlorn figures turned and headed back down the hill allowing their observers a closer look. The skinny one had faded blue jeans and a white denim jacket. Her friend wore a black fur jacket over a button-fronted, dark blue wool dress, thick black tights and long, black winter boots.

'Right, if this is a goer, I want the big diesel burner in the fur jacket.' Barry made his preference clear.

'Look, Barry, I just came out for a beer. I'm done with all this malarkey. I'm getting married in the summer.'

'But you're not a married man yet. Come on... favour to me.'

'You're asking me to go with that scrawny thing?'

'Let's see how it plays out.' The two women were approaching the car. Barry wound down his driver's window. 'No joy, ladies?' Barry flashed his best smile. He was a thirty-two-year-old divorcee, with a pleasant face and a neat side-parting in his light-brown hair.

'Bloody knock-back. Would you believe it?' Fur Jacket told them what they already knew. The Cotton Club, until recently called Maestro's, was one of Glasgow's premier nightclubs, known for its strict weekend door policy.

'I'm Barry and this is Paul. You fancy a coffee? We were going to head up to the club for a few beers but if you want, we can keep you company, go for a bite and then get you home.' Barry laid out their offer.

The two women stepped back from the car for a short

confab. 'Can I jump in the front with you?' Fur jacket made her selection known. It was a yes.

Barry beamed. Paul tried to muster up some enthusiasm.

They drove through the city.

Glasgow didn't need an audition to be a film-noir location. Driving through the city at night, the grey buildings and dim sodium street lighting evoked an image of nitrate film prints, casting grainy light and shade on the magnificent Victorian architecture. The city's wynds and vennels conjured up a black-and-white movie screening in some dark, smoke-filled cinema. They drove through the Merchant City, the dark heart of the second city of the empire, built on tobacco, weaving, commerce and the buying and selling of slaves. A shimmer of frost made the city streets sparkle with the monochromatic resonance of an Oscar Marzaroli print.

They crossed the Clyde and headed for a popular drive-up greasy-spoon joint south of the river. Fur Jacket introduced herself as Clare; her friend was Ellie. They were chatty, not drunk, but they'd had a few drinks. Paul took the order for burgers, chips, teas and coffees and joined a small queue at the counter of the large white trailer. The smell of cooked meat permeated the cold night air. Paul eyed two drunk youths, who'd taken ages with their order, larking about with the oversized mustard dispenser. The taller one squirted the bottle at his pal but some of the yellow paste landed on Paul's jacket sleeve.

'What the fuck?' Paul grabbed the boy by the throat, pressing him back against the trailer.

'It was an accident, big man.' The second youth pushed between them.

'I'm sorry, pal, let me pay for your dry cleaning,' the perpetrator said, fumbling in his jeans for some money, once Paul had let go of his throat.

Barry sprang out of the car and led the two youths away

from the scene. He gave them a piece of his mind, pointing his finger into their faces and ushering them away.

Paul and Barry returned to the car with the food and drink.

'What was that all about?' Clare asked.

'That stupid ned splattered mustard onto my suit,' Paul replied. 'I think I got most of it off with a paper towel and some hot water. Hopefully no lasting damage and no smell.' Paul laughed.

'I hate mustard,' Clare said.

Over stewed tea, scalding hot coffee and tasteless hamburgers, the four of them made easy small talk, chatting about Glasgow's various pubs and clubs and what they did for a living. Clare was a ladies' hairdresser with plans to one day own her own salon in Pollok, where they both stayed. She was curvy, with a lot of cleavage on show under her jacket. The more outgoing of the two, she ran her hand through her long, thick mane of black hair and did most of the talking. She made jokes about having a big bust and how difficult it made it for her to cut customers' hair.

Ellie was wraithlike skinny, with short-cut straw-blonde hair, pretty blue eyes and a shy smile. She said that she knew they were on a knock-back from the club, because of the way she was dressed. The dancing had been an afterthought after a night's drinking in the Iron Horse, but they were grateful for some hot food and a run home on such a freezing night. She talked about her work in a bakery.

The aroma of half-cooked burger meat was overpowering the waning pine scent of the car's Magic Tree air freshener. 'That's actually pretty vile,' Barry said. He tossed his half-eaten burger through his open window. Barry explained they were both car salesmen, working for a major Vauxhall dealership in the city. That fitted with their appearance; smart suits and open-neck shirts.

En route to Pollok, Barry detoured to a remote area known locally as the Barrhead Dams. The Dams had been established to provide a clean water supply to the rapidly developing Gorbals district on the south side of the River Clyde and covered a vast area of green space around the East Renfrewshire and Glasgow city boundary. The three massive reservoirs and their gravitational water system stood as a lasting testament to Victorian engineering.

Barry Rodgers wasn't thinking about Victorian engineering as he drove along the myriad networks of country roads that linked Barrhead, Neilston, Darnley and Newton Mearns. The headlights of Barry's 1982 Ford Escort provided the only illumination on the dark and narrow roads as he searched for the perfect spot. Barry knew his route; he'd driven these roads many times. A single-track road on the south side of the vast Balgray Reservoir was the ideal spot.

Barry kept the car heater running as he stopped in a lay-by. Both couples started kissing. Clare clambered over the centre console to sit astride Barry. In no time he had unbuttoned the front of her dress and unhooked her bra. She seemed untroubled by the two observers in the back. Paul and Ellie were getting it on at a much slower pace and were both distracted by the passion being ramped up in the front seats.

Paul slipped his hand under Ellie's blouse and played with her erect nipples. She rubbed his hard cock through his suit trousers. He unzipped her denims and slipped his fingers inside her knickers. Ellie wriggled and moaned in the back seat; they were catching up with their friends. Barry grew more annoyed as Clare occasionally stopped to glimpse what was happening in the back. These checks unsettled Ellie, as she suddenly pushed Paul off, zipped up her fly and opened her door.

'I'm going for a walk.'

'C'mon, Ellie. It's Baltic out there.' He was in no mood to follow her.

Clare and Barry stopped. She leaned over the seat. 'She wants you to go with her.'

'Go where? It's absolutely freezing out there.'

'You can't stay here.' It was Barry, twisting his head around to speak through the gap in the front seats. He made a face that said *get the fuck out of this car, now!*

'You can't sit there watching us like some pervert.' Clare sat upright, pulling her dress over her breasts to restore some modesty. She urgently wanted to resume her session.

'We can just go and get her and head home,' Paul said.

'No, you go and get her.' Two voices in unison.

With no desire to be a captive audience to the heavy foreplay in the front seats, Paul heard the clinking sound of a penny drop in his skull and realised he only had one option.

'I'll catch her up.' He opened the car door and shuddered as the freezing night air flooded the car's interior before walking off into the darkness.

## 3

Two uniformed figures took up a position in the heart of the junction, observing the patrons as they spilled out of the bar at closing time. The Granite City Inn was one of the first stops for the Gorbals police patrols on the night-shift beat. The pub, one of the few to survive the district's tenement cull, was a Gorbals institution, notorious in police circles for drunkenness, disorder and sporadic violence. Its situation at the five-way intersection formed by Pollokshaws Road, Cathcart Road, Gorbals Street and Cumberland Street was at the very heart of the Gorbals district.

The two cops were busy shepherding large groups of revellers leaving the pub in various states of drunkenness. It was an anti-disorder patrol; the Granite attracted patrons from all across the city as the Gorbals diaspora was drawn back to their old watering holes. Many came from the sprawling, south-side Castlemilk housing estate; the principal reason for the police presence at the junction. The drunken clamour and potential disorder caused by those catching the last number 37 bus home was the subject of a standing complaint from the bus operators.

Constable Chrissie McCartney marvelled at the way her

more experienced colleague handled the crowd. Peter Costello had seen it all, or most of it, before.

'Can you get us a polis taxi, big man?' an inebriated teenager asked.

Costello laughed and pointed out the obvious flaw in the request. 'Polis taxis only run to the polis station and I don't think you want to spend the weekend there.' The big cop's booming, gravelly voice rose above the crowd.

'Hey, doll, can I have your phone number?' Another drunk chanced his arm with McCartney.

'I've already got a boyfriend.' It was her stock reply. 'You're not my type' was another, although a stern glare from Costello would also dissuade would-be suitors. Chrissie knew that other cops at the station would handle this group differently. Inebriated young men didn't need much of a push towards confrontation and Costello had shown her, expertly, how to walk that line. She was very glad he was beside her. McCartney was twenty-four, a former bank clerk from leafy, suburban Bearsden. The contrast between her previous occupation and current role could hardly be more marked. But she loved the variety, the challenge and occasional excitement that police work offered.

Costello and McCartney observed the pub crowd mingling around the pavement outside the bar. Occasionally a patron, the worse for drink, would stray onto the busy roadway only to be steered to safety by Costello. A number would wander around finishing off their drinks, pint glasses in hand. Costello took a stricter line here; a pint tumbler could do a lot of damage in a fight. Transgressors were sternly warned to return the glasses to the pub or face charges. Peter Costello stood six feet five in his socks; very few argued with him.

Chrissie McCartney knew that the secret to a happy work life was having a good neighbour and she had one of the best going. In Glasgow polis parlance, the term *neighbour* denoted a partner. She'd been neighboured up with Costello for around eighteen months and enjoyed being his sidekick. They were chalk and cheese; he was into books, classical music, and old Hollywood movies. She liked nightclubs and was into U2, Michael Jackson and Prince. But they worked as a partnership. With five-and-a-half years' service, McCartney had learned more working with Costello than she had in the previous four years. She was happy to put up with all of his war stories and tales of the old Gorbals.

'You know why the Granite has survived when so many other Gorbals pubs have been demolished?' Costello asked.

'The fact that it's built into the railway bridge, maybe?' McCartney laughed. 'I think you may have mentioned it previously.'

Costello had also insisted on instructing his neighbour on the history of the area's pubs. The old Gorbals was legendary for the number of public houses in the district. Most of them had been demolished over the last thirty years.

'Are you going to start listing all of the pubs that have disappeared?' McCartney asked with a cheeky grin.

'Only the ones I've taken a dram in.' The big cop laughed.

Costello had regaled McCartney with stories about his early days as a Gorbals constable, when the entire night shift would be despatched to oversee 'throwing out' time. Their efforts were appreciated by the staff, landlords and licensees; no one wanted to fall foul of the strict licensing laws governing opening hours, underage drinking and drunkenness. Once the patrons had left and the doors were locked, appreciation was shown to officers by way of a generous measure of whisky.

'I'm pleased the police drinking culture is dying out,' McCartney said. It wasn't why she joined up.

A scuffle broke out near the bus stop. McCartney pushed

through a group of revellers and got between the two teenage protagonists.

'You want to get the bus home or ride a polis van back to the station and lie-in all weekend?' McCartney asked the young men, who were both the worse for drink. Costello stayed close to his neighbour, but she didn't require any assistance from him. She was a little terrier who got stuck in. The two youths took the tiny policewoman's advice and crept quietly away from the scene.

Just south of their location was Gushet Faulds, a historical Gorbals landmark, the name surviving from when it accommodated a public water fountain. Half a mile north was Gorbals Cross, which marked the boundary with the river and the city centre. When Costello started out as a young beat constable, there were more than twenty hostelries dotted between the Gushet and the Cross; the Citizen, the Seaforth, the Cumberland Arms and many, many more. A small number, including Dixon's Blazes, Derry Treanor's, and the Govanhill Bar had survived as final remnants of the old Gorbals. The buildings that housed them had been lost to the post-war annihilation of the Glasgow tenement, demolished to make way for a new Gorbals; communities in the sky with high-rise towers or damp, poorly-constructed flats. But those last few surviving bars had endured the tenement cull. They stood as lone structures, dominating the barren, brown dirt landscapes of their surroundings, like oases in a post-apocalyptic urban wasteland.

Costello had lived in the neighbourhood as a young boy. His family had stayed in a tenement close in Crown Street, just along from the Dixon's Blazes. The pub had been named after the Dixon's Govan Iron Works which, for over a hundred years, had lit up the night sky south of the River Clyde with the red glow of the fire and fumes from its five blast furnaces. Today, the site, once nicknamed 'Dixon's Blazes' was a vast cash-and-carry warehouse.

A gangly young man broke into a run, his sudden movement starting a commotion in the crowd. He was stopped in his tracks by a large hand on his shoulder. 'Sammy boy,' Costello asked, 'where are you off to in such a hurry?'

'I'm sorry, Mr Costello,' Sammy replied, 'I was just trying to catch up with my mates.'

With his massive height and build, a full head of white hair, and a ruggedly handsome face, Costello was a familiar sight in the area. He was one of the longest-serving officers at the station and his local knowledge was second to none. He knew all the criminals, or 'neds' as they were termed by cops; all the various interconnections across and between families, their residences, their vehicles. He was a one-man criminal intelligence system for the area. Local 'intel' was so important in the age-old battle between polis and neds and Costello was a major contributor to the fight.

If McCartney had one complaint, it was that Costello was overprotective of her, often taking charge of situations where he felt she may be threatened or harmed. It was understandable: he was self-confessed 'old school' and his actions were motivated by noble intents. He was the father of two teenage daughters and his protective instincts kicked in when he worked with McCartney. It was partly due to his physical presence; he was a giant, she was a petite five foot six. She'd had that difficult conversation with her neighbour and his response had reassured her. After their chat, she saw a marked change in Costello's behaviour and he allowed McCartney to take the lead in many incidents.

Costello and McCartney were not the only ones watching the crowd. High above them, a dark figure stood sentinel, observing the two constables policing the group and shepherding drinkers towards the bus stop.

The man in the shadows wouldn't be making any moves while the police were in the vicinity. The old, abandoned City Union Bridge that abuts the rear of the Granite City Inn provided him with a perfect vantage point. The trains didn't run there anymore, since the demolition of the grand Saint Enoch's railway station and hotel back in the late seventies.

Up above the street lights he could see but not be seen. Dressed in an ankle-length black leather coat over a black hooded top, the darkness wrapped around him like a cloak. He knew the big cop, Costello, a legend when he was a teenager, but it wasn't the police officer who concerned him tonight. The man he was interested in was not bound for Castlemilk with the jostling queue at the crowded bus stop, but for the Hutchesontown district of the Gorbals.

He caught sight of his prey. Colin Watters was wearing a distinctive, cream-coloured Harrington jerkin and was alongside a second man, who he knew only as 'Moser', from the nearby high flats. Both men looked the worse for drink as they stood chatting by the side of the road. With the Castlemilk bus queue safely despatched, the police headed away along Gorbals Street as the crowd thinned to smaller groups and stragglers, making their way home.

Moving cautiously, he descended the disused staircase, adjacent to the sandstone railway arches on the side of the bridge. Keeping Watters in his sight line, he watched as the two men said their exaggerated, drunken goodbyes. Moser sloped off towards the high flats entrance, leaving Watters, his gait unsteady, heading home.

Colin Watters was scum. He'd completed full research on his

target and was in no doubt about the reliability of his information. He'd checked it and double-checked it. Watters was a drug dealer who'd destroyed hundreds of lives, from the school gates to the street corners. He was also a shitebag. Watters wasn't known for his fighting ability; he'd made his name by putting in the hours. Cannabis and heroin available any time of the day, the former peddled as a gateway drug into the latter. Watters relied on others for his protection. Tonight there'd be none.

Now at street level, he started to close the distance between him and his prey. Watters would have to cut through the derelict E-block of low-rise flats to get home. He quickened his pace, adjusting his clothing; black beanie hat and hoodie, a black scarf covering his mouth, so that the only visible part of his face was his eyes.

Eyes burning with anger.

When Watters entered the foyer of his flat, he was already standing there, waiting for him in the shadows. The faint smell of urine, discarded drugs paraphernalia and the graffiti-marked walls were all too familiar.

'S'cuse me, big man.' Watters' speech was slurred. His path was blocked.

The tall, black-clad figure was still and silent.

'Get out o' my way, pal,' Watters said.

'I'm going nowhere, Watters.' He opened his coat and with a well-practised flourish, drew a long-bladed silver katana which he brandished under Watters' astonished face.

'C'mon, man. What's the score? Do you want some gear?' He steadied himself by grabbing hold of the staircase banister.

He bristled at the mention of drugs. 'That's why I'm here but not in the way you think.' In an expert posture, he wielded the sword two-handed and with great fluidity in his wrists, swung it up, around and down on his target, slicing off Watters' right hand.

Watters let out an anguished, high-pitched scream and fell to his knees next to his severed, bleeding hand. Paralysed by shock, a dazed and confused Watters held the stump of his right hand in his left. He was howling like a wounded animal. Cowering, terrified, he looked up at his attacker. 'What the fuck...? What was that for?' Watters managed to utter through his pain.

'That's justice for all the lives you've destroyed. You can tell Phil Canavan I'm coming for him next.'

'Who... who the fuck are you?' Colour draining from his face and blood pumping from his stump, Watters was sprawled on the damp, grey concrete, looking up at his attacker's cold blue eyes; staring impassively.

'Tell him the Gorbals Samurai is coming for him.' He pressed the tip of his sword into Watters' neck and laughed as he replaced the katana back in its *saya*, the scabbard concealed inside his coat.

It was a hollow, terrible laugh.

## 4

___

Barry and Clare were enjoying a post-coital cigarette, both front windows opened a little to let the smoke out. The back door opened. Paul stuck his face into the rear seat space.

'Where's Ellie?' Paul's question took them both by surprise.

'Very funny. I take it you caught her up?' Barry led the laughter with Clare joining in, both clearly expecting to see Ellie appear from behind his back.

'Seriously, did she not come back?' Paul's tone was apprehensive.

'That crazy girl. She's always pulling shit like this.' Clare seemed unsurprised. 'She's probably walked back to a main road and hailed a taxi home.'

'I obviously walked off in the wrong direction, but to be fair, it was pitch-dark outside and I couldn't see my hand in front of my face. I stayed away from the car as long as I could to give you a chance to finish what you were doing.'

'Let's go and see if we can pick her back up en route but she's got about twenty minutes on us,' Barry said.

Barry drove full tilt, quickly picking up the roadway. A short distance later, as he manoeuvred a sweeping bend, his full-beam headlights picked out the figure of a woman lying on the ground in a lay-by. Ellie Hunter's white denim jacket and faded blue jeans were unmistakeable.

Clare shrieked in horrified recognition as the twin cones of white light illuminated her friend's body. 'What have you done to Ellie?'

'I swear I haven't seen her since she left this car,' Paul replied.

All three hurried from the vehicle and rushed to her side. A light film of frost covered Ellie's clothing as they knelt beside her on the frozen ground. There was no blood or obvious sign of injuries. Illuminated by the car headlights, Barry took hold of her arm, trying to establish a pulse. He noticed heavy scarring on both her wrists.

'She's freezing cold, but I think I've found a pulse,' Barry said.

'Move aside, you're using your thumb, let me try.' Paul leaned in closer to Ellie and slowly tracked the middle and forefinger of his right hand across her right wrist. He, too, noticed the heavy scarring. 'There's a very faint pulse but we need to get her to a hospital ASAP.' Paul traced a stronger pulse in her neck to confirm that she was still alive.

'What did you do to her?' Clare shouted non-stop at Paul. 'Wake up, Ellie, wake up!' She grabbed her friend's shoulders, shaking her and gently slapping her face to no avail.

'I'll say it again to be clear. I haven't seen her since she left the car. This is no time to be hysterical, we need to get her to a doctor.'

The two men lifted Ellie's frozen, limp body into the rear seat of the car. Her slight frame took little effort. Barry carried her by the head and shoulders and noticed a speck of blood on the collar of her white denim jacket. There was a tiny red smudge on her neck. Clare then sat with her, holding Ellie in her lap, her legs laid out across the back seat. She caressed her face, softly speaking her name in an attempt to revive her. Barry closed the rear car door on the two women and pulled Paul to the side for a whispered discussion.

'What happened with you two?'

'Are you dense? I never saw her after she left the car. Do you think I'd leave her lying there like that?'

'There's a wee bit of blood on her jacket collar and her neck,' Barry said.

Paul inspected his right hand and saw a small nick on the ball of his thumb. 'That must've happened just now when I was searching for her pulse.' He lifted the wound to his mouth and sucked away the excess blood. 'I slipped on the ice on my way back to the car.'

'Did you clock her wrists?' Barry asked.

'Yeah, self-harmer. Clear sign of suicidal tendencies. Typical that I end up with the nutcase. Let's get her heated up in the car. Maybe she'll come to en route to the hospital.'

'Right. I'm Raymond and you're Pat, okay?' Barry had a plan.

'Let's just get her to a doctor.' Both men jumped back into the front seats.

'Royal Alexandra in Paisley is the closest A&E and we can't afford to wait around for an ambulance.' Barry gripped the wheel with new urgency and gunned the accelerator on a route through Barrhead. 'How's she doing? Keep talking to her and maybe she'll come around. Pat reckons she must have got hit by a car.' He threw some shade on the narrative.

'She's warmed up a wee bit and she's still breathing. That's the main thing.' Clare continued to stroke Ellie's face.

Paul turned around and looked directly at Clare. 'I notice that Ellie's got old scarring on her wrists. Does she have suicidal tendencies?'

'She had some issues years ago but she's fine now. She's always been a bit of a flake.'

'Her walking off into the night like that wasn't too much of a surprise to you?' Paul asked.

'It's the kind of stuff she does,' Clare replied, stroking her unconscious friend's hair.

'When we get to casualty, can we just say she got knocked down in a hit-and-run accident? Pat never saw her again.' Barry was thinking a step ahead.

'We don't know what happened. Let's see what the doctors say,' Paul replied.

'We could say she got out of the car to do a pee and slipped on the ice and banged her head.' Barry was thinking out loud now as he sped towards the hospital.

'When she wakes up, she'll tell us what happened,' Clare said. 'Why do you want to make shit up?'

*What have I done?* Paul never spoke the words, but the question dominated his thoughts. His stomach was roiling at the prospect of what might happen next.

The Dams to the Royal Alexandra Hospital was a fifteen-minute drive; Barry completed the journey in ten. He brought the car to an abrupt halt outside the A&E entrance, amid a fleet of waiting ambulances. Paul ran into the main reception, alerting staff to the arrival of an unconscious woman. A young porter, wearing a brown lab coat, rushed to help Paul and Barry lift Ellie from the car to a trolley and directed Clare to the reception desk to provide the patient's details.

A&E was busy. Two uniformed policemen were in the waiting area, noting witness details from the family member of a young man admitted with a bleeding head injury. Clare approached the officer who wasn't writing in his notebook. He looked the senior of the two.

'Excuse me, can I have a word please?'

The cop ushered Clare to a quieter corner of reception. It

was clear to Barry and Paul that she was recounting the events prior to Ellie's hospital admittance.

Barry motioned to Paul in the waiting area. 'We should really get out of here, bud.'

'We can't just run off, we need to wait with Clare a bit, see if they can revive her.'

They fell silent as the police officer approached with Clare in tow.

'Gentlemen, what can you tell me about the young woman you just brought here?' The constable spoke directly to Paul.

'I can't add any more to what you've probably heard from Clare. Ellie left the car and I next saw her twenty minutes after that when I picked her up off the ground.' Paul held up both hands in a half shrug.

Barry shot the cop a sceptical glance. He went to his inside jacket pocket and produced a slim, black folding wallet. He flicked it open to show his warrant card. 'I'm Detective Constable Barry Rodgers, Gorbals CID. This is my colleague, DC Paul Kennedy.'

# 5

## Saturday

As the on-call duty DI for Paisley, Ronnie Miller always half expected his home phone to ring in the wee small hours on weekends. It was unusual for a Friday and Saturday night to pass without a call-out for the duty dog. His night shift DS, Gerry Whelan, had briefed him over the phone to confirm that two F-Division detectives had been detained at the hospital and would be conveyed to Paisley police office with a female witness. Whelan, a very competent investigator and experienced supervisor, knew that the identity of the two detainees would have telephones ringing all over the force. This one would quickly escalate above his pay grade.

Whelan updated Miller on the latest medical notice. The victim, now confirmed as twenty-two-year-old Ellie Hunter, was still unconscious. The initial diagnosis had found a fractured skull with a suspected subdural haematoma. Whelan's best effort at translating the medicalese was that a fracture had caused bleeding on the brain and she'd probably need surgery.

Ellie Hunter was in dire straits.

Miller walked his DS through a detailed set of instructions. The car, the place where it was initially parked, the lay-by, the victim, her hair and clothing, and Paul Kennedy himself, were all to be treated as multiple crime scenes and subject to full forensic examination and analysis. DS Whelan seized Hunter's clothing at the RAH, where the medics pointed out the bloodstain on her jacket and the smudge on her neck.

Ronnie Miller was a meticulous investigator by nature but with police officers involved as a suspect and a witness, this case would need to withstand the highest levels of scrutiny. He would not be found wanting. Barry Rodgers' Ford Escort left the hospital atop a low-loader, destined for the forensic vehicle bay at Paisley police office. Paul Kennedy's clothing was seized for forensic examination and his hands were bagged and sealed until swabs and blood samples could be taken by the on-call force casualty surgeon.

Clare Travers' statement was noted by a female detective. Barry Rodgers and Paul Kennedy – who was now wearing a white paper evidence suit – had to endure the humiliation of sitting in separate glass-fronted detention rooms adjacent to the uniform bar at the back office. Kennedy sat on the bench with his head in his hands, trying to avoid the stares of police officers walking past. Rodgers stood at the glass-panelled door trying to attract the attention of a custody officer. No one went near him; they'd been warned by the duty inspector to steer clear.

Once all the main players were safely located at Paisley office, Miller's first order of business was to examine the locus. DS Whelan rescued Rodgers from his detention room hell, and with Miller in the back seat, they set off in a CID pool car to the lay-by where Ellie Hunter was found. The atmosphere in the car was as frosty as the early-morning air.

Miller broke the silence. 'I'm told the girl's in a bad way. How the hell did this happen?'

'I've no idea, boss, I never got out of the car,' Rodgers replied.

'But Paul Kennedy was gone for around fifteen, twenty minutes?' Miller asked.

'Around that, yes.'

'Plenty of time for you to get your end away with the witness. Is that how it went?'

Rodgers groaned. 'I think that's why he got out. He could hardly sit there and watch the two of us.'

'How long before he went after her? Remember, even though you're technically not under caution, you need to think hard about what you say here.'

'I'm sure the girl, Clare, will say the same thing. It was a very short conversation with the three of us. A minute, a minute and a half?'

'So no big gap between her leaving the car and him getting out?'

'Around ninety seconds or so, two minutes max.' Rodgers shifted in his seat.

'So very unlikely that whatever happened to her happened in that short time?'

'Very unlikely. But I think they set off in different directions.'

'Well, we'll see about that. Gerry will get a full statement from you when we get back to the office.'

DS Whelan stopped the car at the lay-by where Ellie was found, leaving the full-beam headlights on to illuminate the scene. The two Paisley detectives added their torch beams as Miller hunkered down to examine the ground. There was nothing obvious to suggest a struggle, but he was too astute an investigator to imagine that this constituted an effective or professional locus search. He would close the road at both ends and have the traffic department set up local diversions. Traffic examiners would inspect the scene to confirm or rule out a road-traffic accident. Meantime, a uniform patrol car would be posted to ensure no interference with the locus.

At first light, he would arrange a full fingertip search by a support unit crew. Miller's experience had taught him to call upon the services of the men and women from Springburn, with their police overalls, welly boots, rakes, poles and professional search techniques. One divisional commander jokingly referred to them as the Peggy Spencer Formation Dance Team, but they would do the business. Detectives never liked to get their expensive Ralph Slater suits dirty.

Back at the office DS Whelan noted a statement from Rodgers that backed up everything he'd already told them. Working from Clare Travers' initial account, Whelan asked him some pointed questions about what he saw as potentially incriminating behaviour; pretending to be car salesmen and approaching her to say Ellie had been the victim of a hit-and-run driver.

'Has DC Kennedy got a bit of a temper then?' DS Whelan asked.

'I wouldn't say that,' Rodgers replied.

'According to the witness, Clare Travers, Paul Kennedy attacked a young guy at the hamburger stall.'

'Attacked is a bit strong,' Rodgers said. 'The guy sprayed mustard on his suit.'

'And he choked him for doing that?' Whelan asked.

'Aw, come on. It was two drunk neds. We chased them down the road. There was nothing in it,' Rodgers replied.

'That's not what Clare Travers was thinking when she watched you from the car.'

The DS also speared him with Travers' claim that he'd started calling Paul Kennedy by a different first name. Rodgers admitted it all in his statement. It all sounded like a cover-up and he knew it looked bad. His career would suffer after this episode. He'd probably get bounced back into a woolly suit or onto traffic duties.

'I never thought the girl was so badly injured. I just wanted to make sure that we were well out of it for when she woke up.' Rodgers realised how shallow and heartless it all sounded. He felt ashamed. They were police officers, for God's sake.

'What if she never wakes up?' Whelan held his gaze.

Rodgers had to avert his eyes. He hung his head in shame. He had no response.

His statement included a confirmation, prompted by his interviewer, that he could not say whether Paul Kennedy was with Ellie Hunter or not. Though it grieved him to say it, he had no idea what happened. He'd been too busy shagging Clare Travers. The dawning realisation that he was unable to help his colleague, to cover his back in the way that detectives always cover each other's backs, meant that a quick and dirty fuck in his car could cost Paul Kennedy his CID career and his liberty.

# 6

Ronnie Miller sat in his room at Paisley police office. He had to check himself. This was a big case; potentially massive. He'd need to stay between the lines on this one; the scrutiny would be intense. But he'd quickly established the known facts and had detained Paul Kennedy as a strong suspect for serious assault or attempted murder. The medics had yet to confirm or rule out rape or sexual assault, the head injury was a clear and urgent priority. It could go murder or culpable homicide; his case would be ready wherever the evidence took him.

Miller and Whelan checked off the salient points from the written statements of Clare Travers and Barry Rodgers as preparation for the Kennedy interview.

'One of DI Kidston's boys looks to be in a wee bit of bother,' Miller said with a sarcastic smile as he finished reading through the statements.

'Former colleague of yours?' DS Whelan asked.

'Aye, and fair to say, no love lost between us,' Miller replied. 'But I mustn't let that colour my judgement. It's not Luc Kidston who's sitting in the detention room.'

The statements were fully corroborative on the material issues; Kennedy had left the car around ninety seconds or two minutes after Ellie Hunter and was gone for an estimated twenty minutes. He was breathing normally when he returned and there was no mud or dirt on his clothes. Travers hadn't noticed any blood marks on her friend and Rodgers explained the transference had occurred when Kennedy was tracking a pulse in her neck.

Travers was able to recall the number of songs that played on the car stereo during their lovemaking. It was Sade's *Diamond Life* album and she was familiar with the track listings. They'd both smoked a cigarette before Kennedy returned, which meant she could be pretty certain about his twenty-minute absence. She also spoke to the fact that the other couple had indulged in foreplay; Kennedy had his hand inside Ellie's pants, she was rubbing his crotch.

'We need a confession for this one, Gerry. Rodgers says Kennedy's getting married in the summer, so we'll focus on the shame and the end of his police career. He'll burst like a ripe melon.' Miller wasn't one for fancy-dan interview strategies; he was more of a blunt instrument when it came to questioning suspects.

Whelan offered a plausible scenario. 'So they leave the car to get it on away from the other two, maybe in the trees or behind a hedge... They argue, or something goes wrong... he pushes her or attacks her, and she hits her head on the ground. He cuts his hand in the struggle and his blood transfers to her jacket.'

'Sounds credible but remember, we'll be on tape.' Miller wanted the confession on the record. He had opted for a tape-recorded interview. They weren't yet a legal requirement as the force was still rolling them out but there was a wall full of memos and standing orders about how they should be used, where available, in serious cases. Detectives were still getting used to the procedural differences in taped interviews; more formality, more structure and a more nuanced style of questioning. Kennedy's detention met the 'serious case' criteria.

The interview room at Paisley police office had undergone a renovation as part of the tape-recording project. A twelve-foot-square room, with off-white acoustic tiles on the walls and ceiling, it was dominated by a five-by-three, wood-topped table against the far wall. The table and four grey metal chairs were all bolted to the floor. The room, by design, was otherwise featureless.

Kennedy sat across from his K-Division colleagues, an empty seat at his right side. He was twenty-nine and had been on the job for almost eight years, three of them as a detective. He could pass for twenty-one with his baby-faced good looks and his winning smile. He wasn't smiling now: a strange, unsettling feeling threatened to overwhelm him as his anxiety increased. He was on the wrong side of the interview table, the wrong side of the interrogation, and the wrong side of the law. He wondered how he would have progressed the exact same case, with the same circumstances, same evidence. The air in the drab little room felt thin and he was grateful for a sip of water from the plastic cup provided. Could his colleagues smell his fear?

DS Whelan made a great show out of stripping the cellophane from the two C90 cassette tapes and loading them into the twin tape deck. He explained the preamble to the taping procedure, but Kennedy knew the drill: one of the cassettes would be sealed, dated, and signed by all three men when the interview was concluded. It would then be entered into evidence and forwarded to the procurator fiscal as a crown production. The second copy would be retained by the investigating detective. Another show was made of the common law caution; words Kennedy had recited hundreds of times, but there were procedures to be followed.

Kennedy eyed his interrogators. He knew Gerry Whelan well from a detective training course at Tulliallan; he was a skilled investigator and a decent guy. Ronnie Miller he knew only through his formidable reputation. Miller was the alpha male, a silverback; a man who thrived in the cut-and-thrust macho culture of CID. An impressive physical specimen, he carried his broad build and wide shoulders well due to his muscular six-foot-one frame. With a ruggedly handsome face, a shock of wavy blond hair and a strong jaw, Miller could turn on the charm. He also carried an air of palpable menace; a fixed stare from his dark-brown eyes could unsettle anyone. The detectives in his team respected him. They also feared him.

Now it was Kennedy's turn to face him.

## 7

A stern Miller asked Kennedy to confirm, for the benefit of the tape, that he understood the reasons for his detention and that he would have no access to a lawyer for the initial six-hour period.

'I won't be needing a lawyer, inspector. I haven't done anything wrong.'

'Okay, Paul, you know how this works. Tell us what happened after Ellie Hunter got into the car last night.' Miller spoke slowly and deliberately in a tone slightly softer than his usual gruff voice.

'Can I ask how Ellie is doing first?' There was concern in Kennedy's voice. 'What's the latest from the hospital?'

*Very clever*, thought Miller. A suspect who understood the nuance of a taped interview. Could be a difficult nut to crack. Miller related the extent of Ellie's injuries, fixing Kennedy with a penetrating stare to gauge his reaction.

'That's worrying, and it's bad for me that she hasn't regained consciousness,' Kennedy said. The young detective was impassive. 'When she wakes up we'll find out what happened to her.'

The initial questioning covered the pick-up in Sauchiehall Street, Kennedy's initial reluctance to get involved, and Rodgers' plea to take one for the team. He walked his interrogators through the trip to the hamburger stall and the conversation in the car.

'Why did you tell the women you were car salesmen?' Miller broke in.

'That was Barry. You both know how it is on a night out, you tell someone you're police and it can go wrong very quickly.'

'But why car salesmen?'

'Well, we were both still wearing our suits from doing a backshift. Made sense, we just took our ties off.' Kennedy picked up his account. 'When Barry stopped, I had no clue where we were. I just knew we were in the general area of the Dams. It all started out fine. I'm in the back seat, Barry and Clare are getting into it. We start to kiss... there's a bit of petting... both ways...'

Miller interrupted him. 'So for the avoidance of doubt and for the benefit of the tape, your hand was inside her vagina? You admit you were fingering Ellie?'

'Look, of course, there'll be traces of vaginal fluid on my left hand from the swabs taken earlier, but that's as far as I got with her.'

'But you had an erection from her petting you? You were aroused?'

'Yes, no doubt. I thought we were going to get it on... make love in the car.'

'So what happened?'

'I think she was spooked by her pal watching her. Clare was sitting astride Barry... she'd mounted him, no other way to put it, and she was facing directly into the back of the car. She kept looking over Barry's shoulder and watching what we were doing. It was awkward, clearly very off-putting for Ellie.'

'No discussion, Ellie just got up and left?'

'She just announced, "I'm going for a walk," and took off into the night.'

'What did you do or say?'

'I said, "Hold on, it's Baltic outside. You need to be crazy to go out there."'

'You wanted her to stay in the car?'

'Well yes, it was minus one or two outside. Freezing cold.'

'Now she's left you with Barry Rodgers and Ms Travers. How did that play out?'

'They made it abundantly clear they wanted me out of the car.'

'But you wanted to stay?' Miller asked.

'Well yes, but I quickly realised it wasn't really an option.'

'How come?'

'Clare said, "I hope you don't think you're going to sit there watching me like some pervert,"' Kennedy replied.

'And that did it? That got you moving?'

'I did consider ignoring them, just sitting there to force them to drive after Ellie but they had unfinished business.'

'So you were angry at having to leave the car and head out in the freezing cold?'

'I wouldn't say I was angry. I might have been a bit annoyed.'

'Annoyed and angry at Ellie. Were you angry when you caught up with her?'

'I wasn't angry, and I never caught up with her.'

'You got angry with the young guy at the hamburger stall,' Miller said. 'What was that about?'

'It was nothing. It was all over in a flash,' Kennedy said. 'He messed up my suit.'

'Flash is right,' Miller said. 'Clare Travers said you went straight for his throat. Did your temper flare up like that with Ellie?'

'I never saw Ellie after she left the car, sir.'

'Let's revisit this stand-off in the car,' Miller said. 'You considered staying put?'

'For a short time, but I decided to leave them to it.'

'How long?' This detail was crucial.

'A minute, maybe a bit longer. No more than two minutes,' Kennedy replied.

'Tell us what happened when you went after Ellie,' Miller asked, fixing his suspect with a cold stare.

'Nothing happened. Well... nothing much.'

'Oh, come on now, Paul. That's not good enough. How did Ellie Hunter end up in the RAH with life-threatening injuries?' Miller's voice revealed its first traces of frustration and hostility. 'How did your blood end up on her jacket collar?'

'I tripped on my way back to the car.' Kennedy extended his raised right hand for his interviewers to inspect. 'The blood came from me feeling for a pulse in Ellie's neck. I kept walking onto the grass verge, that's how I tripped. Look, I honestly can't help you further. It was pitch-dark. I couldn't see my hand in front of my face. I shouted her name, several times. I shouted her name for ages.'

Kennedy straightened up in his chair and made eye contact with both his interviewers. It was a confident performance. That was Miller's problem: it was just too good a performance. Kennedy continued. 'Absolute pitch-blackness, no moon, no stars. I realised within two or three minutes that I'd set off one way and she'd obviously gone the other. It was futile; I couldn't see anything.'

'So what's your theory on how Ellie Hunter ended up with her injuries?' Miller asked.

'I'm speculating here, same as you. Maybe she got hit by a car, maybe she slipped on the ice or tripped on the verge. As I said, it was pitch-black, it was icy... she was taking a chance.'

'How many other cars were likely to be in that area at that

time of the night? Come on, Paul, you were away from the car for twenty minutes. What happened? Did she reject your advances?'

'I'm not disputing the fact that I was gone twenty minutes. I walked ten minutes out and ten minutes back. There were a few cars on the road, very sporadic. When I saw headlights approaching, I thought it was Barry coming back with both girls.'

'So you walked the whole time, you didn't run?' Miller asked.

'I couldn't see to run. It was way too slippy and I had no reason to run,' Kennedy replied. 'As for the time, I wanted to leave Barry and Clare plenty of time to finish what they were doing. I fully expected to find Ellie sitting in the back of the car when I got back.'

'But she wasn't. Did that not trouble you?'

'It did trouble me, but Clare said she was a bit of a flake, her exact words if I recall, and it seemed she did stuff like this all the time. Look, I think it's important for me to point out that I wasn't the one who initiated leaving the car, that was down to Ellie. I had no desire to walk about in the dark, in the freezing cold.'

*Smart arse*, thought Miller. He was making speeches for the benefit of the tape recording. All very plausible and a jury might just buy some of this shit, but he didn't.

'You lied about being car salesmen. You lied about your names. Ms Travers says that your name changed to Pat. You were lying then and you're lying now.' Miller's expression darkened as he eyeballed Kennedy.

'That was all on Barry. He was just being an idiot. He called me Pat a couple of times on the run to the hospital, but I never used any other name for him. I think he panicked after he saw Ellie's wrists.'

Kennedy paused as he picked up the DI's tell. Miller scrunched his eyebrows in a confused expression and looked at

Whelan, who glanced frantically at his notes before shaking his head.

Kennedy continued, 'Ellie Hunter has historical heavy scarring across both wrists. Clear indicator of suicidal tendencies. I go back to Clare Travers' description of her friend as a flake.'

*Bastard!* Miller struggled to conceal his fury. Why was this fact not included in his medical information? Someone would get their arse handed to them tomorrow. This smug upstart, baby detective, who'd been in CID for ten minutes was directing the interview. *Bastard! Bastard! Bastard!* All of it was on tape and it would make them look like amateurs.

Miller recovered his composure enough to pose his next question. He steepled his large hands under his chin and fixed his gaze directly into the eyes of his suspect. 'Regardless of any historical injuries, I put it to you that you went for a walk with Ellie Hunter. We know you've got a temper. You were angry and aroused. When she refused to have sexual intercourse, you struck her or pushed her to the ground in a violent manner, resulting in her very serious injuries. Some of your blood got on her jacket. Then you walked back to the car and pretended to not have seen her after she had left the vehicle. Do you admit to assaulting Ellie Hunter?'

'No. I never did it.'

'Admit it, you did it.' Miller's dark eyes probed Kennedy's expression for signs of his guilt. 'Own up, be honest.'

'No. I never did it.'

'What other feasible explanation is there for what happened?' Miller asked.

'I'm not a religious man, inspector, but I'm sitting here praying Ellie wakes up soon and tells us what happened.'

'Come on, Paul, it'll go better for you if you tell the truth. Think about your poor fiancée, think about the job. Come clean.

Tell us what really happened.' Miller realised he was questioning Kennedy in a manner the younger detective would be familiar with. He had a strong urge to stop the tape and introduce Kennedy to some old-school interrogation techniques. As an up-and-coming detective, Miller had seen great success from his 'good cop, bad cop, sadistic cop routine'. Violence – or even the threat of violence – in an interview setting had contributed greatly to his clearance rates in the past; but these were different times and his suspect was a serving detective officer.

Miller shifted uncomfortably in his chair; the furniture wasn't designed for someone of his bulk. 'Clear your conscience, Paul. Think about Ellie's parents: they're currently holding a bedside vigil at the hospital. Think of them, think about your fiancée. Think about the police. Your job.' Miller laid it on thick, returning to the key themes he believed would secure a confession.

'Believe me, inspector, I am thinking of those things. Everything you said is important to me: Ellie and her parents, Sandra, my job. I just want all this cleared up, hopefully when Ellie regains consciousness. You're looking at the wrong suspect, inspector. I'm not the attacker in this case.' Kennedy remained impassive and defiant.

'You're the only suspect, Paul. Come on now, you're a detective. Faced with this scenario, these witnesses, this evidence, who would you be looking at for the crime?'

'You've got me there, inspector. I can see why I'm in the frame for this, but I'll plead my case until the end. I'm innocent. You need to widen the scope of your investigation. It *wasn't* me.' Kennedy was so emphatic that both interrogators sat back in their chairs.

'We'll see how you're feeling about it tomorrow, after a night in the cells.' Miller glared at his suspect. 'In the meantime, in the absence of any exculpatory information, I have sufficient circumstantial evidence to arrest you and charge you with attempted murder.'

Miller watched as the words of the caution and charge washed over his suspect. As a detective, Kennedy must have known what was coming, but his expression was that of a terrified young man.

Whelan switched off the tape recorder and marked up the tapes. Kennedy selected the cassette closest to him and signed his name on the sealed case. The procedure was so familiar, but Kennedy had never imagined himself in the role of suspect or accused. Miller motioned Whelan to escort a dazed Kennedy to the cells.

Miller sat looking through the interview notes. This case presented him with a delicious sense of irony. Kennedy was a DC in Luc Kidston's team at the Gorbals. Kidston was a former colleague, and a rival. There had been several clashes between them, most notably when they were both detective sergeants in Joe Sawyers' team. DI Sawyers encouraged competition between his investigators but had to step in when they took their rivalry too far. The bad blood between them had lingered, leaving a sense of personal animosity. He would take no pleasure from locking up a police officer but there was just a sliver of perverse satisfaction that the arrest of one of Kidston's protégés would reflect badly on his rival. Miller was still poring over his notepad when Whelan returned from the cells.

'He's not for bursting, boss, is he?' Whelan asked.

'Not yet, but he will.'

'I thought he stood up well to the questions.'

'He had all the answers, all right.' Miller gave his sergeant a sour look. 'Too smooth, too smug, too self-assured, if you ask me. Come on, he's a detective with almost eight years on the job. He's not going to roll over easy.'

'I'm clear on ability and opportunity but what's his motive?' Whelan was going through his checklist for circumstantial evidence in the absence of eyewitnesses and a confession.

'Come on. He was aroused. Clare Travers' statement says he'd a big hard-on for the girl. He wasn't taking no for an answer. He was frustrated and angry at having to get out of the car. He lost his temper. He catches her up, they struggle when she refuses to have sex with him; he injures his hand and gets some blood on her clothing.' Miller looked at his notes. 'Travers stated he wasn't out of breath when he came back to the car. The distance between where Rodgers parked the car and where Ellie Hunter was found is no more than a seven- or eight-minute walk. If she'd been found fifteen minutes away the distance might have alibied him, but it's well within the twenty minutes that all three agree was our time frame.'

'Yes, the distance doesn't help him,' Whelan agreed. 'I'm just hoping the lassie wakes up so we can get a first-hand account.' He hesitated before expressing his doubts. 'You're sure he's our man?'

'I'm certain. Who else could it have been?'

'Maybe she did slip on the ice.'

'Kennedy did it. He'll confess tomorrow.'

## 8

D I Luc Kidston heard his bedroom phone extension on the second ring. He squinted at his radio alarm clock: 3.33am. It was most likely the duty officer at the Pitt Street control room. Kidston was listed on the roster of hostage negotiators held at force headquarters. His normal practice was to take a minute to wash his face and then phone back, pen and notepad at the ready. This ensured that a full description of the ongoing incident, its background, and an accurate locus could be jotted down with minimal misunderstanding. With critical incidents like these, you needed to be fully informed.

It wasn't force control; it was his boss, Detective Superintendent Joe Sawyers. 'Sorry to wake you at this hour, Luc.'

'That's okay, boss, it's normally me phoning you in the wee small hours.' Kidston rubbed the sleep from his eyes. This had to be important.

'I've just taken a call from Colquhoun. One of our guys, Paul Kennedy, has been detained and arrested in K-Division for attacking a young woman over at the Barrhead Dams. Apparently, he was out on the pull with Barry Rodgers.' The warm, measured tones of Sawyers' voice were at odds with the information he was imparting. 'The woman is in the RAH with a serious head injury. She hasn't regained consciousness and Kennedy's facing a possible charge of attempted murder.'

Kidston took a few moments to process. 'What's the evidence against Paul?'

'It seems they were parked up in a lovers' lane and he and the victim were out of the vehicle for twenty minutes. She had a two-minute start on him. He returned on his own, she was found unconscious by the roadside a few minutes later.'

It was a concise summary, which Kidston had come to expect from his superintendent. Joe Sawyers was a man for detail and precision and there was little doubt that the K-Division briefing to Assistant Chief Constable Farquhar Colquhoun would have been relayed verbatim. Any detective phoning the man known as 'Q' in the early hours would need to have all the facts. As ACC Crime, Colquhoun was the force's de facto senior detective.

'Has Q asked you to look at it?' Kidston was aware of the tight relationship between Sawyers and the assistant chief.

'Mostly a courtesy call about DC Kennedy, who'll be suspended from duty. Colquhoun is concerned about the potential media fallout and damage to the force's reputation. Bob Ferguson will look over it and he'll liaise with me, but I'd like you to have a very discreet look at it.' Ferguson was Sawyers' opposite number at K-Division.

'It's Ronnie Miller's case, so just tread carefully. I don't want you to frighten the horses.'

'I'll tread very carefully.' Kidston laughed at his boss's appeal for caution.

'And while I've got you, your night shift is dealing with another serious incident: a sword attack. A drug dealer by the name of Colin Watters had a hand severed near his home in the Gorbals. One of Phil Canavan's crew. He'd been drinking in the

Granite City Inn, so maybe a fallout with another ned, or there's a drugs feud in the offing.'

'It never rains but it pours. I'll head in and see how that one's looking, and I'll make some enquiries into the Kennedy arrest.' He ended the call having arranged to meet Sawyers later in the afternoon.

Kidston had been separated for three years and divorced for two from ex-wife Melanie, so there was no one else to disturb in the house. Their split had been amicable, and with Kidston able to buy out Melanie's half of the mortgage, he'd stayed on in the marital home. She often commented how much she didn't miss those telephone call-outs in the middle of the night. He splashed cold water on his face, slicked back his damp hair, then ran the electric shaver over his stubble and got changed into his work clothes.

Kidston headed for K-Division. He might catch Miller or his night-shift crew and get a sense of what happened. He'd be allowed a welfare visit to check on Kennedy. The drive from his home in Giffnock wouldn't be a long one. His seven-year-old Alfa Romeo was showing its age but following his divorce, a new car wasn't high on his priorities. He loved the little car's Sprint Veloce styling and how its 1.5 litre boxer engine handled, but it was starting to present mechanical issues beyond Kidston's knowhow, and it was rusting up in places. He punched Paul Simon's *Graceland* into the car's tape player.

Kidston was having some difficulty processing Sawyer's shock announcement. Paul Kennedy had been his appointment to the CID. He'd first spotted his work on a uniform patrol shift; a series of housebreakings cleared up and a number of sizeable drugs seizures. His potential really stood out as a plain-clothes officer, when he showed further prowess as a natural thief-taker. Kidston recruited him as a CID aide (a six-month trial secondment and a precursor to appointment), and he hadn't disappointed.

Could he have been that wrong about him? Kidston knew he was in a long-term relationship and due to be married in the summer. It all seemed so out of character. He'd been wrong before; a very small number of cops and detectives, who'd been given second chances, had gone on to let him down. None were given a third chance.

The roads were quiet with mostly taxis and lorries going about their early-morning business. 'Diamonds on the Soles of her Shoes' came on the tape player; it was one of the songs that showcased *Graceland's* ambitious scope with African rhythms, a great horn section, and Simon's unfussy vocals backed by the beautiful voices of Ladysmith Black Mambazo. The music helped Kidston focus and gather his thoughts.

He smiled as he drove, recalling Sawyers' plea for restraint. The die had been cast on the conflict between him and Ronnie Miller when they were both detective sergeants working under Sawyers when he was their DI. Antipathy born out of personal dislike, together with contrasting policing methods, investigatory tactics and management styles, meant they would never be anything but rivals.

Kidston had long considered Miller a bully who ruled his team by fear and coercion, too willing to bend the rules. Sawyers was a natural team builder but realising his two detective sergeants were unlikely to be close colleagues, he encouraged their competitive instincts. It was great for Sawyers' crime figures and clearance rates until it blew up in his face. Both sergeants were skilled and tenacious investigators. Kidston would always concede that Miller got results; it was his methods Kidston found questionable.

Kidston had detained a suspect for robbing a bookmakers. Miller fancied him for a housebreaking he was investigating and interviewed him in his cell without telling Kidston. The suspect was a strung-out junkie, climbing the walls with withdrawal symptoms. Miller, eager to clear up his case, gave him two Diconal pills to barter his co-operation. There was a serious black market for the opioid prescription tablets at the time and Miller had held a quantity back from a stash he'd seized in an earlier case.

Instead of a confession Miller got a hospital emergency admission. The suspect found by the duty officer, foaming at the mouth in his cell, thirty minutes after Miller's interview. An ambulance rushed him to the Victoria Infirmary and there was an anxious three-hour wait while his stomach was pumped. He made a full recovery, but Kidston was furious. The inevitable cover-up commenced with Miller lying that the suspect had secreted the pills on his person, and they'd been missed during the custody search. This didn't sit well with Kidston, as it cast doubt on the professionalism and integrity of the uniform bar staff, but Joe Sawyers smoothed it all over and everything was kept in-house. It was just another example of Miller playing fast and loose with the rules.

Kidston arrived at Paisley office at around 4.20am. On getting out of the car, Kidston stretched his full height to convince his tired body that he should be awake at this time of the morning. An athletically-built six foot two with pale-green eyes and an unruly mop of raven hair, he was wearing a blue Burberry gabardine raincoat over a black three-piece suit.

Miller had gone for the night and there was nobody around the CID room. He spoke to the duty inspector, who escorted him through the locked, barred gate and through the grim, foul-smelling environment of the cell block.

'Turnkey! Turnkey! Ho, turnkey!'

Loud voices, many in unison, came from the cell occupants; drunks, wife beaters, junkies, drug dealers, drink drivers, thieves and petty criminals; the damaged and broken human detritus of Renfrewshire society. Some of them would be released in the morning, many would be doing the dreaded lie-in, detained for court until Monday.

More shouts came from behind the heavy cell doors, some with their inspection hatches open, as the Friday night clientele realised someone was afoot in the cell block corridor. Enquiries about when they were being released, about seeing their lawyer, about address checks, messages to families and requests for medication from the junkies were the norm for weekend detentions.

Kidston was offered twenty minutes with Kennedy in his cell. He noted that Kennedy was wide awake when the door was opened. Dressed in a white paper forensic suit, his young colleague looked haunted.

It felt strange seeing him in a police cell. The grim twelve-by-ten-foot concrete box had a stainless-steel, lidless toilet bowl. A raised stone floor base passed for a bed, with a rubber foam mattress, and coarse grey flea-infested heavyweight blankets. The red-painted floor and grubby white walls were dimly lit by a fluorescent strip light, covered by a metal grille. A high window of glass bricks was protected by thick steel bars.

It was a truly hellish environment.

The DI looked down at his young protégé. Kennedy sprang to his feet and almost hugged his boss. Instead, they went for a handshake, Kidston patting his young colleague's shoulder supportively.

Kennedy looked close to tears.

'How did it come to this then?' Kidston asked. He leaned

back against the cell wall rather than sit on the toilet bowl, which though empty, gave off a nauseating stench.

'It's a nightmare, boss. I've been sitting here trying to figure out how this turns out well for me. The only hope I have is Ellie Hunter wakes up and confirms I had nothing to do with her injuries.' Kennedy looked distraught as he relayed his full account of the trip to the Dams in the same detail he'd given to DI Miller and DS Whelan. He described the levels of foreplay and his account of how the bloodstain ended up on the girl's jacket. Kidston wrote the salient points in his notebook.

'How did the interview with Miller go?'

'Not well. Don't get me wrong, I stood up to the questions, but Miller was expecting me to burst. He wanted a confession.'

'I need to ask you straight up, Paul. Did you do it?' Kidston's pale eyes searched for signs of guilt in his young colleague's face.

'I swear, inspector, I never saw her after she left the car until we found her lying on the road.' Kennedy held his gaze, impassive, defiant. 'I think I upset DI Miller by highlighting that Ellie had scarred wrists and might be suicidal. It was information he wasn't aware of.'

'Never a good idea to upset Ronnie. Someone will get a kicking for that.'

'I know this looks bleak for me. If I was the detective making enquiries, I'd fancy me for it.'

'Did you sleep?' Kidston asked. 'You should try.'

'I tried before you came but I can't. I just run over countless scenarios again and again to try and work out what happened. I don't think I'll get any sleep in here.'

Kidston thought about the old polis adage that a guilty man will sleep soundly, while an innocent man will find sleeping a futile pursuit. It wasn't a hard and fast rule, but it tended to be a very good indicator. 'The duty officer tells me you haven't had a lawyer contacted. We need to change that. I'll get someone on it. What about Adam Sharkey?'

'That would be appreciated.'

'Anyone else? What about your parents or Sandra? They'll all be worried sick. I can make some calls, if you like. They'll allow her to hand in a change of clothes, get you out of that ridiculous paper suit. Thinking worst-case scenario, maybe bring a suit for court on Monday?'

'That would be very helpful. If you call Sandra and ask her to tell my folks? I'd prefer she got my version from you, rather than all the rumours that will be flying around later. Please have her stress that it's all a misunderstanding and it will get sorted.'

Kidston used the remainder of the allotted time to record the details of Kennedy's account in his notebook. When the duty officer cranked open the massive steel door, he allowed them another two minutes to draw their discussion to a proper close.

As the cell door closed behind him, Kidston caught a final glance at his colleague's haunted expression. It was clear that Paul Kennedy was caught in an emotional hell.

# 9

'Good morning, gents,' announced Kidston, as he opened the door to the main Gorbals CID office. 'Someone's had a busy night.' He saw the surprise on the faces of DS Jack Morrison and DC Gordon Hope, who weren't used to seeing their DI at 5.45am on a Saturday morning. An experienced pairing, they were putting the finishing touches to their briefing note on the Watters sword-attack incident.

'Choose your weapon, boss,' DS Morrison said. 'Machete, cleaver or samurai sword. Just another Friday night in the Gorbals.'

The two night-shift detectives had fully covered the incident to their usual professional standard. There were no witnesses, suspects or known motive for the attack, but they had traced drinkers who'd seen Watters earlier in the Granite. The ambulance crew and doctors at the city's Victoria Infirmary told the detectives that Watters' injury was consistent with a sword or machete attack. Surgery was being looked at to reattach the limb, but there was a strong possibility Watters would lose the hand.

Morrison and Hope walked Kidston the short distance from

the police station to the locus of the attack. The foyer of the low-rise block was cordoned off with police barrier tape, the entire scene guarded by constables Costello and McCartney, who greeted their CID colleagues from the shelter of the close entrance.

'It must be serious, the DI's been called out,' Costello said, laughing. 'Scenes of crime not long finished. We're just waiting for a specialist search team before the locus is stood down.'

'Did the SOCOs get much?' Kidston asked.

'Lifted a lot of blood samples and photographed a number of bloody footprints.' McCartney pointed to the gory site of the attack.

'Peter and Chrissie covered the initial call earlier,' Morrison said. 'Their statements are with the paperwork back at the office. Caught a wee bit of door-to-door before everyone went to their beds. Nobody saw anything but a few of them heard the scream.'

'We saw Watters leave the Granite at closing time,' Costello said. 'Told the ambulance driver his attacker was waiting for him in the foyer, behind the stairs.'

'I got a statement from the man that put his hand in the poly bag with some ice cubes,' said McCartney. 'Quick thinking. It might save his hand.'

'You prefer your major drug dealers to keep both their hands, do you?' DC Hope asked her.

'When you put it like that... I suppose...' She tailed off when she saw the smile on Kidston's face, realising she was being teased. Kidston wondered if Hope was flirting with the young policewoman.

'Any thoughts on who or what might be behind it?' Kidston asked, looking directly at Costello, who had one of the best intelligence networks he'd ever known.

'Crazy move, whoever it was,' Costello replied.

'What's this about samurais?' Kidston asked.

'Watters said something to the ambulance crew about the Gorbals Samurai.'

'Come on, Peter. This is the Gorbals. We do chib men, blade artists, junkies, whores and comic singers – we don't do samurais.'

'We did have the Gorbals Vampire back when I was a kid.' The big cop laughed, referring to the notorious 1954 incident when large groups of children armed with blades, crosses, stakes, and dogs descended upon the nearby Southern Necropolis to hunt for a rumoured child-killing vampire that stalked the graveyard.

'Peter told me he was chief vampire hunter that night.' McCartney joined in her neighbour's laughter. The rest of the group did the same.

'There's no doubt, an attack on Watters is a move on Canavan and his people,' DS Morrison said once the laughter ceased.

'Is someone trying to muscle in on the south side drugs trade?' DC Hope asked.

'Who do we know crazy enough to make a move like that?' DS Morrison only had more questions.

'Maybe it was a personal attack on Watters,' Kidston said.

'Revenge,' Costello said. 'An act of vengeance. That makes sense, given the players involved.'

'A fallout in the pub with some retribution,' Kidston continued. 'If Watters knows his attacker, there's a good chance he'll not be telling us. We need to get ready for a retaliation from Canavan.'

'We could be in for some more of the same tonight.' DC Hope laughed at the prospect.

'So young and so naïve,' DS Morrison reproached his neighbour. 'I've had quite enough blood and mayhem for one night shift.'

The detectives left the community cops to finish up at the locus and headed back to the station. Kidston spoke in hushed tones and briefed his two colleagues on the Kennedy arrest. Two veteran detectives exchanged a look of shock and surprise. Morrison shook his head in disbelief. 'How the hell could that happen?' the DS asked Kidston, who shrugged in response.

Kennedy and Rodgers had handed over to them at 10.30pm the night before and they'd heard nothing about Kennedy's arrest. Kidston urged total discretion.

Hope made coffees and the three men sat around the lunch table in the long rectangular CID office. One of the largest rooms in the station, the wall at their back consisted of a floor-to-ceiling bookcase stacked with crime reports packed into A4 box files and indexed in the various crime categories required by the force's statistics department. Discussing the shocking news about their colleague's arrest and the attack on Colin Watters, they speculated further on who could be behind it.

'The main question is whether this is a one-off "ned versus ned" attack, or a precursor to a drugs feud between rival dealers,' DS Morrison said. He was sceptical that any other group would take on Phil Canavan's crew.

'What if Canavan's fallen out with his suppliers?' DC Hope asked.

Kidston grimaced at the thought. Canavan had Glasgow's south side heroin trade sewn up tight in recent years, working with suppliers from Liverpool, and a small band of trusted dealers and a heavy team of enforcers. There would be very few bold enough to mess with Canavan or his people. That would be a bad scene, involving some intercity policing challenges. Kidston wanted to rule out that possibility – quickly. If no one was muscling in on Canavan's turf, he would need to consider the possibility that the attack on Watters was personal.

Kidston thought about the use of a sword. It seemed very

unusual; the victim had been unsure if it was a machete or a meat cleaver, both more familiar types of knives used in Glasgow attacks. But his description of how his assailant wielded the weapon and the words he used when he taunted him all pointed to a Japanese form of weaponry. Whatever lay behind the attack, Kidston knew this would be a difficult and challenging investigation.

Watters would be interviewed later following surgery. Based on initial witness statements from drinkers leaving the Granite and the neighbour who found him, Watters had lain bleeding for around thirty minutes. The neighbour had put the severed hand in a polythene bag with ice before calling an ambulance. The three detectives speculated on the odds of Watters' hand being successfully reattached and came up with a collective estimate of fifty-fifty.

Kidston sent Morrison and Hope home early before the day shift arrived. They'd had a long, difficult night, so he would brief the day shift team on the Watters attack. They would take up the investigation. He had important calls to make. First up for Kidston was DC Barry Rodgers, who was unsurprised to take an early-morning call from his DI ordering him back to the office for a one-to-one briefing.

His next call was to Adam Sharkey at his Burnside home. Sharkey was a former detective sergeant, who'd established a successful criminal law practice after leaving the police on an ill-health pension. He'd sustained a debilitating knee injury when, chasing housebreakers, he crashed through the roof of a cash-and-carry warehouse. Sharkey agreed to visit Kennedy later that morning and would attend any future interviews. Normally a defence agent would arrange to meet a client in the sheriff court cells on the morning of their appearance, but Sharkey would go the extra mile for the accused detective.

Kidston checked the duty roster to confirm that PC Sandra

Holt was likely to be at home. She and Kennedy both had their own places that they planned to sell to fund the purchase of a new marital home in the summer.

'Who is this?' An incredulous Sandra Holt thought one of her colleagues was winding her up with a prank call. A series of expletives followed as she eliminated a list of colleagues she suspected of being the culprit.

Kidston spoke calmly, reassuring the policewoman she could call him back through the office switchboard to confirm his identity.

'I'd like you to come into the office later to discuss the situation,' Kidston said after he'd imparted the basic information. It was clear that Sandra Holt was stunned by what she was hearing. Kidston heard her incredulity change to anger and then tears.

Given it was now nine hours after her fiancé's arrest, Kidston was mildly surprised that he was the one to break the news to her on the phone. Strathclyde Police was a village when it came to scuttlebutt. Polis were sweetie wives for gossip, but Kidston got to impart the facts, rather than the embellished hyperbole that would be doing the rounds later.

Kidston disclosed a fuller version of events, including Kennedy's denial of the allegations. He updated her on his visit with Paul and the arrangement for Adam Sharkey to be his lawyer. She agreed to pass the news on to her intended in-laws, and would call in to see Kidston later, after dropping off a change of clothes and a suit for court.

The Saturday morning CID office tradition was for hot breakfast rolls with pots of tea and coffee for the teams covering the weekend. Sourced from the bakery next door to the police station, there would be a mix of bacon, square sliced sausage, links sausage and potato scone. Rodgers arrived at the station just in time for the roll delivery and Kidston beckoned him into his office. Over tea and bacon rolls, Kidston questioned Rodgers about the incident for over thirty minutes. He made him go over his statement to Miller, again and again. Kidston took copious notes and asked supplementary questions about the victim, the locus and the time lapses between Ellie Hunter leaving the car, Paul Kennedy following her and his return without her.

Rodgers was eager to hear of any improvement in Hunter's condition. The disappointment that there was no good news merged with his acute embarrassment about the situation made it a difficult session for Rodgers.

'I'm sorry, boss. It was just a lumber that went wrong.' Rodgers looked weary.

'What are your thoughts on what happened? Could Paul have attacked her?' Kidston eyed his colleague, who since his divorce was enjoying his reputation as a shagger.

'DI Miller had me between a rock and a hard place. I don't know what happened and Miller knows that.' Rodgers took a swig of tea and swallowed hard. 'If you're asking me whether Paul did it, I have serious doubts. I don't think he's got that in him. Do I think he's in the shit? Yes. Do I think he attacked that girl? No.'

'How can you say that? You've worked with Kennedy, what, coming up two years?'

'Yes. He's just not the type. I mean, he's very good with women; he knows how to behave around them. Women tend to like him, a lot.' Rodgers looked crushed.

'Any other possible scenario you can think of?'

'This is hard for me. Normally you offer your neighbour an alibi or corroborate their story, but I can't do it for this.'

'Trust me, I think it's harder for Paul.' Kidston gave the DC a look that made it clear he was unimpressed.

'I think she could have slipped and fallen or been hit by a car.'

'Her injuries probably rule out the car option. I'm sure Miller will have the traffic examiners check the locus but that's looking unlikely.' Kidston leaned forward with his elbows on his desk. 'So we may have a *no crime* incident, but Ronnie Miller has a body, he has evidence and because it's a cop involved, the fiscal will run with it.'

Rodgers fully understood the term 'body'; police parlance for an arrestee or an accused person, but it was sad to think about his neighbour and good friend in such terms. Kidston instructed the weary detective to get home for some sleep as he was rostered to do a late shift that day. He doubted Rodgers would be doing much sleeping.

Kidston marked the crime report for the Watters attack to himself and DS Gregor Stark. The youngest and least experienced detective sergeant in his team, Stark made up for a lack of supervisory experience with his youthful enthusiasm, a positive attitude and willingness to take on anything. He handed the green investigating officer's copy of the crime report to Stark.

'We can work on this one together, Gregor, see how it plays out. We'll likely have an uncooperative complainer in Watters, but we'll need to find out what's behind the attack.'

'Nice one, boss. Could be an interesting enquiry.' Not daunted in the slightest, the young DS was eager to get started.

Kidston had been impressed by his youngest and most recently appointed DS. Gregor Stark was twenty-nine and had been in the rank for just over six months. With his boyish good looks, many people assumed he was a newly appointed detective constable, and often deferred to his older colleagues who were his junior in rank. Stark had been fired up by his welcome speech. It was the same talk Sawyers had given

Kidston when he was a young, newly appointed DC. He'd passed the mantra on to Stark, who carried the words like a badge of honour: *Youth is no handicap, it's what makes you hungry.*

The Watters enquiry would be in safe hands with Stark. Kidston was aware that his senior DS, John Wylie, would probably have liked to work on what was sure to be a high-profile case, but Stark deserved his chance. Gregor Stark was openly ambitious, something frowned upon by many colleagues, especially the cynical ones like Wylie. The older sergeant would see young up-and-coming officers as a threat rather than an asset; a resource to be mentored, developed and utilised. Kidston had been mentored in detective tradecraft by one of the best in Joe Sawyers and it was time to pay some of that back. Stark had responded well to Kidston's tutorship and he had high hopes for his young DS.

Kidston and Stark discussed the Watters case in detail. Stark confirmed that he'd arranged to interview Watters at the hospital for a full victim's statement after his operation. He'd also arranged a team of CID and uniform colleagues to conduct an evening visit to the Granite City Inn, show Watters' photo to punters and bar staff to see if anyone recalled any altercations that might have led to the attack.

Kidston's extension rang. It was Miller.

'I see you had a wee visit to the Paisley cells this morning, Luc. Did you not realise that the duty officer would mark you through the detention book?'

'I think if you speak to him tonight, you'll find that I told him to mark up my visit. That's the official procedure, Ronnie. Kennedy is one of my detectives. I wanted to check on his welfare.'

If the term 'official procedure' rankled Miller, he did a good job of hiding it. 'I see we've had a hive of activity this morning.

Visits from his fiancée and Adam Sharkey. You've been a very busy boy.' He didn't hide his sarcasm.

'Look, Ronnie, I got a call around 3am from Joe Sawyers. We'd had a sword attack and the Paul Kennedy thing. I was coming out anyway, so I thought I'd check up on my DC's welfare.'

'No doubt he told you he was innocent?' Miller was straight to the point.

'Says he never saw her after she left the car until they found her.'

'There's nobody to corroborate that version. They were about to have sex in the car. She got out. He was aroused, he followed her out. They got back into it and your boy got too rough for her...' Miller tailed off.

'There's no witnesses to that version either, Ronnie. Let's hope she wakes up and we get the undisputed truth about what happened.'

'So you think he's innocent?'

'I think you're the senior investigating officer and I'd like you to at least entertain the possibility he could be innocent.' Miller's unswerving certitude was a benefit and a burden. For his part, Kidston could never conceive of a world where he was right *every* time. Policing wasn't engineering, when he'd worked metal to a thousandth of an inch, cut by eye and feel; that level of precision in policing was extremely rare. 'It's your call as SIO to press charges based on the sufficiency of evidence, but Paul Kennedy won't confess to something he's adamant he's not done.'

'It won't look good for any of you when Ellie Hunter wakes up and tells us Paul Kennedy attacked her.'

'What's her chances?' Kidston asked.

'Not good right now. Swelling means brain injury is inoperable, she's likely to be in a coma for a while longer.'

'We can only hope she comes out of it.' Kidston wouldn't say it, but Ellie Hunter waking up remained Paul Kennedy's best hope.

'I don't want you poking your nose in, Kidston. Is that understood?' Miller's stern voice conveyed a hint of menace.

'It's your case, Miller. I was just checking into the welfare of one of my detectives,' Kidston lied.

Miller hung up.

*Why did it have to be Ronnie Miller?* thought Kidston. The clincher for the total breakdown in their relationship was Miller's unswerving belief it was Kidston who reported him for having an extra-marital relationship with a colleague. It wasn't Kidston, although he knew the identity of the informer and her reasons for coming forward. Miller seemed blissfully unaware that his affair was public knowledge, with colleagues sniggering behind his back.

Miller, supposedly showing a newly appointed detective the ropes in CID, started an office romance. His blatant favouritism of DC Amanda Cowan was disrupting working relationships on the team. It didn't play well with the other detectives that Miller selected her for overtime assignments working alongside him, allocated her the best enquiries and other special duties to the point where he became a laughing stock. One sceptical colleague had remarked about their affair: 'More fanny-struck than love-struck.'

Following an acrimonious falling out between the couple, allegations emerged of Miller's bullying behaviour towards Cowan, and the affair was brought to the attention of bosses. Miller expected Cowan to be transferred out of the team, but it was him who was moved to another station. As the newly appointed DCI it was Sawyers' decision, and he surprised many by finding in favour of a junior female detective. This rankled with Miller. It pushed his promotion to detective inspector back by two years, meaning Kidston made the rank before he did: the true root of Miller's antipathy towards him. The Amanda Cowan affair was the primary reason for Kidston's hard and fast rule about not having romantic relationships with colleagues.

Kidston would dig further; it was in his nature. He wasn't sure Miller would give Kennedy a fair crack of the whip. A nagging voice in his head tormented Kidston: what if Paul Kennedy's presumption of innocence was already undermined due to their association? He was thankful that their first interview was on tape and subsequent sessions would be with a lawyer. The old Ronnie Miller would not have hesitated to verbal a suspect's confession. Kidston couldn't imagine him trying that tactic with a police colleague. He wasn't sure where else he could take the enquiry, but he was determined to look deeper into the arrest of Paul Kennedy.

*Wake up, Ellie Hunter*, he thought. *Wake up.*

## 10

'DI Kidston, Gorbals CID.' He picked up his office phone on the first ring.

'Are you Paul Kennedy's boss?' It was a woman's voice.

'Who is this please?' Kidston asked. His mind frantically raced through the possibilities, Paul Kennedy's mother or maybe the witness, Clare Travers.

The caller wasn't forthcoming. 'You don't need my name, right now. I'm hearing Paul Kennedy was locked up for attacking a woman.'

'What do you know about that case?' Kidston asked. 'If you have information about the case, you need to come to the office and give a statement.'

'No statement, but you need to know, Paul's an animal. I'm glad the law's caught up with him. I'll be watching to make sure there's no cover-up.'

'We don't do cover-ups. Why are you using that term? What did he do to you?'

'I'm an ex-girlfriend,' the woman said. 'Let's just say he's a bit too handy with his fists.'

'I really need to speak to you, whoever you are,' Kidston said.

'Not going to happen.' The line went dead.

Kidston sat back in his chair, his face a puzzled frown. Anonymous calls were the bane of a detective's life. Fragments of phantom intelligence, often without foundation, teased and tormented the investigator. Who and what was behind this call? Kidston had never worked a murder enquiry or major investigation that didn't receive its quota of anonymous calls. Tip-offs about partners, family members, colleagues, neighbours, bosses. Most were crank calls, but some weren't and that was the fear. He would have loved to get the full story on his mystery caller. What was their motive? A grievance against Paul Kennedy? Against Sandra Holt? Kidston called down to the duty desk sergeant, who confirmed that the call had come through the main office switchboard, the caller asking for him by name. Whoever made the call, whatever their reason, Kidston had a bad feeling it wouldn't augur well for Paul Kennedy.

Kidston noticed the redness in Sandra Holt's eyes as she took a seat in his office. Her thin-lipped expression was unsurprising, given the kind of day she was having. Dressed in civvies, Holt was a shapely and attractive young woman, with shoulder-length blonde hair. Four years younger than Kennedy and with five years on the job, she'd met him while working on the same uniform patrol group and before his appointment to CID. They were due to be married that August.

'I'm very grateful for you making time to see me,' Holt said. 'And sorry again for the mix-up on the phone. It's been a bit of a nightmare day.'

'No problem,' Kidston reassured her. 'How did the Paisley visit go?'

'I handed in a suit for court, a change of clothes and a pack of sandwiches but obviously I wasn't allowed to see him. The staff at the uniform bar said that, despite everything, he was in a positive frame of mind.'

They were seated either side of Kidston's desk. Holt bit her lip, her eyes tearing up. Her expression seemed to say, *Please help me understand this nightmare.*

'How are you feeling now, Sandra?' Kidston asked.

'I was raging after I came off the phone with you earlier, absolutely livid, but now I'm more focused on helping him.'

'Have you told many people, friends, colleagues about Paul's situation?' Kidston asked.

'Both sets of parents, that's all,' she replied.

'No friends or colleagues?'

'No, why do you ask?'

'I'm just trying to monitor what's out there,' Kidston lied. 'Sandra, do you or Paul have any enemies that might want to fire you in?'

'We've been a couple for three years,' she replied. 'There's no trail of bitter exes as far as I know.'

Kidston decided she didn't need to know about the call he received earlier. 'How did Mr and Mrs Kennedy take the news?' he asked.

'Shocked and stunned, it's fair to say. Mrs Kennedy was devastated,' she replied. Kidston noticed the puffiness around Holt's eyes. 'Both are confident that he'll be cleared. That's parents for you, I suppose.' There was a forced smile. 'They're very grateful for your intervention with the lawyer.'

'And you, Sandra? Do you think he'll be cleared?' Kidston looked directly into her eyes, trying to determine the level of support for her man.

'Mr Kidston, I can't believe Paul did what they've accused him of. I'd never believe that of him. You know Paul. Anyone who knows Paul will know he's not got it in him to attack a woman.' She returned Kidston's gaze with a strong stare, but he could see her bottom lip quivering.

'So you'll stand by him.'

'Absolutely, I will. Paul's biggest challenge was working with Barry Rodgers. I think you already know he's a bit of a shagger, always looking to go clubbing or out on the pull.' Holt sat up straight in her chair. 'I'm not naïve, inspector, I know what it's like in CID, but Paul is ready to settle down. I can assure you this won't derail us, or our wedding.'

It was a spirited defence of her fiancé's character. Kidston would find himself musing over Holt's declaration for some time to come.

Costello and McCartney walked their community beat, with Chrissie trying gamely to match the long stride of her big neighbour. They were headed for Cumberland Arcade, where there were a couple of likely dosses that would offer a cup of tea. It was a cold, gloomy afternoon and a cuppa would keep them ticking over until break time. Costello had tutored his less experienced neighbour in how to gather valuable titbits of community intelligence over a chat with tea and biscuits in the back of the grocer's, the newsagent's, or the shoe shop. The two cops were making their way through the shopping crowd when something caught Costello's eye. A young couple dressed in garish, matching purple, orange and white shell suits juked into the newsagent's like they were trying to avoid the polis. When they re-emerged three minutes later, two of Strathclyde's finest were waiting to speak to them.

'Are you avoiding us?' Costello asked.

'Naw, we just went intae the shop for some chewing gum.' The young man shot a furtive glance at the big cop.

It took a few moments to sink in, but Costello realised he knew them. The dramatic changes in their features had caused his hesitation. Both had an ugly light-brown growth on their eyeballs, like raised furry veins. Their faces told of heroin addiction; the telltale gauntness of their jaws, the translucent skin stretched over their skulls and their spaced-out expressions. Costello saw his neighbour avert her gaze from the horrific sight of their eyes. It was like a scene from a zombie apocalypse movie. The cops had been briefed that a recent bad batch of heroin had been cut with yeast, but they'd not seen the dreadful outcome until now.

Terry Hinds and Mary Colville were both eighteen. Costello had reported Hinds to the Children's Panel three years earlier for abusing solvents. He'd arrested Colville for shoplifting as a juvenile. The big cop was shocked by their condition. Their descent into heroin had happened fast; from stealing groceries and sniffing glue to smack addiction in under three years. Their habit would now have to be fed and they would be stealing and robbing to finance their next high. Girls like Colville would head to Glasgow Green to prostitute themselves with a quick trick or a blow job to get a fix. Boys like Hinds would be their stick man, pimping them out for a quick knee-trembler up a close or down a lane. The Green was the city's second-tier, bargain-basement, red-light area after the notorious drag in the town centre's Blythswood Square.

They sent the two of them up the road after a cautious frisking confirmed that neither were carrying any drugs or works. Watching them walk off into the afternoon gloom, Costello was struck by their peculiar gait. Even walking is a challenge once your brain circuitry has been fried by narcotics.

'Those eyes are the creepiest things I've ever seen. I hate junkies,' said McCartney.

'I just find it a tragic state of affairs,' Costello replied. 'Two eighteen-year-olds who'll be lucky to see thirty.'

'What can we do about it?' McCartney asked.

'Policing can't deal with it alone,' he replied. 'This is

becoming an epidemic. I've seen kids go from glue sniffing to hash to smack in short order. Heroin could take out an entire generation from the housing schemes. This is a health issue as much as policing or law enforcement. It's just such a needless waste of young lives.'

Costello had felt like the little Dutch boy with his finger in the dyke as a tidal wave of heroin surged through the neighbourhood in the early eighties. Senior managers were incredulous to the problem and caught on the back foot in terms of drugs policy. The force's drugs squad was modelled around tackling anti-establishment hippie dopeheads with their tie-dye T-shirts, joss sticks and Woodstock soundtrack. This was no longer about peace and love and rock 'n' roll; this was commerce, the supply and trade of highly addictive deadly substances. Criminals like Phil Canavan saw their opportunity and weighed in to make their fortunes.

Dealers like Colin Watters would cut the heroin with any substance that could make the powder go further; additives like baking soda, powdered milk, caffeine, household cleaners and now yeast had been used to dilute the drug. Two young women had died in September from heroin thought to have been cut with rat poison. Adulterating the drugs increased the profits for the dealers and the risks for the users.

Once heroin took hold, crime numbers rose, as the users turned to theft, robbery and fraud to feed their voracious appetites. The Gorbals had seen a community and a generation ravaged by heroin. Gangsters like Canavan had created a subculture where drugs were freely available in many of the pubs in the area. In those same pubs, junkies would take orders for any article, within reason, to be stolen to order for delivery the next day; designer clothes, kitchen equipment, white goods. The amount of stolen electrical goods arranged through the pubs could stock a branch of Argos. Much of Glasgow's black market was driven by drug addicts looking to score their next hit.

Costello had arrested his share of junkies and dealers and it hardly made an impact. Big players like Watters and Canavan were always removed from the front-line activity, preferring to use teenagers and kids to conduct the deals and take the heat from the constabulary.

They'd both stood guard at the locus of last night's attack on Watters and stepped over pools of his blood. Despite all the laughter, Costello saw how much the incident had affected McCartney and it had sent shock waves through the neighbourhood with both the polis and ned population trying to calculate the possible motives and potential ramifications. Colin Watters was the victim of a horrific attack and may have lost a hand, but you would be hard pressed to find any police officer with the slightest sympathy for an individual responsible for so much misery in the area. *You reap what you sow*, thought Costello. He had a feeling that things were about to get very interesting.

It was mid-afternoon when Kidston arrived at the Craigie Street Divisional Headquarters in the Queen's Park district of the city. The CID had a generous share of the top floor of the large sandstone, three-storey building. Detective Superintendent Joe Sawyers had a sizeable, well-appointed office at the end of the corridor.

Kidston entered to find Sawyers looking over a stack of papers. He stood up, walked around his desk and the two men exchanged friendly smiles, warm greetings and a handshake. They sat at a small conference table. Sawyers produced a plate of chocolate biscuits and Kidston boiled up the kettle for coffees.

Sawyers' impeccable appearance made no sartorial concessions to the fact it was a Saturday afternoon and officially his day off.

A handsome, slim and fit forty-four, Sawyers typified the new and emerging breed of senior CID manager. Young for the position, he looked more like an accountant than the public perception of a career detective. He wore a navy-blue suit, a pristine white shirt and a wine-coloured tie. The previous postholder had sported a soft hat as part of the senior detective's 'uniform' but times were changing. Sawyers was part of ACC Colquhoun's reform programme that brought through senior detectives who were more than proven investigators. Colquhoun wanted leaders; strategic managers to drive through a programme of structural and cultural change.

Kidston updated Sawyers on his morning briefing from Morrison and Hope, his meetings with Rodgers and Sandra Holt, and his not unexpected call from Ronnie Miller. He withheld reporting the anonymous phone call, wondering if his boss may have received a similar call. He'd wait and see if the woman would contact him again.

The detective superintendent was renowned for his polite articulate manner and refined speaking voice which were as far removed from glottal Glaswegian as you could imagine, belying his humble roots in a crumbling single-end in Bridgeton. No one ever confused his politeness with softness. He was a murder squad veteran; an experienced SIO and known for his quietly spoken character assassinations.

'Ronnie's convinced he's got his man?' Sawyers asked as he sipped his coffee.

'As you'd expect, he's convinced it was Paul Kennedy.'

'You're not as convinced?'

'I looked him in the eyes and I asked him. That was his chance to confess everything.' Kidston looked at his boss. 'You once taught me that a guilty man sleeps like a baby in a police cell. Kennedy never slept a wink.'

Sawyers smiled at the recollection. Even in his early days as a detective, Kidston had been a willing pupil, eagerly soaking up the tools and techniques of CID tradecraft. His uncanny knack of securing some of the most challenging confessions that Sawyers had ever witnessed had earned him the nickname *The Human Lie Detector*.

'Did DC Rodgers add anything to our understanding of what went down?'

'He's embarrassed. Feels bad that he can't corroborate Paul's version. The whole pick-up routine was his idea.' Kidston reached for a chocolate digestive. 'Doesn't reflect well on him. All the stuff about switching names and wanting to flee the hospital. He admitted this morning that was all down to him.'

'Hmm,' Sawyers reflected. 'Once the dust settles, I'll get him rotated back to a uniform post. Ideal candidate for Q's transfer programme.'

At the heart of Colquhoun's reforms was the notion of tenure; for the first time someone was challenging the idea that a police officer could be appointed detective after six, seven or eight years and then coast through a specialised department for a further twenty-plus years, even with a poor staff appraisal record. The man they called Q was going through the CID like a dose of salts, ensuring detectives throughout the force looked to their laurels.

There was no defence Kidston could offer for Rodgers. He was an ineffectual investigator who'd been coasting for years. Paul Kennedy was just the latest in a long line of younger detectives that Rodgers had latched onto, hoping to enhance his own standing in the team. If Kidston could save Kennedy, he would. But that would have to come later.

'DI Miller believes he's got a tight case based on the call I got from Bob Ferguson,' Sawyers said.

'Ronnie's done everything I'd have done if it was my enquiry. He's covered all the bases; eliminated the likelihood of a traffic accident, hit-and-run. But there's no confession. I'd be looking for one and I think if Paul Kennedy did this, he'd put his hands up.'

'What alternative scenarios are there?' Sawyers asked.

'A slip or fall on the icy road is the most obvious but Paul's clutching at straws,' Kidston replied.

'Kennedy really needs the girl to wake up and end his nightmare,' Sawyers said.

'What if she was crazy enough to get into a second car?' Kidston asked.

'Who's clutching at straws now?'

'I know, I know, but her pal says she's quite flaky and wasn't surprised she went walkabout.' There was a familiar glint in Kidston's pale-green eyes.

'How do you even investigate that?' Sawyers asked.

'I'm not sure but I think I need to try. I can't just give up.' Kidston laughed and pointed to the framed *Peanuts* cartoon on the wall.

Sawyers was known for his love of Charles M. Schulz's cartoon strip and pride of place on his office wall was a framed drawing of Charlie Brown. It showed Charlie with his instantly recognisable crumpled and downturned mouth, as he missed the football moments after Lucy had snatched it away from his attempted kick. The original caption had read 'GOOD GRIEF!' but Sawyers had had it overprinted by the graphics department. It now read 'You Could Always Give Up'. Sawyers saw it as a universal, sad cosmic joke. Charlie Brown never gets to kick the football, but he never gives up. He never stops trying.

Sawyers joined in the laughter. 'Yes, you *could* always give up.'

Sawyers knew his inspector's moral code wouldn't allow him to give up on his young protégé, especially since his nemesis, Miller, was in the opposition corner. He was well aware of the hostility between the two inspectors. He'd mentored both as detective sergeants on his team when he was *their* detective inspector. Miller was a man of action; he'd used him as a blunt instrument when he needed a steamroller, but his scattergun approach didn't always work. Kidston was the more measured; just as tenacious, but with a more nuanced approach to investigations.

Sawyers recalled how the sparks would often fly between the two dogged and skilled investigators; distinctive characters with their different methods. He'd said it often back then; Kidston was a terrier, but Miller was a pit bull. More than once, he'd refereed bouts or calmed eruptions between them.

Sawyers contemplated the coming storm.

'Paul Kennedy is one of ours and I know you'll want to take a closer look. It has to be unofficial, unauthorised, and I don't want it blowing up in our faces. You know how volatile Ronnie is. Officially, of course, I must warn you against any possible interference in another division's investigation.' Sawyers laid it on the line. 'Absolute discretion required.'

'Any blowback will be on me, Joe. You've warned me against it in no uncertain terms.' A knowing smile and a nod passed between them. Both men understood how plausible deniability worked.

## 11

Kidston spent late Saturday afternoon catching up on his sleep. He could function for days at a time on little sleep but there was always a reckoning. After four or five days of sleep deprivation he would slumber between twelve and fourteen hours. His 'catch-up' would leave him fully recharged, ready to start the inevitable cycle again. He'd set an alarm to allow himself time to shower and eat prior to a long-standing social engagement.

He cooked up a king prawn pasta, flicking through the Saturday papers as he waited for the penne to boil. There was no mention of the Barrhead Dams incident in the *Daily Record* or the *Glasgow Herald*; more likely it would break in the local *Paisley Daily Express* on Monday. The *Record* had missed the deadline for the sword-attack story, but it would probably be picked up by the *Sunday Mail*. Both incidents would be included in the chief constable's briefing notes on Monday morning, bringing another level of scrutiny.

Feeling refreshed after a shower and a decent meal, Kidston headed to a little-known corner of Glasgow that would be forever Nashville. As he approached the entrance, the dazzling colours of the neon signage illuminated the grey gloom of the damp night sky. The Grand Ole Opry at Paisley Road Toll in Govan may have been around 4,000 miles from its better-known Tennessee namesake, but for visitors to Glasgow's only country and western music club, they might as well have been in a bustling Nashville honky-tonk.

When Kidston entered, he was greeted by the familiar faces of people dressed in cowboy hats, western shirts and rhinestones. He was a frequent visitor and a friend of Grace Cassidy, lead singer of the band, Nashville Skyline. Named after Dylan's country album, the six-piece band's Opry set normally comprised classic country songs. Kidston made his way up to the mezzanine level. The building was still recognisable as a former cinema, with the old projection room visible above the bar.

Kidston had known Grace since early childhood when they were both involved in the traumatic incident that saw Luc survive being thrown out a tenement window by a deranged old woman. They'd gone out together through high school, shared their first sexual experiences and been so loved up that all their friends assumed they were a *forever* couple. But it wasn't to be; Grace was doing her university degree at the time while Kidston was working as an apprentice engineer in the shipyards. They both started hanging out with new groups; Grace at the student union of Glasgow University, and Kidston in the city's clubs and pubs.

Aged twenty, he'd initiated the break-up, wanting more freedom and dead against settling down too young. Even though it was his choice, Kidston handled the split very badly; he'd never fallen out of love with Grace and seeing her out with other guys drove him insane with jealousy. His 'freedom', such as it was, moving from girl to girl, in a series of unsatisfactory romances, turned out to be a false dawn. He'd always conceded that Grace handled the situation much better. Even though she believed he'd abandoned her and broken her heart she had told him back then that the door was open for his return. It just never happened.

The band took the stage to rapturous applause; they were a popular Saturday night draw. They started their set with their version of 'The Night They Drove Old Dixie Down', then followed a bluesy twist on the Creedence standard 'Have You Ever Seen the Rain?' Grace then shared vocals with lead guitarist Matt on a cracking version of 'Lyin' Eyes'. Grace and Matt looked good singing together. Matt taught at the same school as Grace, and Kidston had met him a few times. He wondered if they were a couple.

The next run of songs leaned heavily on Grace's wonderful voice and her vocal dexterity. From Dolly to Emmylou with some Anne Murray thrown in for good measure, she led the band through their set. Kidston watched her from the balcony; a woman in the spotlight, commanding the stage and holding an audience in thrall with her singing and guitar playing. She looked beautiful in a button-fronted, dark blue, floral-patterned dress and her brown cowboy boots. Her Martin guitar strap slung over her shoulder, Grace ran her hand through her thick mane of long red hair as she chatted and smiled through the song introductions. Her warm personality and love of the music shone through. Kidston was in awe of her talent.

Music had been their thing as kids. She'd grown up in a house full of country and western records. Her dad was big into Hank Williams, Johnny Cash and Glen Campbell. Her mum was a massive fan of Patsy Cline and Jim Reeves. She'd been singing these songs since she was a little girl. Kidston came from a house of blues music. As kids together, they'd experienced the early days of rock and roll with Little Richard, Elvis Presley and a childhood illuminated by the music of the Beatles. Luc found his own groove with soul music, especially Tamla Motown and Stax. Their shared love of music was a hallmark of their relationship and they attended live gigs together every chance they got.

Luc sat on his usual place in the balcony; well back from the barrier to ensure his acrophobia didn't surface. He acknowledged Grace with a discreet wave. Shielding her eyes from the dazzling stage lights with her hand, she looked up to him as she introduced the next number.

'This one's for a very dear friend of mine. This one's for Luca.'

Her pet name for him went back to their Gracie and Luca days at high school. He knew what was coming next. Luc watched in wonder as she led the band through their version of the Jim Reeves classic, 'He'll Have to Go'. He'd first heard her sing the song at their school qualy dance as a shy, awkward twelve-year-old. Back then her shyness was obvious but there was no doubting the quality of her singing voice; strong and steady, exquisitely pitched. The song featured again at her first impromptu public gig when Luc and Grace formed part of a group of underage drinkers trying to be inconspicuous in a hotel bar in Rothesay. Their low-profile cover was blown when Grace joined the house band for a rendition of her favourite party piece. That was the night the two sixteen-year-olds had made love for the first time.

*Put your sweet lips a little closer to the phone.* The song stirred such evocative memories of them as a couple. He sipped his orange juice, reflecting on how they'd both ended up married to different people. First him to Melanie when he was twenty-seven. Grace was thirty-one when she married Gary, four years later. Grace's marriage had ended in divorce a year ago. By all accounts, her experience of married life turned out badly with a controlling partner who expressly forbade her to continue singing in Nashville Skyline. Finding himself divorced at thirty-five, when he'd hoped to be starting his family, Kidston had given up on the institution.

He was jarred from his reverie by a vibration pulsing through his belt. His pager flashed a message to contact the control room at Pitt Street. Force control had oversight of all serious incidents across their policing area and managed the call-out of specialists and senior officers. Kidston was rostered for the month as a hostage negotiator. With everything else going on, he'd given some thought to standing down from the list but, if he was honest, he was scared to miss out on a decent shout. He used the office behind the reception desk to phone in.

*Deep joy*, said the sarcastic voice in Kidston's head. A suicide intervention call and it sounded like a tricky one. A young man had climbed to the wrong side of the Erskine Bridge and was threatening to jump into the River Clyde. The duty officer confirmed that he'd already despatched a second negotiator: Inspector Harry Thompson, who was on duty at nearby Govan. Negotiators were always deployed in pairs. Kidston knew Thompson well; he was a seasoned negotiator, a solid and dependable operator. They'd done a few shouts together in the past and trained together on exercise programmes. Thompson was as reliable as they came.

Kidston had been fortunate to avoid too many suicide intervention call-outs in the past. Most of his shouts had been sieges or barricade incidents. These tended to be massive police operations; the so called 'three-ring circus', with firearms teams, public order units, and media support in attendance.

Aware of the risks of not performing at his absolute best in critical incidents, Kidston was content that, aside from a few vertigo-like symptoms, he could control his acrophobia. He didn't disclose it when he trained as a negotiator but as he saw it, the course he completed was advertised as 'hostage negotiation'.

The suicide intervention aspect had been something of a later evolution in the role as it became redefined as 'crisis negotiation'.

Back in his car, he flicked through the cassettes in the glove compartment and opted for Deacon Blue's *Raintown*. It was an advance bootleg copy provided by Grace. They'd caught them live a few times and had tickets for their upcoming Pavilion gig as part of Mayfest. The music soothed Kidston's anxiety; call-outs for jumpers were always tense.

As expected, the bridge was closed on the approaches. The vast, illuminated river crossing that linked Renfrewshire and Dunbartonshire was one of the top suicide locations in the west of Scotland. A cordon officer in a fluorescent yellow jacket directed him to the Dumbarton-bound carriageway and Kidston walked over the crest of the bridge to a cluster of officers formed up as an inner cordon.

It was another freezing cold night with the temperature pushing into minus numbers. He spotted the bulky figure of Harry Thompson off to the side. He was listening in to a discussion between a veteran sergeant and the subject, who was clinging on to the top of the barrier, on the wrong side of the safety railing.

'Hello, Harry.' Kidston greeted Thompson warmly with a handshake and a pat on the shoulder.

'Hi, Luc,' Thompson said. 'I hope you've got something warmer to wear. It's Baltic up here.'

Kidston, dressed in denims and a casual tailored jacket, went to the boot of the Alfa Romeo and dug out a thick, heavy, three-quarter length coat, pulled a dark woollen tammy over his ears and slid his hands into a pair of padded gloves. 'What's the story, Harry?'

Thompson briefed him on how the discussions had been going. The man, who'd given his name as Russell Maitland, said he was twenty-nine, and had told the police an age-old story of domestic strife and mishap due to a serious gambling addiction. Thompson explained further that Maitland had been thrown out of the marital home after gambling away anything of value in the house. Drink had been taken.

Kidston nodded; it was a familiar lament. They quickly decided that Kidston, the more experienced in negotiator terms, would take the lead or 'number one' role. Thompson took on the 'number two' position.

Their subject was perched precariously on the parapet, with only the slimmest foothold on the ledge. The dark, murky waters of the River Clyde were 180 feet below him and at this point of the river the currents would sweep his body miles out to sea. He hadn't allowed the police officers to come any closer than fourteen feet, threatening to leap off the ledge if they took another step.

'Russell, my name is Luc,' Kidston said loudly so his voice would carry. 'I'm with the police and I'm here to help you.'

'I don't know why you're wasting your time. What can you say that the other police haven't said already?' Russell was politely spoken and seemed to have been waiting to speak to a trained negotiator. Kidston had learned an early lesson about live negotiations: the cops at the scene can't wait to tell the subject that a trained specialist is en route. It got them off the hook and could sometimes de-escalate a situation, or at least buy some precious time.

Kidston and Thompson needed to get closer. The opening gambits were all about decreasing the distance between the two inspectors and their subject. The two men inched forward, Thompson directly behind Kidston, whispering suggested approaches and cautious advice under his breath. Thompson had a tight grip of Kidston, his overriding priority the safety of the number one negotiator. Face-to-face negotiations were always challenging but suicide interventions left negotiators most exposed. Colleagues had lost jumpers in mid-dialogue and any negotiator would struggle to recover from an outcome like that.

With Thompson's hand gripping Kidston's belt, holding him back, they looked like a shadowy ventriloquist with an oversized walking doll as they crept forward in step sequence closer to the barrier.

Kidston felt the freezing night air nip at his exposed nose and cheeks and burn his eyelids.

Russell allowed them to advance to around eight feet before demanding they stop with yet another threat to jump. It allowed them to get their first decent look at him. Around five feet ten in height and sturdily built, he wasn't dressed for straddling bridges on a freezing cold February evening. He looked frozen stiff in a pair of jeans and a pullover. He also looked terrified.

Alarmingly a film of frost had formed on his hair, face, and clothing. The more he spoke with Russell, the more Kidston feared that his end would not come from jumping, but from falling. Any attempt at moving his frozen limbs would be fraught with danger.

The negotiation hooks were the obvious ones. With a seven-year-old daughter and a six-year-old son, Russell was every bit the proud father. Kidston got him talking about his kids' achievements in reading, swimming and football. His wee girl, Beverley, was learning piano and little Dennis was attending football coaching.

'But I pawned Beverley's electric piano to put a bet on the football,' Russell said, his anguish clear to both negotiators. 'I'm a fuckin' disgrace. I've hit a new low.'

'You can get help for gambling addiction these days. I know some cops who've been helped,' Kidston said. 'I'm told it works really well. You shouldn't give up hope. You can get back on your feet and buy Beverley another piano.'

'That's why I was chasing a win at the bookies. I'm in deep wi' a money lender. The interest is killing me... I've no chance of paying it back. I'm as well jumpin' in the Clyde.'

'Who is it?' Kidston asked.

'Why would that matter?' Russell said with an air of despondency. 'I can't pay the guy off.'

'Whoever it is, it shouldn't push you to something as drastic as this.'

'...Phil Canavan...'

'Fuck,' Kidston whispered under his breath. *That bastard Canavan has tentacles everywhere*, he thought. 'You can't let scum like Phil Canavan be the reason you never see your kids again. Come on, Russell, think about your children.' Kidston kept pressing the positive outcomes that lay ahead in Russell's life – but only if he changed his mind about jumping.

'Russell, are you really telling me you can contemplate the thought of never reading another bedtime story to your kids?' Kidston measured his every word with great care.

'You'll always be their father, Russell, no matter how much debt you're in or whatever happens in your marriage. There are people, qualified people, who will help you clear your debt and help with your gambling addiction. We can get the money lenders like Canavan off your back. Do you understand what I'm saying to you, Russell?'

'I understand,' Russell said.

Kidston knew then that Russell wasn't going to jump. He could still fall, but he wouldn't be jumping.

Not tonight.

Step by step they edged closer. This was no time for stealth; no false moves. Trust could dissolve in an instant, like melted snow. They would not rush him or grab him. Everything from this point forward would be negotiated, patiently, painstakingly by agreement. One step, one movement at a time.

'Russell, I don't want you to jump, and I think you've decided not to jump.' Kidston wiped his frozen runny nose with the back of his glove. 'But, Russell, I fear that you're now so cold that any attempted movement brings a risk of you falling off the bridge.'

Kidston imagined Russell's frozen limbs causing him to stumble or fall into the dark, freezing river below. 'You look frozen solid, Russell,' Kidston said. 'Are you maybe too cold to even risk moving?'

'I think I must be,' Russell said quietly.

'Now, Russell, this is very important.' Kidston spoke loudly and clearly. 'Please don't try to move. Just in case your legs or your feet have frozen up. We'll come to you, Russell. Is that understood?'

Now realising the full horror of his predicament, Russell attempted to move his ice-covered feet along the ledge. As he shifted his weight, his legs faltered.

He slipped.

Both policemen rushed forward but couldn't close down the last remaining paces to secure the falling man. For Kidston, the final few seconds seemed to happen in slow motion. As he reached the barrier, Kidston leaned over and peered into the darkness. He was just in time to hear the faint splash of Russell Maitland's body hitting the dark, icy waters far below.

He was gone.

Kidston braced himself against the barrier. His head was spinning, nausea rising, even though he was too high up and it was much too dark to contemplate the scale of the drop, he was overcome by a failing sense of equilibrium.

'That's not on you, Luc.' Harry Thompson placed a reassuring arm around the devastated Kidston's shoulder. 'You told him to stay still. Falling's not the same as jumping.'

Kidston felt the nausea subside. Gripping the barrier rail, feet on solid ground, he felt the strength slowly return to his body.

*Falling; not jumping*, Kidston thought, taking no consolation whatsoever.

# 12

## Sunday

A clear blue sky.

*The sensation of nothing beneath his feet. He's flailing around, trying to grab hold of something, anything. Anything to find a foothold in the merciless, empty air. Hurtling fast towards the ground.*

*No trace of Superboy.*

*Kryptonite.*

His eyes now wide open in terror.

*Falling; not flying.*

Kidston woke up with a start. The tightness in his chest made him gasp for air. The nightmare had returned. It had been over twenty years since his dreams featured the terrifying slow-motion horror of being pushed from a third-storey tenement window. He sat up in bed, drenched in sweat, his face a troubled frown; the events of last night had plagued his sleep. The face of Russell Maitland had occupied his thoughts, preventing him from falling over. Kidston had held his acrophobia in check but was unable to save the man's life. The survivor guilt of his childhood had resurfaced.

There would be an enquiry and they'd probably withdraw his negotiator credentials until the outcome was clear.

Maitland fell rather than jumped. That fact didn't help with Kidston's overwhelming sense of failure and despondency. Loss of reputation within his cadre of negotiator colleagues was one thing but it paled into insignificance against the loss of a young father's life. Added to the Paul Kennedy case and the conflict with Ronnie Miller, Kidston had a lot on his mind. Interfering in Miller's case had presented a dilemma he could have done without. The strange anonymous call that cast doubt on Paul Kennedy's character was also troubling him. Maybe it was the very real threat to his own reputation and career presented by this extraordinary case. Kidston knew that pursuing an unauthorised investigation into Paul Kennedy's arrest would require him to recalibrate his own moral compass. Breaking the rules didn't come as easily to him as it did to Miller. Even if such an investigation presented itself, there were no other obvious lines of enquiry. He would look at it fresh again tomorrow. For now, he needed to catch up on some sleep.

He tried Grace's number and as he suspected it might, it rang out. She would be at her parents' house for Sunday breakfast with her sister's family. He left a sleepy message explaining his call-out to the Erskine Bridge, apologising for missing the end of her Opry set and that he was going back to bed.

When he woke up again it was after 2pm. A call from his ex-wife, Melanie, wanting to drop by. Kidston took a quick shower and dressed in a faded grey marl T-shirt with a Stax records logo and a pair of black jogging pants. He gave the bungalow a quick tidy up, made himself some toast and put on a pot of coffee. Kidston heard a familiar low howling when the doorbell sounded. Tallulah, the Siberian husky, pushed past Melanie and leapt on Kidston, who dropped to one knee and nuzzled the dog's neck. Tallulah's enthusiasm knocked him sideways and he continued clapping her from a lying position with the dog on top of him licking his face.

'Hello, beautiful girl.' Kidston got to his feet. 'And hello, other beautiful girl.' He kissed his ex-wife on the cheek.

At thirty-five, Melanie was two years younger than him and wore tight blue jeans that showed off her petite figure, shapely hips and slim waist. She worked hard to maintain her looks and it showed. Her lustrous dark-brown hair complemented her big hazel eyes. With a natural Mediterranean glow to her skin and the sweetest smile, Kidston had often wondered about the gorgeous babies they could have made.

'Smooth talker.' Melanie smiled. 'I know who you're most pleased to see.'

They sat on the large brown leather sofa with Tallulah positioned between them enjoying the fact that her two favourite humans were in the same place. The striking grey-and-white husky with her piercing ice-blue eyes and lupine face was lapping up the affection. She was the child of their marriage; a rescue dog they'd picked up from the pound when she was still a puppy.

'You look knackered but you're looking great, if that makes sense.' Melanie ruffled Tallulah's belly with one hand and sipped her coffee with the other.

'I've had a bit of a nightmare Friday and Saturday. It's all down to a lack of sleep. A man fell off the Erskine Bridge last night, while I was talking to him. Added to that, one of my DCs has been arrested for attempted murder and it's Ronnie Miller who's the SIO. But you look fantastic.' He flashed his best sardonic smile.

'For goodness' sake, Luc,' Melanie said. 'Why don't you give up all that negotiator stuff? You've always understood the risks.'

'I suppose so,' Luc said absent-mindedly. 'Ronnie Miller's the SIO for my detective that's been jailed. I did say.'

'Yeah, Ronnie Miller, you said.' Melanie Bridges was married to a cop long enough to know the shorthand for senior investigating officer. She also knew the contempt the two men held for each other. 'Anyone I know?'

'One of my newer detective officers; a great young DC, very promising and supposed to be getting married in the summer, to a lovely young policewoman that I met for the first time yesterday.'

'Poor girl. That crazy, fuckin' job of yours. Sounds like it's claimed another victim... two victims.' Melanie shook her head.

'You always hated my job, Mel.'

'In the end, yes. I truly detested it. It took you from me and I could never compete with anything as all-consuming as a CID career. You know you were married to the job.'

'I might not have much of a career left, Mel, the way things are going.'

'You'll work it out, you always do,' Melanie said. 'The work's too important to you.'

'I think we were both distracted by work. You can't build up a baby clothing empire without being single-minded.'

'Three shops are hardly an empire, but that's why I'm here.' Melanie produced a thick brown envelope from her Gucci handbag and handed it to Kidston. 'This is long overdue.'

'I told you when we divorced I didn't want any of your money.'

'You gave me that first £5,000 when I opened the first shop. I said I'd repay it, so there it is, with a little bit extra, as a thank you.'

'How much?'

'Eight thousand pounds in total.'

'Whoa, way too much. But wait, that's a grand for every year we were married. Is that how you calculated it? Compensation?'

'It's long overdue and I needed to get it off my conscience. You know I hate being in debt.'

'Technically it wasn't a debt. It was a gift.'

'Down, girl.' Melanie scooted Tallulah off the sofa, sidled over to Kidston and kissed him lightly on the cheek. 'Well, I'm gifting it back with interest. Thank you. Have you made your bed yet?'

He recognised a familiar twinkle in her eyes. 'What are you after?'

'I was hoping to seduce you and drop the cash on the bed, but if you're too knackered...'

Her smile was hard to resist but Kidston would pass – this time. 'I thought we were going to stop all this?' Visits like this had become code for catch-up sex. They'd both agreed that it had to stop but, in the absence of other partners, it had continued as an occasional and enjoyable distraction.

'We do need to stop,' she replied. 'But as long as neither of us is seeing anyone.'

'Still no one on the horizon for you?' Kidston asked.

'Nah, too set in my ways now,' Melanie replied. They sat side by side on the sofa. 'I tell them early I've no interest in kids and that seems to cool their jets.'

'I suppose we're at an age where we bring a lot of baggage,' Kidston said.

'What about Grace? I always thought you two would work together.'

'She's my best friend. She held me together after our split and she works damn hard to make sure the job doesn't consume me.' Kidston adjusted his position so he could see her face. 'I was at one of her Opry gigs last night until I got called away to that shout on the Erskine Bridge. Great set, they're a really tight band and you know she can sing.'

'Star-struck or love-struck? Come on, Luc, you know you two still love each other.'

'We both came through bad marriage break-ups. Grace's was horrendous. Neither of us was exactly looking to jump into another big relationship.'

'Seriously,' Melanie continued. 'With all the stuff you two do together; movies, gigs, tennis, you sound more like a couple than most of the couples I know. If I'm honest, I was always a bit jealous of what you two had.'

'All ancient history. We had our chance and we blew it. Or at least I blew it.'

'But you'll always love her.'

'Yes, but not in the way you're thinking.'

Melanie smiled. 'You should give each other another chance.'

Kidston kissed his ex-wife goodbye at the door. She would be hurt by his knock-back, but she would be even more wounded when she discovered that he'd slipped the cash envelope back into her designer handbag before she left. He wondered about Mel's attempts at matchmaking but he'd learned a long time ago that the universe was indifferent to his marriage break-up and his complicated love life.

Kidston sprawled back on the sofa trying to remember what a good night's sleep felt like. There was a lot to think about. Harry Thompson's statement about the Erskine Bridge incident would be supported by the cops on the cordon. If only Russell Maitland had waited, they'd have gotten him off the bridge safely. There would be talk about a jumper. The inaccuracy would be irksome, and it would be a stain on his reputation, but he knew he'd given the incident his best shot.

Kidston's thoughts turned to the Kennedy arrest. The

anonymous telephone call bothered him. It placed a huge question mark over Paul Kennedy's character. Had Kennedy told him the truth? He put himself in Miller's shoes. With honest reflection, in all the same circumstances, and ignoring the fact that it was one of his detectives, he'd have followed the same detention and arrest procedures. But the little voice in his head niggled at him: there was no confession. He'd looked straight into Paul Kennedy's eyes and given him the chance to own up to his guilt.

But still that little voice said *leave it*; wait for Ellie Hunter to wake up, let the fiscal or a jury decide what happened. Grappling with his motivation for getting involved in the case, Kidston realised that he had no choice. In a situation like this, someone like Kennedy would confess his guilt. He would assume the girl would wake up and tell them what happened. Why prolong the agony? Why delay the inevitable? Was it blind faith, optimism, naivety in the extreme, or was it an acting masterclass?

Kidston thought about the risks of his planned course of action and working against Miller. There was no way they'd both come out of this as winners; reputations and careers were on the line, and there could be no tie. One of them would be damaged irretrievably. Miller would be enjoying the fact that it was one of his guys who had been arrested; it might even have provided extra impetus. Could Miller's schadenfreude undermine his case?

## 13

Monday

Barry Rodgers was very uncomfortable. Monday mornings in the CID room would usually be buzzing as detectives caught themselves up with the crimes and misdemeanours of the weekend. Police incidents vied with football results and social engagements as the chatter jumped from one topic to the next. Monday day shifts meant that, except for late-shift and night-shift detectives, the full CID team was present. Today, the office was noisier than normal as the news about the Kennedy arrest filtered through. Rodgers was being sought out by his colleagues but was under strict instruction not to talk about it. 'The boss is going to hold a briefing,' he explained. The clamour for more information added to the noise in the room.

But they would wait.

John Wylie, the senior detective sergeant, held court meantime, in his role of investigations manager. There were the usual serious assaults, stabbings, sexual assaults and high value housebreakings to be allocated and Wylie relished his role as he assigned crime reports for investigation. But the Kennedy arrest loomed large in the room, hanging in the air like a nasty odour. Could it be true – one of their own was in custody for attempted murder?

Rodgers saw the sour glance directed at him by Wylie.

The buzz and chatter in the room quietened down as Kidston entered. Telephone calls were suspended to be returned later, detectives swung around in their chairs, facing away from their desks to hear what *the boss* had to say. Kidston always commanded a room, but the anticipation was at a higher level than usual. A low hum of expectation pulsated through the CID office as Wylie offered a confirmatory nod to his inspector.

Rodgers' stomach churned as Kidston took up his favoured position in the centre of the room and scanned the group of detective officers, which in addition to DS Wylie, included DS Gregor Stark, DS Sally Draper, DC Alison Metcalfe, DC Anthony 'Zorba' Quinn, and DC Robyn 'Mork' Williams.

'Good morning, all. DS Wylie has informed me that today's enquiries have all been allocated but I need ten minutes of your time.' Kidston footered with his cufflinks as he spoke. 'Everyone knows by now that DC Paul Kennedy was arrested in the early hours of Saturday morning and has been charged with attempted murder. He did a lie-in over the weekend and will appear at Glasgow Sheriff Court later today.'

There were some whispered mutterings across the room.

'I want to take a few minutes to separate the facts from the fiction. I need this to stay tight, people. Paul is one of our own and I don't want scuttlebutt in the station or between here and Paisley division. I'm expecting him to be remanded in custody at Barlinnie.'

There were audible gasps as the enormity of the news sank in.

'Holy fuck.'

'Jesus, imagine one of us going to Barlinnie.'

Kidston motioned for silence and continued, 'The victim is a twenty-two-year-old woman named Ellie Hunter. She's a baker from Pollok and is currently in a coma in the Royal Alexandra Hospital in Paisley. At one point we didn't expect her to survive the weekend. Currently her condition remains critical but stable. When I visited Paul in the early hours of Saturday, he was very calm, obviously distraught but relatively hopeful given his situation–'

'He'll be distraught now, heading to the Big Hoose.' It was a typical intervention from DS Wylie, an officer renowned for his caustic sense of humour. Nobody laughed. Wylie was trying to lighten the atmosphere, but his use of Barlinnie's nickname was off colour. Kidston caught the eye of his DS with a withering look.

'DC Rodgers is a witness in this case and let me be clear: I don't want everyone pestering him about what happened on Friday night. I would like Barry to say a few words about what he can speak to. Barry...'

A sheepish Barry Rodgers spun his office chair around so everyone could see and hear him. He wondered if Kidston was making him do this as some form of punishment. Kennedy was one of the DI's favourites, something of a protégé, but it was hardly his fault that he was locked up. He was wearing a mid-green, double-breasted suit with a pale-yellow shirt and a floral tie. As he looked around the room, he couldn't help noticing the number of detectives dressed in dark business suits. It was a Kidston thing and before that it had been a Sawyers thing. Clones, Wylie called them. In Rodgers' days in the cloth, detectives were glad to get out of wearing black serge and white shirts and add some colour to their gear. This new breed was so fuckin' corporate-looking and much too funereal for Rodgers' tastes.

Rodgers swallowed hard and related the Friday night encounter, omitting the fact he had intercourse with Clare Travers. He described the front seat, back seat arrangement and told his rapt colleagues how Ellie Hunter decided to leave the car and go for a walk. He estimated that Kennedy hung back for a minute or two, complaining about the freezing cold night, before realising his only other option was to sit and watch.

Rodgers' discomfort was clear. This was not an easy address for him to deliver. He told the group that he assumed Kennedy would catch her up quickly but no one in the car was certain what direction Hunter had set off in. He recounted how both he and Travers had joked about Hunter's non-appearance, expecting her to materialise behind Kennedy, who looked surprised to find that she wasn't already in the car.

Rodgers emphasised that Kennedy had told him he hadn't seen Hunter since she left the car.

'But neither you nor the girl Travers can speak to that?' It was Wylie, voicing what everyone in the room was thinking.

'And that's the problem, John. I can only speak to what she speaks to. We were together the whole time until we found Hunter.' Rodgers looked crushed.

'Is there anything else that might help us understand what happened?' asked Kidston.

'Travers was unperturbed by the thought of her friend walking home from the middle of nowhere on a freezing cold night. She said she did flaky things like that all the time. It was only when we found her lying in the lay-by that she lost her shit.' Rodgers grimaced before he continued. 'She was frozen when we found her lying there. I honestly thought she was dead. When I looked for a pulse, I noticed that there were multiple scars, old scarring, across her veins. Same on both wrists. Paul noticed, too, and we gave each other a look. He found a pulse in her neck and got some blood on her jacket collar from a nick on his hand.'

There was a collective sharp intake of breath at the mention of the bloodstain. The detectives knew this looked bad for Kennedy.

'In essence, this is the statement Barry gave to Ronnie Miller,' Kidston said. Rodgers gave an embarrassed nod to his boss. 'Travers' statement will cover the same ground, but she's jumped to the belief that our colleague attacked her friend.'

'The same belief as DI Miller?' It was Wylie again.

'Given the witnesses, the forensics and the close time frame, it's probably the call we would all make.' Kidston pulled at his cufflinks. Rodgers had seen him do it many times when he was in serious mode. 'In a situation like this someone like Paul Kennedy would admit their guilt, offer some explanation by way of mitigation. Paul is sticking to his story; he's not admitted it and I don't expect him to confess.'

'Where does that leave us, boss?' asked DS Stark.

'Well, Gregor, in an ideal world, Ellie Hunter wakes up, remembers everything and fully exonerates Paul. But, if we flip that, the prosaic fact of the matter is that she succumbs and he's facing a murder charge with no alibi and strong evidence against him.' Kidston outlined the dilemma that had disturbed his sleep over the weekend.

'She could have been hit by a car or just slipped on the ice,' DS Stark replied.

'That was something I put to Paul on Saturday morning,' Kidston continued. 'He reckons that three or four cars passed him going towards Stewarton but can't recall makes or models or plates because of the dark. DI Miller has his suspect locked up and we can't change that. He has the evidence he needs for his case and we won't be able to influence another division's investigation. However, if anyone can think of anything that might help Paul's case, please come and see me.'

'So you think he's innocent?' It was Wylie again.

'Innocent until proven guilty was what I was taught at Tulliallan.'

Kidston called the gathering to a close and returned to his own office. He sank back into his chair, John Wylie's question running through his head. It was the same question Ronnie Miller had asked. *So you think he's innocent?*

# 14

'Can I have a quick word please, boss?'

Kidston signalled DC Alison Metcalfe to close the door and ushered her to one of the two chairs in front of his desk.

'Can I speak frankly?'

'When do you not speak your mind, Alison?' Metcalfe was a seasoned DC, one of a group that smashed through the glass ceiling for women appointed as detectives. With her preference for short, cropped hair, smart business suits and sensible heels, Metcalfe had won a reputation for being tough, dogged and pragmatic. But she'd had to fight for equal status in a male-dominated CID. She and Kidston went back a long way.

'This is some business. First up: that clown Rodgers. He's been leading young Kennedy astray since his divorce. He's looking for a shagging partner and Kennedy's engaged to Sandra Holt. He's out for an after-work drink but his mad shagger of a neighbour's always looking to hook up.' Metcalfe's exasperation was evident, and Kidston let her go on. 'Ironically, Medallion Man can't even offer him an alibi or any defence. What're the chances for Paul?'

'They're bleak, Alison, very bleak. Ronnie Miller's got a body, he's got his witnesses and the evidence he needs. He'll not get a confession, but it will go to a jury because the fiscal will run it. It's a perfect storm.'

'Can we do anything?'

'It's in the hands of the procurator fiscal and they'll need to go full tilt on the prosecution. There can be no suspicion of half measures or going easier because the accused's a detective. Plus, the chief constable, ACC Colquhoun and Joe Sawyers will all be looking at this in forensic detail. Just imagine the media shitstorm when it gets out.'

'There must be something we can do,' DC Metcalfe said.

'Alison, we need to at least consider the possibility Paul is guilty. I'm not saying that's what I believe but we need to keep an open mind.'

'I don't believe that for one minute. Surely, there must be something we can do,' DC Metcalfe persisted.

'I've been thinking a lot about that. I can't be seen to be doing anything overt, and officially I've been warned off by Sawyers.' Kidston smiled. 'So he's got full deniability if I fuck this up.'

'If we fuck this up.' Alison Metcalfe pointed to the switch on the wall that operated the red, engaged light outside Kidston's office door. 'Can I light this for a few minutes? I'm going to tell you something.'

'Yeah, sure.' Kidston was intrigued.

'I know you don't approve of office romances but around three-and-a-half years ago, before he linked up with Sandra Holt, I had a brief relationship with Paul. It lasted around four months and I can tell you there's no way he would attack or take advantage of a woman. He's a genuine, decent guy. In many ways too good for the CID. I always thought this department would destroy him. As far as I know, no one from here knows about it.'

'Okay.' Kidston took in the news. 'Well done keeping it under the radar. I certainly never knew.'

'I think he was scared of you finding out. Worried that you'd transfer him out of the team. He looks up to you a lot. Hated the idea of disappointing you.'

'So you're speaking to his character?'

'Yes, and the way he treats a woman, romantically and physically. He never pushed anything, very gentle, a very considerate lover.' Metcalfe cradled her forehead. 'You know this is difficult for me, right? There's a sixteen-year age gap between us but he handled that brilliantly.'

Kidston looked at his colleague. 'So you were quite taken?' She appeared much younger than her years and had worn her blonde hair short for as long as he'd known her. With her androgynous build, clear blue eyes and prominent cheekbones, she was a striking woman.

'We never got to that stage but yes, I was falling for him. Even a woman at my age, who should know better.'

'Should I be questioning your impartiality as a character witness?' Kidston teased.

'You've always trusted my judgement in the past, Luc.' Metcalfe smiled. The two detectives had started out in CID at the same time and had worked many cases together.

Kidston leaned back in his chair, his fingers steepled under his chin. 'Okay, we need one more to make this an effective unit. Who else can we trust to work under the radar on this?'

'How about Gregor or Sally?' They've both got a high regard for Paul and believe he's innocent. It can't be John Wylie or Barry Rodgers. They'd be about as covert as a giant pink flying elephant.'

Kidston laughed at the colourful metaphor and considered the merits, characteristics and current workloads of his detectives. Rodgers was a definite no; he was already mired in it and would be a witness for the crown.

'Gregor's working with me on the sword attack. The media are all over that one, calling it "The Gorbals Samurai", would you believe? Sally Draper's a career officer. Will she be comfortable working off the books?'

'I'm sure she'll be sound.'

'Okay, I'll speak to her, and get her thoughts. I wouldn't like her to feel she's been ambushed by the two of us. Can you send her in please?'

Kidston considered the character support Metcalfe had just given to Paul Kennedy. It contrasted starkly with the anonymous call he'd received on Saturday morning. Metcalfe's motives were clearer, she was supporting a colleague she'd just revealed to be her ex-lover. Alison Metcalfe was an experienced detective and nobody's pushover. Kidston had relied on her professional judgement on numerous investigations, but he recognised the potential bias in this instance.

DS Sally Draper took the seat vacated by DC Metcalfe. She was considered a high-flyer with a background in specialist child protection work and headquarters' postings in crime policy, working closely with the big bosses in CID and the executive corridor of Pitt Street. She was a tall and slender redhead, her height disguised by her liking for sensible, flat work shoes.

Draper was riding the wave of cultural change that was sweeping through policing. Equal opportunities were driving shifts in policy, particularly changes around gender inequality. ACC Colquhoun's agenda for change was not only focused on tenure but also a major drive to increase the number of female detectives. Sally Draper was an intelligent woman; she could see that the age of the dinosaur was coming to an end. Relics like John Wylie belonged to a different time. He'd insisted on calling her 'hen' when they first worked together. The practice stopped after she reprimanded him for his politically incorrect language.

Kidston recalled the spat between Wylie and Draper as she settled into the chair. Maybe she would be a bad choice for this kind of task, but he would sound her out... gently.

'What's your take on Paul's arrest?' Kidston asked.

'To be honest, I'm disappointed in his behaviour,' she replied. 'Out on the pull, six months before his wedding to Sandra. She'd be quite entitled to kick him into touch.'

'Do you think he's the type of character who would leave an injured woman lying at the side of the road, in the freezing cold?'

'Is he a love cheat? Yes, but that's the way of the world in CID. Do I think he's a sexual predator? No. But I'm a detective. I'm trained to keep an open mind and at least consider the possibility Paul did this.'

'I just said the same thing to Alison. I'm not blind to the possibility, but I spoke to him, Sally. I told him to confess. All of my instincts tell me he never did it.'

'You think we're looking at a potential miscarriage of justice?'

'I do, and it doesn't sit well with me.' Kidston didn't sugar-coat what he wanted to ask of her. 'This conversation never happened. What I'm about to propose to you is high risk, completely unauthorised and could get everyone involved into serious bother. I want you to assist me investigating the Dams incident and see if there's any other line of enquiry that might take us away from Paul Kennedy.'

'Can I think about it?' Draper asked.

Her hesitation threw him. 'Of course, but I need to know by close of play today.'

'Would it help you?'

'It would be a great help. With the sword attack and all the other stuff going on, I'm going to need a small team to work on this. However, if you're uncomfortable with the nature of the enquiry, no harm, no foul, I'll ask one of the others.'

'I've thought about it. I'll do it.' Draper smiled at him. 'You believe he's innocent and I'm willing to back your judgement.'

'Thanks, Sally. I'll take any backlash, all of the heat if it misfires. You and anyone else will be following lawful orders from me and following my direction. Complete discretion required.'

'It's the right thing to do,' she replied. 'I understand the need for discretion.'

'I don't want you having any run-ins with DI Miller. If he comes up, you need to refer him to me. Is that understood?'

'Totally, boss.' Draper knew Miller's reputation.

'It'll be you, me, and Alison Metcalfe. We'll meet back here this afternoon, once Paul's had his court committal. We'll need to confirm that he's being remanded. I can't imagine there's any way he'll be granted bail.'

As she left the room, Kidston saw her smile. She looked pleased to be part of his clandestine enquiry. Draper and Metcalfe were the only two women in the Gorbals CID team. The numbers were similar in the other stations; women detectives remained something of a rarity across the force.

Kidston sat alone in his office rubbing his temples. He pushed his hands back through his hair. The red *do not disturb* light was still on and he didn't switch it off as he sat back in his chair. He had just enlisted two colleagues to work on an unauthorised, parallel investigation into a major, high-profile case. A case that may yet end up with a police officer being charged with murder.

The way Alison Metcalfe had spoken about her colleague had helped Kidston make his mind up. He'd need to be careful. Softly-softly and all that. Two women had so far come forward to speak to Kennedy's good character. A mysterious anonymous call had hinted at some dark deeds in the detective's past but hadn't provided hard evidence of bad character. He would want more on that front. Sally was more sceptical than Alison or Sandra Holt, but that was a good thing; she would counterbalance any bias. As ever, he would rely on his own gut instincts and his own judgement. The young detective he knew didn't seem capable of the act he was accused of, but Kidston had been wrong before. And besides, how well did he really know Paul Kennedy? The biggest challenge he faced was the lack of any credible, alternative lines of inquiry, but he wouldn't be giving up so easy.

For Kidston, policing wasn't about the simplistic, polarised extremes often represented. That missed the light and shade of police work. It was never all virtuous morals versus dark intent, but more about the grey areas that endured between the lines and limits of good and bad, right and wrong. Sawyers had taught him that 'truth' was a singular concept; all other accounts were perceptions or versions. Mistruths. The search for truth – amidst the various, competing and conflicting versions that are presented – was the most difficult aspect of an investigating detective's work.

The Kennedy case had sent his own moral compass spinning out of control. He was not a natural rulebreaker; shortcuts weren't his thing. *Let the evidence fall where it may.* Kidston was an evidence man, no matter how long it took to collate it. Experience had taught him not to rely on abstract intangibles such as luck, coincidences or hope.

For someone like Ronnie Miller, the end always justified the means. Miller was blinded by his obsession with results. Kidston asked himself one simple question: if he'd arrested one of Miller's team, would he be questioning the sufficiency of evidence, the suitability of the suspect or the fitness of the charges being brought? He didn't much like the answer he came up with.

Setting aside the personal dislike and mistrust the two men held for each other, there was enough evidence for a case against his young colleague. Even if Ellie Hunter did wake up, she may have serious brain damage or amnesia. In the absence of miracles, Paul Kennedy may be reliant on a judge and jury to believe his version of the truth.

## 15

---

The man who the *Sunday Mail* had dubbed The Gorbals Samurai stood in front of the full-length bedroom mirror, admiring the taut muscle and sinew of his lean body. It was a physique honed by long hours of dedication, harsh discipline and military training. The tattoo emblazoned on his muscular chest read '*Legio Patria Nostra*'. His long, chestnut-brown hair was tied back, fashioned into something between a ponytail and a topknot and he was naked except for the braided *sageo*, belted around his waist, that held the *saya*, or scabbard of his katana.

He drew his sword from the *saya* and swept it back in one continuous move. The *sayabiki*. He would repeat this manoeuvre again and again until he'd perfected it. It looked good, fluid and clean. He could wield the sword with one hand or both and had the strength and fluidity in his wrists to arc his katana overhead into an expert downstroke.

The name in the newspaper had not been part of his plan. It was more of a throwaway comment and he found it amusing that Colin Watters had passed it to the press. He hadn't expected a front-page headline. The publicity concerned him; it might mean that the police would be more engaged in seeking him out. That might make it more difficult to carry out his plan.

After his attack on Watters, he'd experienced an exhilarating high. The method and location had worked out exactly as planned. Punishment by amputation was preordained; the penalty fit the crime. He'd thought about killing Watters. He knew his sword could have cleaved the drug dealer's head clean off, but he had no desire for murder; only vengeance. Murder was too good for the likes of Watters and Canavan. He preferred that their chosen punishments would echo through their lifetimes. He heard the news reports and read in the Sunday papers about doctors managing to reattach Watters' hand. He hadn't factored the skill of the surgeons into his planning. He would need to make some adjustments next time. On his bed lay a Glasgow *A to Z* street guide with several pages marked in coloured highlighter pen.

He smiled at the picture tacked onto the mirror; it was of a young woman of twenty-six with long brown hair, big hazel eyes and an enchanting smile. Carefully peeling the photograph off the mirror, he gently kissed the smiling face before returning it to its original position. He watched himself in the mirror. The katana was wielded expertly, his practice strokes performed with a satisfying flourish. He shouted a loud, emphatic '*kiai*' as he cut and thrust at an imaginary opponent.

Like all the great swords he'd read about in mythology, literature and history, he wanted to name his katana. Like *Excalibur* or *Durendal* – the sword of Charlemagne's paladin Roland that was said to have been passed through the ages by Hector of Troy – or the great Islamic scimitar *Zulfiqar*, one of the swords of the prophet. He'd even visited the Wallace Monument in Stirling and seen the massive two-handed claymore now known as the Wallace Sword. His magnificent katana wasn't a cheap replica bought in a high-street shop; it was the real thing, forged by tempered and folded steel. A replica samurai wouldn't cut through butter, whereas this sword had easily severed the hand of a drug dealer.

He liked the name *Dojigiri*, or *Monster Slayer*, from the tenth century clan Minamoto, one of the most renowned samurai swords in history.

He'd taken care of one monster.

Canavan would be next.

His katana was a sword of vengeance.

He would call it Revenger.

## 16

'Zorba, your detection rates for January are well down, son,' Wylie announced as the detectives returned to their desks after their lunchtime card school. 'You'll need to seriously up your game this month if you want to stay in the premier league.'

'Remember, gaffer, I was at Tulliallan on a training course.' The young DC wasn't impressed by his DS singling him out for criticism, especially in front of his colleagues. He should have expected it after beating Wylie in a tight game of nominations whist.

'Well, Anthony, that's fewer CRs allocated, so if anything, your numbers should go up.'

Joe Sawyers had introduced CID league tables across the division. It allowed the management team to look at detection rates across the various crime categories and more importantly, individual detective officers. Kidston was a fan because it offered an at-a-glance summary of who was pulling their weight and who wasn't.

Wylie, who wasn't a fan, was key to the entire process in his role as crime allocator; if criminal enquiries weren't assigned on a fair and equitable basis, an officer could see his percentage numbers drop. Too many dead-end enquiries, with no likelihood of a detection could bring down a detective's stats. The fear for some detectives was bosses tying in performance figures with the dreaded tenure; an excuse to bounce a detective back to uniform. Wylie assigned crime reports – CRs – as he saw fit. He allocated the most easily detectable ones to either himself, his own group of detectives or his favourites. The 'deaders', with no witnesses, no suspects, or no forensics were dealt to those who'd pissed him off most recently. Zorba wouldn't be complaining too much.

DC Anthony Quinn, known as 'Zorba', had been awarded the label by Wylie, the self-appointed curator of nicknames and it was based on Hollywood actor Anthony Quinn's starring role in *Zorba the Greek*. The young DC was so enamoured of his new name that he signed his notes with a solitary florid 'Z'. Nicknames formed a significant element of police humour, with officers allocated new handles based on acts or omissions, physical or behavioural characteristics or in the case of Zorba and his neighbour, Robyn 'Mork' Williams, similarities with celebrity names. Wylie also had a nickname for Sally Draper. He called her 'Red Beaver' – but never to her face.

Zorba was too early in his CID career to fret about tenure; he had other things to worry about. He'd struggled with the transition from uniform to CID and the move to a new station, having worked as a cop in the Rutherglen office. It felt like starting over again. And he'd clashed with Wylie over football.

The first litmus test for any new cop was the Rangers or Celtic question. With one of the fiercest rivalries in world football, fans of the two Glasgow giants tended to divide along religious lines. As a devout Catholic and a fervent Celtic fan, Zorba never hid his allegiance. Some colleagues chose to feign non-interest in the game or claim one of the 'neutral' Glasgow teams like Partick Thistle or Queen's Park. It was an indicator of the ferocity of Glasgow's religious sectarianism.

Wylie was Rangers; a dyed-in-the-wool bluenose who enjoyed his football banter. Zorba had accused him of crossing the line with comments he'd made about bead-rattlers and Taigs. Wylie had attempted to play it down, but Kidston had been alerted to their blow up and had laid down the law: banter was acceptable – anything with religious overtones was not. Kidston wasn't into football but made it clear he had zero tolerance for bigotry.

Wylie viewed it as another sign of the creeping political correctness that was ruining the job, but he would mind his language.

CID folklore told of an era when Wylie went by the nickname 'Mr Bojangles', a reference to the song of the same name that was his chosen party piece as a young detective. The name had faded, and it seemed such an unfitting tag for Wylie's current persona that it was unlikely to be resurrected.

DS Gregor Stark, who sometimes went by 'Starky', saved his young colleague any further tongue lashing from Wylie with the announcement he made as he hung up the phone. 'I've got a slot later this afternoon to interview Watters.'

'The DI has the Watters enquiry.' Wylie reminded his fellow sergeant of the allocation.

'He's asked me to work on it with him.' The young DS seemed pleased to announce this to his colleagues, viewing it as a vote of confidence in him, for what was sure to be a high-profile enquiry. In typical tabloid style, the *Sunday Mail* had carried a front-page headline: 'Gorbals Samurai Sword Attack.' The story had described the suspect as a masked assailant. The article's speculation around possible drugs feuds was making the big bosses in Pitt Street very nervous.

Wylie's curiosity was piqued by Stark's comments. Kidston

had spent much of the morning locked in his office with Draper and Metcalfe, or Cagney and Lacey as he referred to them. He had little time for his female colleagues; Metcalfe had way too much to say for herself and he suspected she was probably a dyke. Draper was another high-flyer who wouldn't be around too long as she shagged her way to her next promotion. Whatever these two bitches were cooking up with Kidston, he would get to the bottom of it.

Wylie was forty-seven and had come up through a CID where page three pictures of topless women were part of the office surroundings. There were very few women detectives back in those early days, and that's how Wylie liked it. He did a bad job of hiding his attitude to women, a fact that did not endear him to female colleagues. Wylie was feeling the icy blast of the winds of change, losing touch with the rapidly shifting culture of policing and policy changes within the CID.

If his colleagues had to sum up DS John Wylie in three words, there was a fair chance 'moaning', 'faced', and 'bastard' would feature prominently. Once feted as a dogged investigator and thief-taker, Wylie was now coasting in the detective sergeant rank that he'd been stuck in for eleven years. With career advancement passing him by, he was now known more for bitching about junior colleagues overtaking him in the promotion stakes and ranting at senior management for broken promises.

The Watters enquiry had potential to be a huge investigation. Wylie felt it was unlikely to be an isolated incident. If the division had a drugs feud, there would be more attacks. Revenge and retribution were core beliefs for drug dealers. 'You hit us, and we hit you back.'

'I'll go with you to the hospital, Gregor. You'll need a neighbour.' Wylie was in two minds, as he'd hoped to slip away to the bookies and catch a swift half at the Elizabethan at lunchtime, but this would keep him in the loop. Wylie viewed the young DS as a Sawyers/Kidston clone, copying their style of dress, their speech and mannerisms. In truth, Wylie considered his fellow sergeant too young and inexperienced for the rank, but he couldn't criticise his work ethic.

The hospital was expecting the CID's visit and the detectives were met by the smiling, businesslike manner of ward sister Kitty Kelly at the nursing station. She stressed that thirty minutes, no more, had been allocated with her patient. In the presence of so many pretty nurses, Wylie sucked in his gut and constantly ran his fingers over his forehead, attempting to cover his Bobby Charlton comb-over. Stark's vanity took the shape of straightening his tie, smiling at nurses and preening himself in any available reflective surface. One was as bad as the other.

The sister escorted the two detectives to a private side room where they found Watters sitting up in bed. He was dressed in a hospital-issue gown, his right hand wrapped in a heavy dressing and resting in a medical sling attached to the bed. Watters rubbed at the heavy stubble on his chin with his good hand.

'How are you feeling today, Colin? Great news that the surgeons managed to save your hand.' Stark was keen to establish a positive tone from the outset.

'I'm a wee bit out of it to be fair... The drugs 'n' that. I'm not sure I can help youse guys too much.' Watters had spent a lifetime not co-operating with the police.

'I understand that, Colin. We've got the initial statement you gave to the officers on Friday night. We need to go over that with you.' Stark had Watters' first statement attached to a clipboard along with two pages of drugs convictions. 'This description you gave: you stated you don't know your attacker.'

'No idea. The guy was in a hoodie, wearing a tammy and a polo neck or a scarf or something covering half his face. Long, black leather coat. Scary motherfucker... fast... bright blue eyes.' Watters was repeating his previous version.

'But why, Colin? Why would someone attack you like that? We know your criminal history.' Wylie pointed to the papers affixed to Stark's clipboard. 'We know you work for Canavan. You can't expect us to believe this was some completely random thing. Who have you fallen out with?'

'Honest,' Watters continued. 'If I knew who done this to me, I would tell youse. I want him jailed. Bastard ambushed me when I was half-cut.'

Wylie bit his tongue so hard he could taste blood. His joke could wait.

'But he knew where you lived. He had a Glasgow accent. He knows you so you better not be holding out on us, Colin.' Wylie pushed it a bit more, but he felt the urge to grab hold of his heavily bandaged hand and twist it until the little drug-dealing bastard gave up what he knew.

'What about the sword?' Stark asked. 'You told the guy from the *Sunday Mail* something about the sword. Where does this "Gorbals Samurai" patter come from? Do you know what a samurai sword looks like?'

'He said "I'm the Gorbals Samurai" just after he done me,' Watters disclosed. He wouldn't give up the threat against Canavan. That wouldn't be a police matter.

'So not a big "steakie" or a cleaver or a scimitar; the sword had a curve?' Stark probed further.

'Look, I know fuck-all about swords. It was a long, curved, shiny fucker. He pulled it out of a sparkly silver sheath thing. I'm still having nightmares about it.'

They left it at that and reported to the nursing station. The interview had lasted just over thirty minutes. Stark quizzed

Sister Kelly as they were leaving. 'What's the prognosis for our man?'

'The operation was successful inasmuch as he has two hands again. However, there's a chance his right hand will never fully function. Microsurgery is a comparatively new procedure. The tendons and nerve endings may never fully heal. He'll no doubt learn to do most things left-handed, but his other hand will feel like a zombie limb. I've seen it a few times. Sad, but there you go.'

As they walked back to the dark blue Mini Metro parked in a restricted hospital zone, Wylie quizzed Stark about Kidston's absence.

'He's doing something with Sally and Alison. Urgent thing for headquarters to do with recruiting more women detectives.'

'Really?' Wylie shot a sceptical glance. 'Must be urgent and very important for him to skip this enquiry.'

'Trusts me to get on with it. I'll bring him up to speed.' Stark smiled.

As they sat in the car, Wylie started to roll a cigarette from the tin he carried. He was known for his brown, liquorice-flavoured rolling papers, and made such a palaver of collecting the Golden Virginia shag that colleagues were unlikely to tap him for a smoke. Stark, a zealous non-smoker, wound down the driver's window before setting off. The distinctive aroma of Wylie's roll-ups couldn't mask the nicotine smell and Stark despaired as smoke wafted through the car.

'Shut that window, it's Baltic,' Wylie ordered.

'I'll close it when you've finished your cancer stick.'

Stark never took any snash from Wylie. He looked at his older colleague and the trail of fag ash collecting on the lapels of his camel coat. His rheumy eyes looked to have borne the brunt of his nicotine and alcohol lifestyle. Wylie's shambling appearance had gotten worse in the last year. He'd piled on weight; his current suit was at least one size too small. He'd grown his hair longer to disguise his thinning mane. His lunchtime visits to the pub and the bookie had become more frequent. After the pub, Wylie smelled of his favourite Gold Spot breath freshener, masking the stench of whisky and clashing against the waning protection of his Brut aftershave. Stark wondered if, despite all his talk of promotion, Wylie had chucked it and just given up on the job.

Wylie took a long draw on his roll-up and, with a slow exhale, wound his window down enough to flick the butt end out. Stark reciprocated by winding up the driver's window.

'As suspected, Watters doesn't know the difference between a meat cleaver, a steakie, or an ornamental cutlass,' Stark said. 'It's down to how his attacker described himself.'

'So a real samurai sword?'

'It must be to do damage like that.'

'But he was only half-cut.' A sniggering Wylie had waited for his moment. 'Laugh? I thought my knickers would never dry in.'

'Boom, boom.' Stark laughed. 'I think this is personal. A drug dealer attacked by a sword, it's got to be a revenge thing, someone with a vendetta. I think we've got a vigilante on our hands.'

'You read too many comics, Gregor.'

'I've told you before, they're graphic novels,' said an indignant Stark.

Wylie lifted his left arse cheek off the car seat and blasted out a noisy fart. 'Ooft, sorry, Kemosabe, that's rancid. I'm Abraham Lincoln.' Glasgow rhyming slang formed a key component of Wylie's comedy repertoire. Stark had heard most of the terms and knew the slang for stinkin'.

'For fuck's sake, John, I think something has crawled up your arse and died.' Stark rolled down the driver's window immediately. Wylie followed suit in a gesture of conciliation.

Once the air purity was restored to a breathable level, the two detective sergeants closed the car windows and returned to discussing the case.

'Do you intend to interview Phil Canavan?' Wylie asked.

'The DI's keen to trace him but he's gone to ground,' Stark replied.

'Could be someone's out to get him? Could still be a feud.'

'Or another revenge attack. He might be lying dead somewhere. Bladed by the same guy who did Watters.'

'We can only hope.' Wylie laughed. The thought of a dead drug dealer elevated his mood and he broke into a well-known Glasgow street song:

*'Murder, murder, polis, three stairs up,*
*The wummin in the middle hoose hit me wae a cup,*
*Ma heed's aw broken, ma face is aw cut,*
*Murder, murder, polis, three stairs up.'*

Stark groaned at his neighbour's singing attempts and drove towards the office wondering what other ditties Wylie might unearth en route. Despite his colleague's comic turn, his thoughts would remain focused on the investigation. He would rule nothing out. The main lines of enquiry were to interview other dealers, speak to known drug users, check with other police divisions, speak to police informants and assess what came back. Every detective officer cultivated their own network of informants, known as 'touts', who would trade information for cash or favours.

For the moment, the identity of the dark-clad swordsman would remain a mystery.

# 17

D raper and Metcalfe were installed in Kidston's office. The door was closed, and the red light was on. The meeting, to discuss possible ways ahead in the Kennedy case, was restricted to the three attendees. Draper confirmed that Kennedy had been refused bail, was remanded in custody, and been taken to HMP Barlinnie.

It was a sobering thought. At the start of the year Barlinnie had seen a long-running siege in its B-hall with five prison officers taken hostage. Convicts in balaclavas and improvised hoods had got on the prison roof and hurled down slates. Fires had been started and massive damage was done to the hall. After five days the authorities negotiated a surrender. Kidston had been part of a police negotiation team advising the prison service on siege tactics.

The three detectives contemplated the immediate fate of their colleague. Prison was a hellish experience for anyone, a daunting and frightening ordeal. For a police officer it would be a living nightmare. They were in agreement: being processed through the hellhole that was Glasgow's 'Bar L', today would be the worst day of Paul Kennedy's life.

Kidston directed that no notes would be taken and there would be no use of the whiteboard on the office wall. He read out the salient points from Kennedy's statement that he'd noted on his cell visit. The two women took in Kidston's words and discussed Kennedy's version of events.

'Very similar to what Barry Rodgers gave us,' said Draper.

'Yes, but we know from Paul's account, Miller pushed for a confession and he stands up well to it.' Metcalfe offered what she saw as an important element.

'I still feel if Paul was guilty of this, he'd just put his hands up.' Kidston looked at both his colleagues. 'That's the missing piece for me. He'd be anticipating that Ellie Hunter wakes up and tells the police what happened. What do you think?'

'I agree. A clever or devious ned would just say we had a wee bit of a struggle and she lost her footing, fell and struck her head,' said Draper.

'Totally, but Paul's not a devious ned,' Metcalfe said. 'I agree, he would confess to this if he was responsible.'

'Miller's more or less ruled out a road accident. He put the traffic examiners in at first light and there's no road markings to support that theory,' said Kidston.

'Yes, basic tyre markings on the frosty road surface from Rodgers' car where it stopped on finding Ellie but no skid marks or heavy tread patterns.' Draper had been in touch with her traffic department contact.

'We know how thorough Miller is,' Kidston continued. 'He'll have looked at the timescales and distances involved. We have to assume Ellie was found at a distance within that twenty-minute return journey.'

'What else have we got to go on?' Metcalfe asked.

'One thing I discussed with Joe Sawyers on Saturday...' He paused and looked at Draper and Metcalfe. 'What if Ellie Hunter was flaky enough to get into a second car?'

'Go on,' Draper said.

'Well, if there was no RTA, we can only really argue that she slipped and fell–'

'And that would be a case of medical testimony from the defence to argue her injuries are consistent with a heavy fall,' Metcalfe interrupted.

'Exactly,' Kidston continued. 'Unless we can cast doubt that Paul wasn't the last person to see her. Maybe she accepted a lift from another man.'

'Paul and Barry both talked about other cars on the road that night, so it's a possibility,' Draper said.

'It's a hell of a long shot though.' Kidston played devil's advocate.

'Yes, but we can sit back and twiddle our thumbs and wait, hoping and praying that Ellie Hunter wakes up.' Metcalfe was more animated now. 'Or we can be more proactive and look at alternatives.'

'I'm not really one for hoping and praying. If we're not waiting it out, what else can we do?' Kidston asked.

'Can we do a vehicle check on that route around the same time as the incident? Stop cars and check out the occupants, see if they've got a record?' Metcalfe suggested.

'We'll need to use uniforms for that but it's worth a shout,' Kidston said. 'I'll see if I can recruit a couple of community cops to help out.'

'What about a lie detector test?' Draper asked.

'A polygraph? In the USA maybe but unlikely to be permitted here.' Kidston was doubtful. 'We can raise the question with Adam Sharkey, I'm not ruling anything out.'

'What about hypnotism?' Metcalfe asked. 'I believe that's been admissible evidence in other cases.'

'We can run it past Adam and get a legal view,' Kidston replied. He was pleased with the suggestions. Nothing was off the table. In a situation like this one, there were no bad ideas. He brought the meeting to a close.

On his return from the Victoria Infirmary, Wylie passed Kidston's door several times looking for an opening, keen to update his DI on the Watters interview. The red light had been on for some considerable time. He quizzed Gregor Stark.

'What's going on with the boss and Cagney and Lacey? They've been in there for ages.'

'He told me they're working on an urgent strategy paper for Q. That thing I told you about, something about recruiting more women detectives.'

'Seems to be taking up a lot of their time,' Wylie said. 'We need to update him on the hospital interview.' The older DS's annoyance was evident. He wasn't buying the cover story. Something was going on in the long, secret session behind closed doors. He was determined to get to the bottom of it.

## 18

Tuesday

The door to the second-floor tenement flat didn't look that sturdy. The two men knocking knew better; a closer examination of the door jamb revealed a steel plate fitted behind the Yale lock, offering extra security and protection. There was no nameplate but pencil markings on the fading whitewash on the adjacent wall suggested that the current inhabitant went by 'Bruce'.

'Willie Bruce, you better open this fuckin' door or I'll kick the fucker in!' The smaller of the two men was screaming through the letter box.

No response.

'Bruce, ya bam. I know you're hidin' in there. If you don't open this door, it'll go much worse for you.'

No response.

'Right, ya cunt. Phil Canavan's here. You don't want to push it that far, dae ye?'

They heard a lounge door slowly opening and light footsteps coming towards the front entrance.

'Right, Willie, open up,' the booming voice of Phil Canavan called through the open letter box. The door was cautiously opened, and the two callers pushed past a cowering Willie Bruce.

The Canavan effect. Phil Canavan offered an enduring image of one of the greatest of all Glasgow legends: the authentic hardman. Now thirty-eight, Canavan relished his hard-fought reputation as a vicious bastard. It helped when his main henchmen were thugs like Johnny Boy McManus. Tall and lean with close-cropped dark-brown hair, Canavan's defining characteristic was the two-inch scar that ran off the left side of his mouth. The deep wound from being bottled by a rival had left a ragged gouge on his otherwise handsome features. He wore his battle scar with pride; it gave him the authenticity he craved and struck fear into his enemies. And terrified debtors like Willie Bruce.

'I'm sorry, Mr Canavan. I didnae know it was you. I widnae leave you waiting.' Bruce was spluttering apologetically, his hands and elbows raised closer to his shoulders; the stance of a man who knew he was about to take a beating.

'But you'd leave me rattling your letter box all fuckin' morning, ya bam!' The smaller of the two men was Johnny Boy McManus, driver, chief enforcer and occasional bodyguard for Canavan. A squat, menacing five foot six, Johnny Boy was all-out aggression; a man who loved his work. He made his displeasure known by cracking Bruce's jaw with a forearm smash.

'I'm sorry, Johnny Boy. I hoped you'd just leave.'

'You were taking the piss.' Johnny Boy kicked Bruce the full length of his hallway and flung him onto the lounge sofa. Bruce was bigger than McManus but there was little fight in him. He looked terrified.

'You owe me three hundred nicker, Willie lad.' Canavan spoke more slowly and deliberately than the other two men.

'Two hundred, Mr Canavan. Two hundred,' Bruce stuttered, more in hope than realistic expectation. He knew he'd defaulted.

'You're late, Willie lad. Interest rates. You know how it works.'

'I havnae got it but I will get it for you. I'll have it for you soon. I promise.'

'I can't wait for one of your horses to come in, Willie lad. You'll get me a bad reputation.' Canavan nodded to McManus who slung the navy Adidas sports bag he was carrying off his shoulder onto the bare floorboards. 'What's it going to be?' There was a chilling malevolence in Canavan's smile.

'Ball-pein hammer or Hilti gun?' McManus seemed to relish either option.

'Oh, dear God! No that, please God no that!' Bruce screamed in protest.

'Go with the gun, Johnny Boy. If we smash up his hands and feet, he'll no be able to earn the money he owes me.'

'Right bucko.' McManus held down a compliant Bruce and flattened his left hand onto the floor. Bruce was sobbing uncontrollably now, blinded by tears and snotters. Canavan stood on his other arm to stop him wriggling. With a look of menacing glee, McManus shot two industrial size staples through the palm of Bruce's hand. The screams were horrendous.

'Just the one hand for now, Johnny Boy.' Canavan was in a benevolent frame of mind. 'Three hundred pounds before next Saturday, Willie lad.'

'Fuck youse,' Bruce muttered amidst his moaning. 'I'm going to get masel a guard dug.'

'A dug? You think a dug's going to stop me?' Johnny Boy stood over the groaning Bruce. 'I'll gut yer fuckin' dug. I'll slit its throat and rip its heart out. That's why they call me the Tasmanian Devil.' As a parting shot Johnny Boy wheeled around and aimed a kick at Bruce's face, catching him full on the mouth and taking out his front teeth.

They left the flat with the front door snibbed off the latch. There was a good chance a neighbour would hear his cries for help and phone an ambulance.

When Costello and McCartney arrived at Willie Bruce's home, the ambulance technician was meticulously removing the two industrial staples from the stricken man's bleeding hand with a metal tool. Neighbours had heard his cries for help and phoned 999. The two community cops weren't buying the victim's ridiculous explanation that he'd fallen.

'Where's the staple gun then, Willie?' Costello asked.

'I passed out wi' the pain,' Willie Bruce said, his mouth battered and bloody. 'Somebody must have nipped in and stole it.'

Costello looked around the flat with its bare floorboards, peeling wallpaper and threadbare old sofa. A tiny black-and-white portable TV sat on a low coffee table – no doubt to catch the horse racing. The big cop remembered that Willie Bruce had lost his job as an upholsterer a few years back and hadn't worked since.

'Who did this to you, Willie?' Costello asked. 'Do you owe Phil Canavan money?' The big cop knew the MO used by Canavan and McManus but getting victims to testify against them had always proved problematic. It was clear that Willie Bruce had no intention of discussing his predicament further with the police. Canavan and his crew ruled by fear.

'C'mon, Willie, someone has to break the cycle,' McCartney

said. 'If you make a complaint, we can at least start an investigation.'

'I've telt youse both, I fell.'

～

'Phil Canavan and Johnny Boy?' McCartney asked as they resumed their patrol duties.

'Almost certainly,' said Costello, 'that's their MO and it's likely that Willie's into the money lenders for non-payment and big interest.'

'Well, going by the flat, he's got nothing else to pawn or sell,' McCartney said, 'so he's just putting off his next beating.'

'He'll end up stealing or robbing somebody to pay off his debts or he'll move out of the area if it gets too bad.'

'Can it be any worse?'

'It can get worse than that,' Costello said. 'A lot worse.'

McCartney grimaced at the thought. 'So where does Canavan get his power?'

'Phil achieved notoriety in his youth as the leader of The Hill. There used to be massive running battles with the Gorbals gang, The Cumbie,' Costello explained. 'Essentially, you've got a young team from Govanhill versus their Gorbals enemies. The two gangs would fight with sticks, bricks, cleavers and steakies, or steak knives if you're from Bearsden.'

McCartney laughed. 'You mean a big butcher's knife, rather than the type my mum would put out for Sunday dinner?'

'Yes, the big ones.' Costello laughed. 'If The Cumbie was the home team, the battle would take place in Glasgow Green. If The Hill was hosting, it would be in Queen's Park. Innocent shoppers on Victoria Road would scatter as two tribes of youths, some of them souped-up on cheap wine, sped towards each other, brandishing their weapons on the approaches to the Queen's Park gates. It was quite a sight to behold.'

'What? You've policed those gang fights?'

'Absolutely. Often, we'd jump out of a van and they'd all disperse. I think that's what they all secretly wanted to do – run away.'

'Not Canavan?' McCartney asked.

'No, Phil had a reputation for being fearless,' Costello continued. 'He became an enforcer in his late father's money-lending business. Big Davie Canavan was a real hardman, an old-school gangster, but he was on the way out when the drug dealing was taking off. Canavan took over the south side heroin trade. He was never a user but figured out if people wanted to borrow money to pay for their drugs, it was as well to have both markets covered.'

'He can't be untouchable,' McCartney said.

'No one is,' Costello began. 'Kidston put him away a few years ago for knifing a guy. He's a blade artist; notorious for the levels of violence he inflicts on his victims.'

'And he's got that scar – bet there's a tale behind that,' said McCartney, engrossed by the story.

'When he was seventeen, after an argument over a girl, he was bottled by a rival,' Costello explained. 'A sneak attack on Canavan's blind side while he was walking home alone. The Canavan legend and his reputation as a blade artist started with his revenge attack. Glasgow gangland folklore relates a tale where a vengeful Canavan gutted his opponent with a big commando knife and left him bleeding out in a back close. The guy needed surgery to save his life.'

'A real charmer,' McCartney said.

Costello laughed. 'The thing I find strange is that he could have been legitimate by now. Before Big Davie died, Sarah Canavan, the younger sister, started to set up tanning salons. It was easy enough to launder the profits from drugs and money lending through her cash businesses. That's how they rinse the money and that's why Sarah can claim to be a respectable businesswoman.'

McCartney headed back to the station for her piece break. As a pairing they tried to stagger refreshment periods so as to maintain a uniform presence on the streets. Costello's young neighbour was a quick study; she always sought information about their policing area, people and places, past and present. Their community policing beat covered the entirety of the 'new' Gorbals. The area's evolution had subsumed the old districts of Lauriston and Hutchesontown and was now bordered east and west by Oatlands and Tradeston, and north and south by the River Clyde and by Govanhill. Costello was a proud son of the Gorbals, an area that had given the world Sir Thomas Lipton, Allan Pinkerton, Hannah Frank, Benny Lynch, Jimmy Reid and James Stokes VC. Chrissie McCartney would never get to know the Gorbals he'd grown up in. He wondered what other changes she would see in her police service.

The big community cop often reflected on the old Gorbals and the loss of place that resulted from the urban desolation and planning blight inflicted on a once vibrant community. Where had all the people gone? In his raggedy-arsed childhood, the Gorbals had been a city within a city; Cumberland Street, Caledonia Road and Crown Street had been busy thoroughfares, bustling with a variety of shops and traders, cafés, public houses and cinemas. Gorbals Cross had resembled a grand gateway to the city centre.

The ghosts of old Gorbals whispered in his ear: *where is your community?*

*Gone*, he would tell them, living in multi-storey high flats. Gone the way of the steamies or communal washhouses, visited daily by the washerwomen with their dilapidated prams piled high with laundry. The shops were gone forever, the communities of tenement dwellers that sustained them scattered to the vast housing estates on the outskirts of the city; all gone, leaving nothing behind but the whisper of dusty wind between high-rise tower blocks.

Costello played a game in his head where he tried to reimagine the narrow, sharp-cornered streets of the old Gorbals from the few remnants that survived. From the boundary walls of the sprawling Southern Necropolis you could still see the ruins of the imposing Greek Thomson church with its iconic portico and high square tower. A right turn just before the church, heading northwards, would have been the beginnings of what was once a bustling Crown Street, with the imposing Hutchesons' Grammar School and the fondly remembered George picture house, where he'd seen his first Bond movie.

Crown Street had disappeared, the roadway realigned and redesignated. No housing and no shops survived. For all the acts of municipal vandalism committed on the Gorbals, the abolition of the street was perhaps the greatest crime. Housing associations elsewhere in the city were cleaning up blackened, soot-stained buildings to extend their lives. Costello had no doubt that much of the slum clearances were necessary; the horrors of living six or eight to a room, four to a bed, with thirty people sharing an outside lavatory. These levels of poverty and squalor needed to be eradicated, but he questioned whether the city fathers had gone too far. He smiled at his attack of nostalgia for tenement life; in the original Greek, the word 'Nostos' defined the idea of returning home after a long journey, 'Algia' translated as pain. The twinge in his heart was real; he was walking the streets of his childhood, but the memories were harder to find.

## 19

Satisfied that Willie Bruce had been dealt with in an appropriate manner, Canavan's next order of business was to catch up with Colin Watters in the Victoria Infirmary. Watters looked after the drugs sales side of his business, while Johnny Boy McManus took care of money lending and enforcing debt collections. McManus doubled up as his driver and liked to class himself as his bodyguard, not that Canavan needed one.

Canavan knew the polis had been up at the hospital yesterday and the family were doing the night-time visits. He wanted to speak to his drugs lieutenant, get a sense of what might be behind the attack. He had checked with all the dealers in his network to ensure no one had got involved in a dispute. The weekend sales had all tallied and there was no word on the street about a rival muscling in. He had an understanding with the Barlanark team that they wouldn't trade south of the Clyde. He was baffled.

McManus slid the long black German saloon into a waiting space, and they found their way to the ward. Both men took a seat at Watters' bedside. Canavan dropped a punnet of grapes on the small pedestal table that hovered above the bed. It was a private room with pastel-blue décor and a personal television. The visitors were impressed. Watters was pleased to see them and eager for news.

'What the fuck, guys? What have you heard?'

'We've got nothing, no clue. Nobody's taking it,' Canavan said. 'I thought someone was moving against me but nowt doing.'

'What's the story wi' the guy that done it?' McManus asked. 'Did you no get a look at him?'

'Big lanky shite suckered me when I was half pissed. His face was covered up and he had a hoodie on. I never saw anything.' Watters shuddered at the memory. 'The fucker ran away laughing.'

'What did you tell the cops?' McManus asked.

'They were back yesterday. A bit o' pressure to spill who done it but I told them I had no clue. One thing though, Phil: he said he was coming for you next.'

'What the fuck? What do you mean?'

'Namechecked you. "Tell him the Gorbals Samurai is coming for him."'

'What about me?' McManus asked.

'Never mind you, he's no looking for you,' Canavan replied. 'Who the fuck is this guy?'

'Let's find the cunt and do him in,' McManus proposed as he munched on Watters' grapes.

'Who do we know that's into Jap swords?' Canavan was already shaking his head.

Both men offered nothing but more blank looks.

'I'll put the word out,' Canavan said. 'Make this bold cunt sorry he ever tangled with me or my team.'

## 20

Kidston took a call from Sawyers. It was what he classed as a 'good news and bad news' call. The bad news was that he was likely to lose one of his very good detective sergeants. On the plus side, Sally Draper was being offered an opportunity to take up an acting inspector role in charge of the child protection unit at force headquarters in Pitt Street. Sawyers had highlighted her suitability with her background in the specialist discipline.

She'd previously worked on a high-profile, joint police and social work task force on enhancing child protection arrangements. The task force's report, and Draper's contribution to it, had been well received by both police and social work chiefs. This was her reward and a chance to work closer to Colquhoun and the other CID bosses in FHQ. It would be for an initial period of six months with a chance, if successful, to make it substantive. Even though Draper was enjoying her stint as a divisional DS, there was no chance she would turn down an opportunity like this.

Kidston and Draper had arranged to meet Adam Sharkey at his Carlton Place offices as soon as he was clear of his trial commitments at the nearby Sheriff Court. Draper was delighted when Kidston announced the news on the drive over.

'When would I start?'

'A week on Monday but you'd be expected to drop in, spend some time with the team before that. A few hours. I expect you'll know most of them?'

'Yes, it's mostly the same small team from when I was there as DS. But I'd like to help you with the Kennedy case before I leave.'

'Of course, thanks. I'll be sorry to lose you from my team.' Kidston offered a supportive smile. 'Not just for the Kennedy thing, just overall, you've been brilliant in your time with me and it's been refreshing to have a female DS on the team.'

'Helping to flush out some of the dinosaurs?' Draper laughed as she lapped up the fulsome praise of her boss. She was still smiling at her good news when they entered Adam Sharkey's legal practice, located in a basement office a stone's throw from one of the busiest working courts in Europe.

Sharkey greeted them both warmly and showed them into his cavernous offices. His own suite was the largest room and he seated them at a dark wood conference table next to an impressive library of leather-bound law books.

Kidston knew Sharkey well. He had been a respected detective sergeant before he left the service and completed his law degree as a mature student. He'd also done a stint as a procurator fiscal, prosecuting criminal cases before turning to the 'dark side', earning a reputation as a very talented defence agent. The irony for this consult was that his client was a police detective rather than a seasoned criminal.

'What a situation. Poor Paul, but he was in reasonable spirits when I saw him yesterday.' Sharkey pulled out a legal pad and a thick mound of papers. 'No chance the fiscal was allowing bail. How did it all come to this?'

'It's a horror show. He's caught in a perfect storm,' Kidston replied. 'Thanks for taking the time to visit.'

'No worries. No way was he confessing, despite Ronnie Miller pushing it.' Sharkey had worked with Miller during his time on the job. 'We know Ronnie's relentless with a suspect.'

'I think the taped interview helped us. Ronnie's still coming to terms with the technology.' Kidston smiled. 'What's your sense of it, Adam?'

'My overall sense is that he's innocent. Whatever happened to Ms Hunter that night, it wasn't as a result of Paul Kennedy attacking her.' Sharkey doodled on his pad. 'By the way, your boy was very appreciative of your visit in the wee small hours. Took a lot of hope from that. What else have you got?'

'We're assuming worst-case scenarios here,' Kidston replied. 'Ellie never wakes up or wakes up with a severe brain injury and amnesia. Looks like a road accident has been ruled out.'

'So we argue a slip-and-fall head injury.' Sharkey played defence advocate.

'Then it's a matter of credibility for a jury – too chancy.'

'Other options?' Sharkey asked.

'Well, we met yesterday to look at possible options,' Kidston said. 'There's not too many available. We're going to conduct vehicle checks, same time, night of the week, etc.'

'Look for possible witnesses?' Sharkey asked.

'Witnesses, maybe suspects,' Kidston replied. 'The real long shots were lie detector tests or hypnosis for Paul to bolster his testimony.'

'Okay... a bit off the wall but that's good. Lie detectors are junk science, great showboating for American lawyers but no credibility or standing over here.' Sharkey continued sketching on his pad. From his upside-down view Kidston thought it looked like a large monkey's head. 'Hypnosis has some legal standing in UK courts and there is a precedent for using forensic hypnotists.'

'Could it work in this case?' Draper asked. 'We thought the cars that passed by on the night... Maybe he could remember more information, if he was in a trance.'

'I know a very good forensic hypnotist, Max Van Zandt, based in London. A colleague consulted him on a child molestation case. He put a young boy under and managed to access various repressed memories. Memory is such a complex area, but the therapy managed to gather a ream of new evidence.'

'And did it help the court case?' Draper asked.

'Well, it helped build a solid case against the accused, who was the boy's father.' Sharkey was filling in the monkey's ferocious teeth. 'In light of the fresh evidence the father hanged himself.'

'Not quite the outcome we're looking for,' Kidston said dryly.

'Do you think it's worth a try in this instance?' Draper asked.

'Worth looking at. Even if it never makes it to court it could identify other areas for you to investigate.'

Sharkey agreed to consult with Max Van Zandt to get an assessment of the case and check his availability.

When Kidston heard back from Sharkey it was another 'good news, bad news' call. Van Zandt was certain that hypnotherapy would be appropriate in the circumstances, but he wouldn't be available until Thursday. The trail on the Kennedy case was already growing cold. They were officially locked out of this investigation and there were no obvious alternative lines of enquiry. Any further delays would not be helpful to Paul Kennedy's cause.

## 21

News spread like wildfire in police stations, especially news about promotions. Wylie was in a dark mood, avoiding Draper. Congratulating her on a promotion, albeit a temporary one, would stick in his craw. A full promotion was all but guaranteed. She would be an inspector with just under five years in the sergeant rank. It was a real sickener, another one leaving him behind. The job was fucked, well and truly fucked. His anger was rising and the urge to lash out was irresistible. Somebody would be getting it today.

Wylie knocked on Kidston's open door.

'Come in, John, have a seat. I take it you've heard Sally's good news.' Wylie's dark expression told his boss everything he needed to know.

'Aye, great news for her. But where does it leave me?'

Kidston moved around his desk, closed the door and put on the red light. It was going to be *that* kind of conversation. 'C'mon, John, you're the senior sergeant here, you've got the right assessment grade. Promotion could happen for you any time.'

'It feels like I missed my turn.'

'So you fancied a job in child protection? You know Sally's a specialist. With her background and experience, she could fly through the ranks.'

Wylie cut an unhappy, brooding figure. Kidston's words were not having the desired effect.

'John, you know promotions are decided by headquarters now. The old days of dead men's shoes are long finished. Sometimes you need to be more proactive. You could try applying for a promoted post at detective training or the Scottish Crime Squad. These applications get your file pulled by personnel and even if you don't get the post, you can still end up with a move.'

'I want to be a divisional detective inspector, like you.' His eyes were sad and heavy with disappointment. 'There's plenty of those posts around, I'd just like to be considered for one.'

'I'll have a word with Mr Sawyers. Maybe he can use his influence to get you in front of a force panel,' Kidston began. 'You know that a good panel performance would all but guarantee a promotion. Interviews are normally conducted by a panel of three senior officers selected by headquarters personnel department.'

'That's the hard route to go.' Wylie was aware of the amount of work that went into preparing for a panel and how difficult they were to negotiate.

'Well, let's see. In the meantime, just be happy that you're a key member of this team. I rely on you as crime allocator and continue to appreciate all the support you give me,' Kidston said.

His inspector's words sounded too much like the usual platitudes. It would take more than that to placate Wylie.

Wylie returned to the main CID office and made an excuse to leave the station, stating he had an errand to run in the nearby Cumberland Arcade. Colleagues were used to his mood swings and could read him like a weathervane. Dark and stormy saw him head down; shoulders hunched. Fair and sunny saw the loud and comical Wylie, cracking jokes, singing his wee ditties in loud, comic singer schtick.

He visited Ladbrokes and had a flick through the form guide in the *Racing Post*, but nothing caught his eye. He decided to give his cash to the publican rather than the bookmaker and walked to the nearby Elizabethan.

'A half and a half.'

The pub was dead apart from a few local worthies seated at the bar. Hughie, the barman, set aside the tea towel he was using to dry pint tumblers and pulled a half pint of Tennents, then drew a half of Grouse from the optic on the gantry. 'One of those days, is it?'

Wylie's face was set hard, his shoulders slumped. No other clues required. He added two fingers of water to the whisky and raised his glass in a toast. 'One of *those* days.' He was a regular and knew he'd be left in peace to enjoy his drinks.

He thought about this latest kick in the baws. The first belt of whisky delivered a pleasant burn to the back of his throat. He savoured it, letting it play a while longer on his palate. How could a lassie that'd only been a divisional DS for two years be ready to be a detective inspector? Granted, she'd been a DS in child protection for three years before that, but everyone knew that wasn't real CID. Was she sleeping with Kidston? For fuck's sake, was she sleeping with Joe Sawyers?

Consumed by hatred and bitterness, Wylie wondered what had happened to the old ways of doing things. By his reckoning, he'd missed at least four slots for detective inspector promotions, and it ate away at him. In the old CID world, detectives could work out who was next to get a move up. Kidston had termed it 'dead men's shoes' but the system worked; it brought through the right men, ready and prepared for promotion.

Wylie thought about the old certainties as he sipped the last of his whisky: there was the Church of Scotland, the Boys' Brigade, Glasgow Rangers, the job, and the Craft. The old BB maxim *Sure and steadfast... an anchor tried and true* had been a motto for his life. Church attendances were down; he'd stopped going himself after Janice died. But after a long time in the doldrums, the Rangers were on their way back. The Souness revolution was in full swing, Ally McCoist was banging in the goals again. The Hamilton Accies result in the Scottish Cup was a real shock, but hopefully just a blip on an otherwise fine season.

The cold lager rushed to soothe his bitter heart. He drank it down in one draught.

The job was changing. Sometimes it felt like it was changing too fast for him. Women were being recruited in large numbers and making their way into CID. Catholics too, rising up the ranks and making it into CID. The Craft didn't have the pull or influence it once had and many of his masonic colleagues were leaving the lodge. It felt like the world was playing a cruel trick on him; all the old certainties were crumbling.

He caught the barman's eye. 'Same again, Hughie. On second thoughts, make it a pint and a double.' He felt like making a session of it and giving the office a miss for the rest of the afternoon. He didn't like the way everyone was looking at him after the news of Draper's promotion broke. Were they really expecting him to be jumping for joy? He could pick it all up again tomorrow. The second whisky went down in one. He was getting a taste for it. Another double Grouse hardly touched the sides.

The job was eating him up from the inside, heartsick from disappointment. He was a bitter, twisted man. It hadn't always been like that. Before his heart turned to stone John Wylie had been a very capable detective, with local intelligence second to none. Following a violent sexual assault on a young girl, one of Wylie's touts had provided the name every detective was looking for. Maybe he'd rested on his laurels too long: the Carly Benson investigation was over six years ago.

Recalling the Benson case gave him a small spark of satisfaction, matching the glow from the whisky. He could still face those fuckers; he had his pride and he would come good again. The refreshing lager provided the jolt he needed. Shoulders squared, chest out, Wylie headed for the office in better spirits. He administered a wee skoosh of Gold Spot to freshen up his breath, with a couple of polo mints as backup.

Entering the office via the back door, he made his way past the custody bar, where prisoner processing took place, and continued up the stairs. The blue vinyl floor with the white swirls seemed to be out of focus as he squinted his eyes and grabbed onto the banister, surprised at how tipsy he felt. He should have eaten breakfast or had something more substantial at lunch. *Fuck it!* To the tune of Perry Como's *Magic Moments*, he sang one of his most familiar ditties, in full comic singer style:

*'It wasn't the grass,*
*that tickled her arse,*
*it was my finger.*
*Magic moments,*
*When two hearts are sharing.'*

Colleagues heard him before they saw him as he made his way to the main CID office.

'Somebody's in a better mood,' said DC Robyn 'Mork' Williams.

'Well, Mork, you can't keep a good man down. Well, not for long anyhow.' The scent of Gold Spot mixed with the smell of peppermint told Mork that Wylie was just back from the pub.

He was known for having a swift one at lunchtime, but it was 3.30pm and long liquid lunches didn't happen on Kidston's watch.

'I've been used, abused, and penalised. I've been fucked with the blunt end of the ragman's trumpet.' Wylie was in full flow. Colleagues had heard this soliloquy before.

Many times.

Wylie could be extremely funny. He could also be very loud and annoying. The space between amusement and irritation was a tricky area for him to negotiate. He sat on the long worktop desk and began to regale the room with a selection of war stories. He was recounting his role in the Carly Benson case to Mork Williams, Zorba Quinn and Alison Metcalfe when Gregor Stark entered.

'Good grief, John.' Alarmed by Wylie's glassy, bloodshot eyes, Stark steered him through to the vacant DI's room. 'Give me your car keys and I'll get you up the road before the DI sees you half-cut.'

'I'm okay. I promise I'll be fine.' Wylie put a grateful hand on Stark's shoulder. 'I appreciate it though.'

'I'm not taking no for an answer.' Stark held the rheumy gaze of his fellow sergeant. 'I'll arrange for the night shift to bring you in in the morning. I'll put your car keys in your drawer for tomorrow.'

The journey to Wylie's Burnside home found the older sergeant thankful for his younger colleague's intervention. Cops and sergeants convicted of drink-driving offences were being sacked and fewer officers were willing to risk their pensions. The job was changing. Stark had some sympathy for Wylie following his wife's death, but he wasn't helping himself. Stark's short time at the Gorbals had coincided with a gradual deterioration in Wylie's appearance, performance and character.

In a job full of piss artists, few could piss longer, higher or further than John Wylie. He'd recently taken up the practice he called 'a wee gamble'; driving back from the pub when he was over the drink-drive limit. In days past, a fellow officer would wave you on your way on the production of a police warrant card. Not anymore. The job *had* changed.

'Used, abused, and penalised. I've been fucked with the blunt end of the ragman's trumpet.' Wylie repeated his favourite lament about thwarted ambition and broken promises.

Gregor Stark smiled. He knew how this particular monologue went. 'I knew today would have been tough for you, after Sally's news came through, but you can't let it affect you like that.' Stark offered Wylie some sage advice.

'I know... I know, I was going to wait until five o' clock and then get blootered, but I needed to get out of that office.'

'You know, John, if you let it, this job will chew you up and spit you out.' Stark gave a little cough to clear the tension in his throat. This was a difficult conversation to have with a colleague. 'This job can consume us, but only if we let it.'

'The job's all I've got left, Gregor. I'm going home to stare at four walls.' His eyes were filled with sadness. 'It's not been the same since Janice died.'

A childless couple, the Wylies had always enjoyed a decent social life, with a wide circle of friends and two foreign holidays a year. Breast cancer. Horrible, but quicker than Wylie could ever have imagined. Angry with the world, sore, sad and sorry with himself, Wylie had eventually realised most of his friends away from the job were actually Janice's pals from her work.

'Get a grip of your life, John,' Stark continued. 'Get a new hobby, take up swimming or bowling or badminton. The answers are not going to be found in a whisky bottle. C'mon, John, what would Janice say?'

Wylie's silence spoke volumes.

Stark stopped the car outside Wylie's semi-villa in a quiet

Burnside street. As his colleague walked up the garden path, fumbling for his house keys, Stark wound down his window and shouted a reminder that the night shift would pick him up in the morning.

Without turning around, Wylie, his shirt tails flapping under his suit jacket, held his house keys up to the sky in a one-handed triumphant salute.

'Thanks, Kemosabe.'

## 22

Johnny Boy drove his boss to Sarah Canavan's plush Busby home. Canavan enjoyed the sound of the Merc's tyres on the wide driveway's abundant gravel as his driver brought the car to a stop. Phil Canavan often sought the counsel of his wee sister when he was faced with crises or difficult decisions. At thirty-seven, Sarah Canavan was the younger sibling but with her strong personality, decisive manner and maternal instincts, she'd become something of a mother figure in her big brother's life.

Sarah had been the brains behind the Canavan family's criminal enterprises long before her parents passed away. Big Davie had used her as a family *consigliere*, taking her advice on property deals and other investments. She'd built up a chain of tanning salons, located in select Glasgow housing estates, and had worked hard to legitimise her part of the family trade. Her days of screwing delivery vans were long behind her.

Sarah had been part of Phil's group as a young teenager. She made a name for herself with a scam to rob the vans delivering goods ordered from catalogue companies to her housing scheme. Noticing that the delivery van sat unattended while the driver traced the addressee for the package, often in multi-storey flats, Sarah had screwed the van, making off with all the other parcels. These were later offered at the door of the original purchaser at a knock-down price in the knowledge that the original order could be cancelled. It was a great little scam, repeated across other housing estates until the catalogue company got wise and started to double-crew their vans.

'Well, that's it started then. I've been warning you about this for years, Phil,' Sarah reminded her brother. 'It's time to put your money into non-criminal enterprises like used cars, car washes, a pub, or even a restaurant. There's plenty of other cash businesses that offer lucrative returns and don't have the police or sword-wielding maniacs breathing down your neck every day.'

'Everything will be fine,' Phil Canavan said. 'Things will settle down again when we find out who's behind the attack on Wattie.'

A chain of tanning salons had been ideal for laundering money, and Sarah had constructed an impenetrable firewall between her shops and Phil's drugs and money-lending operations. Her long-term aim was to become a fully legitimate businesswoman and she ran a zero-tolerance policy, urging her brother to get out of the drugs business. She'd previously appealed to him to switch from heroin to cocaine: 'It's a better class of clientele, Phil.' Glasgow's cognoscenti, all the party people, professionals from all walks of life were heavily into their coke.

Canavan wouldn't hear of it; he said he didn't like those people. His true reasons were more prosaic; he enjoyed being a gangster too much.

They sat in Sarah's fashionably-appointed lounge with its modern décor, textured wall coverings and large glass coffee table, supported by colourful ceramic elephants. Over tea and a plate of teacakes, she helped her brother rationalise who might have been behind the attack on Colin Watters and the threat made against him. They ran through the usual list of suspects; rival dealers, disgruntled clients from the money-lending side but they were at a loss. The fact that the swordsman had mentioned Canavan by name gave them little doubt he was to be targeted in a personal attack.

'Watters might have made up the bit about your name being mentioned to make sure you were out hunting for his attacker.'

'There's no way, absolutely no way he'd do that.' Canavan was emphatic. 'He knows I'd cut his other hand off.'

'What about your enemies?' Sarah asked.

'We've gone through all the obvious possibilities. I'd prefer to know who was out there looking for me, especially if he's running about with a big fuck-off sword.' A flicker of fear flashed across Phil Canavan's eyes.

'I'm thinking out loud and I'm thinking motive here.' Sarah sat back in her comfortable cream leather armchair. She was an attractive woman. Johnny Boy ogled her long, lean, tanned legs as she kicked off her expensive high heels. 'What about the two girls that died from overdoses in Govanhill back in September?' She folded her legs up onto the chair.

Canavan shook his head. 'There's nothing linking me or my people to those deaths. Polis have got nothing on me for that.' He'd acted swiftly when customers started overdosing. A whole consignment of heroin had had to be destroyed. It cost him a fortune but kept the cops away from his door.

'Okay, just for the sake of argument,' Sarah said. 'Let's accept the dogs on the street knew it was your gear that killed those poor lassies, and that Watters was the dealer.'

'Okay... Where are you going with this?'

'Let's say one of the girls has a father or a brother or a

boyfriend, who wants to even the score.' Sarah shifted in her seat. 'Revenge, pure and simple.'

'Not a father,' Canavan responded. 'Colin says it was a young guy.'

'Wait a minute.' Johnny Boy came to life. 'The girl, Maria Conway, did she no go out wi' that big guy, used to hang wi' Tombo at the paper corner back in the day?'

'Well, did she?' Canavan asked.

'Aye, she did.'

'Now you're getting close to it.' Sarah was encouraged.

'He was into karate, taekwondo, kung fu and all that shit.' Johnny Boy recalled one particular incident that brought the face to mind. 'The bastard's name was Vinnie Davis.'

'So he can handle himself?' Canavan asked.

'He was never a hardman back then but based on what he used to be like wi' martial arts and what he did to Wattie, I think it's a fair shout that he can handle himself.'

'I don't know him. Why would he come for me?' Canavan looked perplexed. 'Where does he live?'

'I told you: revenge, big brother,' Sarah said. 'He blames you for killing his girlfriend. Should be easy to find him before he finds you.'

'He was off the scene for years, moved away,' Johnny Boy said. 'I'd heard he was in the army; commandoes, special forces or something like that but he'd gone down south. His name popped up when Maria Conway overdosed in her pal's flat in Govanhill. I think I heard something about him living wi' Maria in a flat in Mount Florida. I'll make some calls and check around. We'll soon track him down.'

'You're telling me some maniac who's been in the SAS is coming after me with a samurai sword?'

'But he's lost the element of surprise,' Johnny Boy said with an evil grin. 'We'll be ready for him.'

Sarah Canavan bit her lip and shot a scornful glance at Johnny Boy.

Phil Canavan caught a familiar glint in his little lieutenant's eyes. Johnny Boy was already relishing the thought of the pursuit. But he wasn't so sure. Was this guy crazy enough to come after him?

The line between hunter and hunted was more blurred than Canavan liked.

## 23

The man rose to his feet and put his dukes up as Kidston entered. This was their common greeting as the old boxer adopted his favoured southpaw stance, swaying at the hips, rolling his shoulders and throwing left and right hooks, jabs and uppercuts into empty air. A lean sixty-two-year-old, Eddie 'Banjo' Bridges looked as if he could still go twelve rounds. Kidston threw a flurry of combination punches into Banjo's big hands held up like training mitts.

'That's me, all punched out,' Kidston joked as they greeted each other with a warm handshake.

'I ordered you a plate of mussels,' Banjo said.

They were in the Loch Fyne Shellfish Bar on the edge of Glasgow's famous Barras Market. Both were east-end institutions in the city and regular haunts for Banjo, who was enjoying a large bowl of whelks, picking the tiny molluscs from their shells with a pin.

'Thanks, Eddie, these look lovely,' Kidston replied. He eyed the old man devouring his whelks. The characterful face carried traces of his time in the amateur boxing ranks; a cauliflower ear and a boxer's nose were the most obvious giveaways. The old two-inch scar on his forehead was a more recent injury. It had been inflicted by Kidston's ex-wife, then aged nineteen, when she struck her father with a glass ornament.

Eddie Bridges had been off the drink for six years now but back in the day had terrorised his family with his drunken, violent rages. Youngest daughter, Melanie, had intervened when Eddie was dragging his wife about the living room of their Alexandra Parade tenement home, threatening to kill her. The police were called, Eddie was hospitalised, then jailed, and then divorced from Sheila Bridges, who never looked back. The couple's two older daughters had started their own families and a newly sober Eddie had been permitted to spend time with his four grandchildren.

He was a changed man with a much brighter future these days, and a new woman in his life. A friend had offered him some shifts driving a taxi and he took on other driving jobs, a bit of carpet fitting, and some labouring work. But it was his past that interested Kidston; in his heyday Banjo Bridges had provided muscle for Glasgow gangsters, including Phil Canavan's late father 'Big Davie'. He knew the family well and retained very good links with the Glasgow underworld. He'd never broadcasted the fact that his youngest daughter was once married to a police officer climbing the ranks of the CID. Kidston had always joked that Banjo was every bit as much a guilty secret for him. Over the years, the old man had provided him with some vital intelligence.

'All the taxi boys are talking about the sword attack on Watters but nobody's moving on Phil Canavan,' Banjo said. 'No word on old scores or disgruntled punters.' He sucked an oily mollusc off his pin. 'Canavan's asking around too, so he doesn't know who it was.'

'That's what we're picking up,' Kidston said.

'Canavan will take revenge as soon as he finds out who's

behind it. Big Davie Canavan was a vicious bastard, Phil's just the same,' Banjo continued. 'Johnny Boy McManus is a total animal. Whoever's done this is poking some very nasty bears with a big stick.'

'I'm relieved to hear we don't have a drugs war on our hands, but it seems I may have a murder in the offing.'

'Why would the attacker go for amputation rather than just running Watters through?' Banjo asked. 'By the way, he's a snivelling wee shitebag. He couldn't handle himself the way the other two can.'

'It's a strange one,' Kidston replied. 'My DS thinks it's a revenge attack.'

'Could be,' Banjo said. 'Back in the day, swords and machetes were common enough but I'm hearing it was a samurai sword?'

'That's what we suspect going from Watters' statement and the way his hand was sliced through.'

'Helluva thing.' Banjo laughed. 'Something else I want to raise with you.' The old man's expression changed dramatically, which intrigued his lunch companion. Banjo looked around the restaurant to assess if there was anyone within earshot. They had the place to themselves. 'Don't shoot the messenger. DC Paul Kennedy, he's one of yours, aye?'

'Yes, he is,' Kidston replied. 'What about him?' The old man now had his rapt attention.

'I hear he got locked up at Paisley over the weekend for attacking a lassie.'

'How the hell did you hear about that?' Kidston asked, stunned at the revelation.

'You're not the only one with touts, Luc,' Banjo answered with an enigmatic smile. 'DI Ronnie Miller on the case too. Does that not make it even more fucked up?'

'It makes it a bit more complicated for me, yes.' Kidston sighed. 'What do you know about it?'

'Not too much,' Banjo replied. 'If he did that young girl, he deserves everything that he's got coming.'

This was a bit rich coming from the man who, prior to his sobriety, had battered Kidston's ex mother-in-law for years. 'What do you know about Paul Kennedy?'

'He had a brief fling with Sarah Canavan a few years back,' Banjo said. 'Lifted his hands to her too, busted her mouth and nearly broke her nose.'

## 24

'He's a lucky boy she didn't get her big brother involved or tell his bosses,' Banjo said.

'Well, I've been his boss for the last few years and it's the first I've known about it.' Kidston was flummoxed. 'What the hell is he doing getting mixed up with that family?'

'She stabbed him in the arse wi' a corkscrew. Maybe that's why nobody reported it. I think he came off second best.'

The two men sat in silence for some time, picking at the remnants of their seafood.

'She's a stunning woman. I can see why your DC would hook up with her. Sarah Canavan's not a daft ned like her da or her big brother. She's got a good head on her shoulders and has the makings of a decent businesswoman with her salons. Sends her two sons to private school.'

'We're definitely talking about the same Paul Kennedy?' Kidston asked, still reeling at the news.

'If he's the same guy who got the jail at Paisley, then aye, definitely him.'

Kidston finished his mussels in silence, spooning up some garlicky brine with his final mouthful.

'You still seeing Melanie these days?' Banjo asked.

'We meet up occasionally, still share Tallulah,' Kidston replied.

'Aye, the husky. Her sisters tell me she's a cracking dog. I was hoping you two were going to have some grandkids so I could weevil my way back into her life.'

'I'm pleased Laura and Evelyn have let you back into their lives, Eddie. It's great you can see the wee ones, but I think Mel will be a tougher nut to crack. She's dead against kids.'

'I hope it wasn't my drinking that caused that.' Banjo looked reflective.

'More to do with the customers in her baby-clothes shops,' Kidston said. 'Don't be too hard on yourself.'

'Anyhow, I'm pleased to see you're both doing well in your lives,' Eddie said.

Kidston paid for the seafood and slipped Eddie a twenty-pound note as they said their goodbyes. His former father-in-law had given him a lot to think about. Banjo's information was always on the money and he'd been a brilliant tout over the years. He was well connected in the Glasgow underworld with an intelligence network that would rival any police version. He struggled to process the information Banjo had given him. Paul Kennedy and Sarah Canavan would be a challenging match-up for both parties. Her family would have denounced her being involved with a cop. For him, it was even more straightforward; police regulations forbade his association with criminals. Kidston would dig into it some more. Was Sarah Canavan behind the anonymous call he received on Saturday morning? Had he completely misjudged the character of Paul Kennedy?

It was a fifteen-minute walk back to the office if he crossed the Clyde at the St Andrew's suspension bridge. The walk would help him clear his head. Kidston strode through Glasgow Green. He passed the former Templeton Carpet Factory with its iconic red terracotta façade and vivid glazed brickwork. Its yellow enamelled mosaics reflected the weak midday sunshine. He thought about his former father-in-law, a carpet fitter in his youth and a man who could wax lyrical for hours about the quality of the chenille Axminster weave and how Glasgow carpeted the world.

He reflected on Eddie's alter ego 'Banjo' and the cult of violence that had permeated his young life. The man's criminal history had caused some awkward moments for Kidston, but it had never compromised him. On the contrary, Banjo had become his informant, contributing valuable intelligence in numerous investigations. Banjo's characterful face was like a Peter Howson artwork with their visceral depictions of violent-looking muscular male figures, with menacing, brutal faces. Men like Eddie Bridges. If you looked at their faces more closely, you could observe their vulnerability, see the fear in their eyes. The man known as Banjo would make a great study for Howson.

As Kidston skirted the impressive red sandstone People's Palace museum, he spotted the smiling cartoon features of Mr Happy adorning a large banner on the museum's façade. *What have you got to smile about?* he thought, as he considered the latest bombshell added to his growing list of problems. As if the Erskine Bridge tragedy and the Watters case were not enough, he could now add a possible link between Paul Kennedy and the Canavan family.

He managed the smallest of smiles for Mr Happy. The city had undergone a major rebranding through the 'Glasgow's Miles Better' campaign and cultural perceptions were changing. Planning for next summer's Garden Festival was well underway and Glasgow had been announced as the European City of Culture for 1990. The city had washed its face; cleaned up many of its magnificent Victorian heritage buildings and deployed floodlighting to highlight other architectural gems. The mood was changing to a climate of optimism and Kidston, a proud Glaswegian, liked what he was seeing and was eager to hold his natural scepticism in check. Glasgow was about to attempt the transformation from a tough industrial town, the *'No Mean City'* and murder capital of Britain, into a cultural mecca.

A new Glasgow style was emerging; bold and confident. In Glaswegian parlance: gallus. He didn't want it to be some superficial trendy makeover limited to a yuppie adman's slogan. If they invested enough money into music and the arts, Kidston believed the city could change for the better. So long as they kept visitors away from the urban wastelands of the housing schemes with their teenage wildlife, glue sniffers and drug addicts, the broken glass and religious graffiti, everything should be fine.

Kidston smiled, recalling Banjo's comments about grandkids. Mel's decision not to have children wasn't due to his drunken violent past or absence for long periods of her life. Mel had simply changed her mind about having kids. Approaching the suspension bridge, he looked up into the distance and saw the dark, looming towers of the Queen Elizabeth Square high flats. Turning his coat collar up against the cold air, Kidston shuddered as he recalled the last straw in their marriage. He remembered Mel's anger. With a planned summer holiday in Lido di Jeselo and a scheduled trip to Venice, Kidston suffered the body blow of a high court citation; a murder trial that clashed with the first week of their trip.

Quite understandably, Mel had expected that he would be excused, or the trial would be postponed. When Kidston explained that a gang fight incident with two murder victims and five accused made that an unlikely outcome, she completely lost it. It was the biggest argument of their married life. There was no way that Kidston could be excused witness duty. An unhappy compromise was reached, with Mel spending the first five days of the holiday on her own. The force met the extra costs of rearranging Kidston's flights, but Mel never forgave him.

That was the beginning of the end of their marriage.

As he crossed the low suspension bridge at the edge of Glasgow Green, he glanced down on the River Clyde below him. The same murky waters had claimed Russell Maitland three nights earlier. It sent a shiver down his spine. Banjo's revelations about Paul Kennedy and Sarah Canavan had knocked him for six. The woman behind the anonymous call had described Paul Kennedy as an 'animal' and it seemed her main intention had been to pile more trouble and suspicion on the young detective's situation, but without revealing her identity. Why did she not call Ronnie Miller or Paisley CID? It was their case. If it was Sarah Canavan, what was her motivation?

How could Paul have been so stupid? A romantic entanglement with Sarah Canavan could only compromise his integrity as a police officer. And the violence was at complete odds with how Alison had described Paul. He had little reason to doubt Banjo's information; he was well connected and knew the Canavans, and their circle. Banjo had known Sarah Canavan since she was a toddler. He would need to make further enquiries into the connection between Paul and Sarah.

## 25

McCartney was putting the finishing touches to a crime report and Costello was confirming the ten-digit crime reference number from the relevant file kept at the uniform bar. Tam Baillie, the desk sergeant, was regaling the young policewoman with his favourite Peter Costello stories.

'Has he told you the one about his marriage licences?' Baillie asked her.

'I don't think I've ever heard that one.' McCartney shook her head.

'Young Gorbals loon walks into the front bar a few years back,' Baillie began. '"My mammy says I've got to get a marriage licence from Inspector Costello." Inspector Costello, mind you: two promotions for the big man. "I want to marry Betty Murray frae Hutchesontown, and my mammy says aye, so long as you get a signed licence and permission from Inspector Costello at the polis station."

'I got him to fill in some old, random form and said I'd pass it on to Inspector Costello. I sent it through despatches to Peter with a note saying maybe he'd want to conduct the wedding ceremony as well.'

Costello was chuckling as he remembered the sergeant's despatch.

'What happened? Did they get married?' McCartney asked.

'Sadly, no.' Costello took up the story. 'I met his mother in the street and she told me, "That eejit is no marrying anyone." His girlfriend was late with her period and they panicked.'

'Another tale to add to my Costello's greatest hits collection.' McCartney laughed. 'I'm saving them up.'

It was no wonder the man was a legend in the Gorbals. Funny stories aside, the anecdote hinted at the big cop's standing with the community and how he policed his bailiwick. Costello was treated like an old-school village bobby. The Gorbals, with its rough and tumble and its criminal underclass, was no village, but through his presence in the community, his policing methods, his work in schools and youth clubs and the fair way he dealt with the people, Costello had reduced or elevated the place to village status. It was a remarkable achievement.

Their laughter subsided when the office phone rang. Tam Baillie raised his hand for silence. 'I'll send two of my best officers right away, Mrs Callaghan.' The look on Tam's face hinted at the grave and urgent matter at hand. 'Right, you two, step to it double quick. Baby crawling on the balcony ledge, ten floors up at the Queen Elizabeth Square flats. You'll need to go to Mrs Callaghan's flat to get access to the balcony. She's incapacitated, on crutches, so her front door is on the latch.' He wrote the flat and floor numbers on a call sheet and handed them to Costello. 'I'll call up the divisional van, but you guys will be there quicker.'

The multi-storey flats were a stone's throw to the police station and overlooked the backyard of the office. The old joke went that no suspect was ever beaten up in the Gorbals yard because there were hundreds of potential witnesses to any improper acts. Exiting the back door and cutting across the yard, the flats were upon you as soon as you stepped onto the street.

McCartney cast an anxious glance upwards; the intimidating tower block buildings scraped the sky. She tried to imagine an imperilled baby and how, in the name of God, it could access a balcony ledge.

'I don't understand these flats, Peter, they're like a bloody maze.' McCartney was entrusting the location of this call to her more experienced colleague.

'They are a maze, but don't worry, I know my way through it. All the houses are two-level flats, with internal stairs, stacked one on top of the other, designed to share a balcony with one of your neighbours.' He pointed skywards to the offending balconies as they sped towards the lift foyer. 'You'll see when we get up there.'

The Queen Elizabeth Square high-rise flats dominated the Gorbals skyline. Glasgow was renowned, at one time, for having the highest concentration of multi-storeys in Europe. None were as visually imposing or audacious in their design concept as *The Hanging Gardens of the Gorbals*. Characterised by their monolithic design and rigid geometric slab block style, they were inspired by the work of French architect, Le Corbusier.

Twenty storeys of striking brutalist architecture raised up on giant stilts; the sloping pilotis that meant you could walk underneath the massive buildings. For architects and designers, poured concrete had never looked so beautiful. Sir Basil Spence, the architect, had envisioned that when the residents hung their washing out on the expansive communal balconies, the tower block would take on the appearance of a mighty Spanish galleon sailing in the wind.

Those balconies presented additional hazards. Any cops cutting through the square would lift their gaze to the skies, because it wasn't unknown for items like toys, toasters, microwaves and even fridges to be thrown over the side of the flats. But it was the enormous 'flower box' balconies attached to either end of the block that caught the observer's eye; ten gigantic window boxes, running the full width of the gable, each seemingly centre-balanced on top of a single oversized concrete strut that resembled a giant carpet tack.

'Baby on a ledge. Jesus, what kind of call is that to get?' McCartney could feel her heart racing.

'The balconies have all got big, broad ledges, pretty substantial and designed to accommodate window boxes, but nobody uses them for that,' Costello explained. 'The big problem is the barriers are only about three feet high and a child or a toddler can easily clamber up onto the wide ledge.'

'So it's like some crazy adventure playground for Gorbals weans?' McCartney was not reassured by her colleague's description. She found herself wishing that the lift would travel quicker as it climbed steadily to their floor. That it did so without stopping at any intervening levels, was a blessing.

They raced out of the lift, McCartney running as fast as she could to keep up with her big neighbour's long stride. She had to slalom between two eight-year-old boys, who were using the long corridor as a cycle racetrack and three little girls who were playing with their dolls. Mrs Callaghan's voice greeted the officers as they pushed open her front door.

'Downstairs, quickly please.'

The officers descended the steep stairs with Costello's giant stride straddling three steps at a time. They immediately saw the extent of their reporter's incapacitation. An anxious, agitated woman in her mid-thirties was propped up on the couch, looking out through her patio windows to the unbearable and inaccessible drama unfolding on the veranda beyond. Both legs and one arm were in plaster casts.

'Thank God you're here. Quick, quick, through that veranda

door. Wee Jamie from next door's out on the ledge.' She was talking in enormous, gulping breaths, a mix of blind panic, shock, and fear. The external wall between the lounge and outside balcony was constructed primarily of glass panels forming full height sidelights, either side of a hinged metal door. The Callaghan flat had curtains fitted along the glass wall, but they were fully drawn to allow light into the lounge.

Costello swept past the invalided householder, threw open the door and saw the sandy-haired toddler, dressed in a light-blue snow suit, crawling along the balcony ledge. He scooped the oblivious tot into his giant hands and carried him in his arms back into the lounge.

'Not yours then?' Costello cradled the contented toddler, rocking him back and forth in his arms and onto his shoulder. It was many years since he'd performed the manoeuvre.

'My two are at school, thank goodness. My husband's at work.' Mrs Callaghan gave her name as Nan and, as her breathing and speech returned to normal, explained that she'd fallen downstairs after a drunken works night out. 'I can't even manage my own veranda door, the state I'm in. I'm sitting here paralysed wi' fear watching this wee tearaway clambering along that ledge, thinking I need to get to my feet and get out there to save him, but I can hardly stand to make a cup of tea or open a bloody door. What if he wriggled or I dropped him?' Tears of relief started to stream down her cheeks. 'That was the longest five minutes of my life.'

'Is his mother at home?' McCartney asked.

'She is. Her name's Alice Bell, but she'll be lying stocious on the couch. A mix of jellies and Carlsberg super lager, no doubt,' Nan scoffed. 'I can't talk about other people being drunk, given my stair-diving exploits but that wisnae in the middle of the day and the lassie's got a serious habit wi' Temazepam.' The reference to 'jellies' was no surprise to the officers. The city was in the grip of an epidemic of the small yellow opioid tablets, with a healthy black market for the prescription medication.

'Is she a heroin user?' Costello asked. He was aware of the trend for users to mix jellies and heroin to increase the hit rate of their fix.

'No. The lassie's got a hard time of it. Carlsberg and jellies are her thing. It just wipes her out. The wean's faither bailed out when he was a newborn and she's struggled. I don't like to fire anyone in but this lassie's only twenty-one or twenty-two and she needs some help.'

'How old's the little one?' McCartney enquired.

'Fourteen months, I think, and up walking, into all sorts of trouble as you can see.'

'It'll be a tough time for her, but he shouldn't be out on the balcony unsupervised at that age,' McCartney said.

'God, no. I didn't let mine out at any time. Those balconies are way too scary. They're supposed to be drying greens; "patios in the sky" they called them, bloody ridiculous. You know some people have laid a proper lawn to make it like a real garden. The weans just treat it as a big playground but those ledges have always given me the heebie-jeebies.'

The two cops, with Costello still carrying baby Jamie, explored the long, wide and generous balcony space that Nan Callaghan shared with the toddler's mother; her 'veranda neighbour'. It was obvious how the tot had accessed the ledge: Jamie's pushchair was lying on its side, wedged into the corner of the balcony on top of a toddler-sized play car. The little guy had constructed a mini climbing frame, enabling him to push himself onto the broad welcoming ledge to crawl and explore his world further.

They entered Alice Bell's home through the veranda door to find her sleeping on the couch covered in a blanket. Dead to the world. Nan Callaghan's assessment was on the money. The coffee table bore the evidence of her latest session; three empty tins of Carlsberg super lager and a tub of Temazepam.

McCartney roused Bell from her deep slumber. She sat up rubbing her bleary eyes and squinted at the two police officers standing over her. One of them was a giant and was holding her baby son in his arms.

'What is it? What happened?' She pushed herself up into a seated position, sobered by the sight of her toddler son cradled by a big polisman.

'The wee fellah here managed to crawl up onto the balcony ledge. How did that happen?' Costello asked.

'What?' She hadn't quite achieved the level of sobriety or awareness required to fully comprehend the question. 'You mean the outside balcony?'

'The very one,' Costello replied.

Alice Bell's pretty young face registered the shock just dealt to her system. Paralysis. Momentarily, her mouth seemed incapable of creating any words before forming into a full O-shape. 'I left him out on the veranda, strapped into his buggy in the fresh air.' She stared blankly at the two officers, as if confused by her own words. 'He had his wee harness thingy fastened and I could see him through the window. I wanted to grab a wee sleep on the couch.' She started to sob. 'Can I have him, please?' She reached up and Costello handed the tot to his mum, who held him in a close embrace.

'But it looks like you wanted more than a wee sleep, Alice. Super strength lager and jellies are not a good mix. You're increasing your chances of alcohol poisoning.' Costello had dealt with too many overdoses involving drugs and alcohol. 'These don't look like they were prescribed for you. Where did you get them?'

'My pal gave me some to help me sleep.'

'And where did your pal get them?' Costello asked, stern-faced.

'Ah don't know.'

'You're close to seeing your wee boy put into care. You need to think before you tell any more lies. Where did these jellies come from?'

'My pal, Margaret, and me got them off Colin Watters,' Alice said, holding her infant son closer.

'What else does Colin Watters supply you with?' Costello asked.

'Sometimes he's got DF118s or Dicanol tabs but mostly jellies,' Alice replied. 'He can get ye hash or smack but ah'm no intae that stuff.'

'Well, Colin Watters will not be doing much dealing for the foreseeable future,' Costello said.

Alice gave a blank look.

'You need to be careful taking this stuff, Alice. Especially with a young child,' Costello admonished her. 'You can't take them like Smarties.'

Suspecting that Alice Bell was surviving on scarce resources, Costello directed McCartney to check the fridge and food cupboards to assess how the two of them were living. His fears were confirmed; an empty fridge apart from two tins of Carlsberg and a half pint of milk; no baby food in the cupboards, except half a plain loaf and a box of Frosties. Costello gave a confirmatory nod to McCartney and she radioed the control room to call out the social work standby service. Alice Bell needed help and if her toddler son was to have an even chance of surviving his childhood, that help would need to be arranged soon.

Costello was grim-faced. Separating a mother and child didn't sit right with him but he couldn't contemplate exposing an at-risk toddler to further potential harm from a self-abusing, neglectful mother. Alice's mother lived ten minutes away in Oatlands and, based on the social worker's assessment, it looked like Jamie would be placed with his gran until his young mum could be helped.

What would Alice Bell's odds look like stacked against the market capitalism of Thatcher's Britain? Costello knew how hard it was to get out of the schemes: he'd made that journey. The 'new' Gorbals, built largely in the early sixties, was envisioned as a flight from poverty and squalor. Families escaped the overcrowded, rat-infested, crumbling tenements to move to the sprawling new council estates at the edge of the city; Castlemilk, Easterhouse and Drumchapel. Many yearned for a return to the Gorbals they'd left behind but that place didn't exist anymore. Like a Brigadoon, lost in the mists of time, it could never exist again.

He recalled the joy of the families moving into the various new Hutchesontown developments. A new home and a new hope. But it didn't last long; the notorious 'Hutchie E' blocks, a series of low-rise, deck-access flats – around 200 yards from where he was standing – were coming down after only fifteen years. Declared unfit for habitation due to design flaws. Who knew? Apparently building materials designed for a Mediterranean climate don't thrive in the west of Scotland's cold and damp.

Costello was not an overtly political animal, but it was unavoidable; policing happened in a political realm. His moral conscience was pricked by the social conditions he encountered performing his duties. He saw the best and the worst of people and in his experience, people needed a purpose. That meant jobs with decent wages and the safety net of adequate welfare provision when they were out of work. Despair and hopelessness fed the perfect social conditions for crime, drug abuse and suicide. As a police officer, part of his role was to hold the thin line that maintained societal order but at times the job just felt like chaos.

With the social work arrangements in place the two community cops walked back to the office. Costello was quieter than usual.

'Colin Watters ran quite a pharmacy according to Alice,' said McCartney. 'Where will the druggies go now that he's... er... indisposed?'

'Canavan will just have the next guy step up. It never stops,' Costello said with an air of resignation.

'How much longer can he get away with it?'

'Nobody gets away with it forever,' said the big cop. 'This sword attack may draw Canavan into the open. I've got a feeling his time might be coming.'

## 26

D raper pushed the 'go faster' button on the treadmill. Running quicker would focus her thinking, address the mild anxiety she felt about going back to her old unit as the DI. It would also stop her daydreaming about her boss. She'd always found Kidston attractive, with his wild black hair and pale-green eyes, but he was her boss. She knew all about his 'rule', but it hadn't stopped her developing a crush on him.

He was pretty untypical as cops went; into his music, art, and books. Over the two years they'd worked together, she'd enjoyed spending time in his company, in the office and socially. Police work and romance were difficult bedfellows. There were lots of office romances, many of them extra-marital affairs. The divorce rate for cops was shocking. Paul Kennedy and Sandra Holt were just the latest casualties and they hadn't got as far as a wedding. Now that Kidston wasn't going to be her boss, it would be less complicated. And besides, she had her own rule, one she'd never shared with colleagues: she didn't go out with cops.

She would make an exception for Kidston.

Kidston stood by his principles. He didn't just talk about equality, he actively promoted it. He had no issues with her promotion; he could have blocked the move or resisted giving her the opportunity. Instead, he'd encouraged her promotion, talked her up to Sawyers, saying she was ready. He believed in her ability, unlike dinosaurs like Wylie who assumed she was sleeping her way to promotion. How she'd love to slap that man.

The timer display read twenty minutes; she was at the halfway point of her session. Draper adjusted the incline settings so the second half would be uphill; she enjoyed the burn from the steeper slope. Sally knew she was one of the best investigators on Kidston's team. She was curious, tenacious, fearless, principled and carried out her duties in a professional manner. It was a fact rarely commented on by her male colleagues. For a woman in a man's world, it often felt like an uphill battle.

She had just under two weeks to help Kidston on the Kennedy case. It was one hell of a long shot, but everybody believed in his innocence. There were no dissenting voices. She wondered whether that was due to Kidston's unshaken belief in his young protégé. Few would speak out against the DI, but she had to trust her own instincts. He might have cheated on his fiancée, but her gut was telling her that Paul Kennedy was facing a miscarriage of justice.

Johnny Boy McManus spent the evening knocking on doors and making calls. He was struggling to locate Vincent Davis. One lead took him to a second-floor tenement flat in McLennan Street in Mount Florida, reputed to be a last-known address. It was a tidy close in a blond sandstone block near the railway station. As he climbed the stairs a fragrant antiseptic aroma confirmed that he wasn't in the Gorbals anymore.

Johnny Boy gave the door a vigorous knock and rattled the letter box. 'Vinnie, Vinnie!'

No response.

He wedged the letter box open and held his ear to the slot. He couldn't hear a thing. On the verge of kicking the door in, McManus was only prevented from doing so by the next-door neighbour. The blonde woman in her early forties, alerted by the noise he was making, looked posh, middle class; the type that would call the polis in a heartbeat. He eyed her up and down; quite shaggable in her tight black sweatpants and cream V-neck sweater that showed a very nice cleavage.

'Nobody there, I'm afraid. The landlord emptied out the flat last week.' She eyed McManus as she leant on her door frame. 'Who are you looking for?'

Always a vocal chameleon, Johnny Boy modified his voice to a more refined accent. 'Vincent Davis. This is the address I was given for him.'

'Yes, Vincent Davis was the last resident,' she confirmed with a broad smile. 'But he's moved to his sister's home in Donegal.'

'I'm sorry to miss him. We were school friends and I've not long moved back to the area,' Johnny Boy lied. 'Did he leave any forwarding address?'

'No, I'm sorry, that's all I know.' She'd moved the door to a half-closed position and retreated behind it, awaiting his departure. He imagined pushing past the door, getting his hands on those shapely tits and riding the arse off her. Posh birds were such a fuckin' turn-on. His fantasy evaporated like snowflakes in a puddle when he heard the safety chain being attached to the locked door.

McManus wouldn't be put off the scent so easily. Davis may have left a false trail. He would be tracked down.

Tracked down and sorted.

## 27

'You're a wee bit far off your usual beat, detective inspector,' Sarah Canavan said. 'What can I help you with?'

Kidston was seated on a cream leather sofa and he took in the opulent surroundings of Sarah Canavan's well-appointed lounge. *Crime must pay,* he thought, as he checked out the décor and high-quality furnishings. They were either side of her large glass coffee table, supported by ceramic elephants. She'd made a pot of coffee and had produced a plate of sponge fingers, which neither of them was troubling. Canavan was barefoot and wearing stone-washed blue jeans with a loose-fitting yellow cotton blouse. She folded her legs up onto the chair, and Kidston noticed her toenails were painted a vivid crimson. As he studied his host, it was obvious how Paul Kennedy, or any man, would fall for her. She was a stunning woman.

'It's a delicate matter.' Kidston was calculating how much information to impart.

'Is it about my brother?' Sarah Canavan asked.

'It's actually about a colleague of mine.'

'Detective Constable Paul Kennedy, Gorbals CID, by any chance?' She smiled at him.

'Actually, yes.'

'My ex-boyfriend. What about him?'

'When was this and how long did you two go out for?'

'Around four years ago and we lasted for three months.' Sarah Canavan ran her fingers through her lustrous light-brown hair and flashed Kidston a generous smile.

'Can I ask how it ended, Sarah? Is it okay to call you Sarah?'

'Of course, let's be grown-up about things. It's Luc, isn't it?'

'Luc's fine.'

'First of all, Luc, I didn't know that Paul was a cop and he didn't know who my family was. I went by McWilliams then, just after my divorce,' she continued. 'It was after three or four dates when we found out more about each other.'

He was listening intently to her voice. As a hostage negotiator, he was trained to differentiate voices, through pace, pitch and tone. Did she make the anonymous call on Saturday morning? Her voice sounded familiar, but the call had been a short conversation.

'And then?' Kidston asked.

'Then we realised we might have an issue with our compatibility,' Sarah Canavan replied with a broad smile.

'Is that what split you up?'

'That, plus other stuff.'

'This is the delicate bit, Sarah.' Kidston paused to take a sip of coffee. 'Did he ever beat you up or attack you?'

'Let's cut to the chase, inspector. Paul Kennedy's been locked up for attacking a woman in Paisley and you know that I might be one of his previous victims.'

'How could you know about that case?' Kidston asked.

'Come on, Luc, think about it. Eddie Bridges is like an uncle to me. He babysat me and my brothers as toddlers.' She pulled her knees in and adjusted her weight on the armchair. 'Police stations are full of cleaners, turnkeys, civilian typists. We get to hear things.'

Kidston shook his head in disbelief. 'You've got a better intelligence network than we have. You'll no doubt know about my links to Banjo.'

Sarah Canavan laughed. 'It wasn't the worst kept secret in the world, Luc, but nobody gave Banjo a hard time because Melanie married a cop. You see, our worlds are more closely linked than you'd imagine.'

'What about Paul assaulting you?' He was keen to get back to the reason for his visit. He wondered if she knew that Banjo had touted for him over the years. That wouldn't have played well with her big brother.

'Your colleague liked his sex rough,' she explained.

'How rough?' Kidston asked.

'You need to understand, I won't be making any formal complaints about being assaulted.' Sarah wagged a finger in the air. Her nail varnish was the same crimson shade as her toenails. 'And, I won't be giving evidence in any court of law... so long as you accept that.'

'Absolutely,' Kidston said. 'I'm looking for a bit of background on his character.'

'Paul's a bit of a Jekyll and Hyde character. You know how smooth and charming he can be.' She took a sip of coffee and cradled the mug in both hands. She stared intently at Kidston. 'He can get a bit wild in the bedroom, especially after a bottle of red wine.'

'He hit you?'

'I don't want to embarrass you, Luc, but I quite enjoy a wee slap on my arse.' She patted her backside. 'It's a more than ample target, almost as big as East Kilbride.' She laughed heartily at her own joke. 'The problem was that Paul always took it too far. He started choking me, started hitting my face. That's when I told him to stop.'

'Did he stop?'

'I made him stop. He slapped me across the face during sex. We were both drunk. I punched his jaw, he hit me again, harder. He burst my nose and my lip. That's when I skewered his peachy arse with a corkscrew. He was bleeding like a stuck pig. Spoiled a nice set of bedsheets.'

'And without drink?' Kidston asked.

'Not as rough, not as mean. But he's got a quick temper on him.'

'Give me a for instance,' Kidston said.

'For instance, the time he dragged me off the sofa by my hair because I slagged him about his massive ego. Do you think he attacked that girl?'

'Do you think he could have done it?' Kidston asked.

'Absolutely, he could have. Is he going to get done for it?'

'I really don't know,' Kidston replied. 'He was the last person – that we know of – to see her before she was found unconscious.'

'You think somebody else done it?'

'That's what I was hoping for. Or, she wakes up and tells us she had a fall.'

'He'll go to trial?'

'Most likely. Is there anything else you could help me with to get a handle on Paul's character?'

'He had a lot of women,' Sarah Canavan said. 'I heard he's engaged now, but back then Paul always had a number of women on the go.'

'Did he ever pass any information to you?'

'Are you serious?' Sarah Canavan's bright blue eyes glared angrily at Kidston. 'You think I was recruiting polis to work for my big brother? You've got me all wrong, inspector. I'm a legitimate businesswoman. I don't have a criminal record and I'm sure you could check that out. Paul and I met in a nightclub and he rarely spoke about his work. I won't let my two boys anywhere near my brother's business.'

'I'm sorry, no offence. I had to ask that.' Kidston took a final swig of his coffee. He'd heard enough. 'How long have you known about the incident?'

'I only just found out at the start of the week,' Sarah replied. 'Why do you ask?'

'Someone called me at my office on Saturday morning, alleging Paul Kennedy had a violent past. Was that you?'

'Why would I do that, detective inspector?' She smiled, her face inscrutable.

'Unrequited love maybe?'

'Our split was mutual,' she replied. 'I was a bit too old for Paul. So you and Melanie are divorced now, what, three years?' Sarah ran her fingers slowly through her hair, a coquettish tilt in her head, and looked directly into his eyes. 'Are you with anybody just now?'

It was the flirtatious way she asked the questions that spooked him. 'I'm in a relationship with a colleague,' he lied. 'It's tough in this job, you know.' He momentarily visualised the most dangerous liaison with the woman whose brother he was looking to put away.

She laughed at his obvious discomfort. 'A DI would be a substantial upgrade on a DC.' Sarah Canavan walked towards him. She came closer and he was briefly transfixed by the look on her face. 'I'll take that,' she said, smiling sweetly and reaching for his coffee mug.

'Of course, thank you.' He snapped out of his reverie. 'Thanks for everything.'

'I hope I was able to help,' Sarah said. 'Good luck with everything.'

As he drove away from the house, Kidston was reasonably sure it had been Sarah Canavan who'd made the anonymous call, though he didn't expect she'd ever admit to it. He was unable to reconcile the Paul Kennedy described by Alison Metcalfe with the character related to him by Sarah Canavan, but he better understood two things: he realised how difficult it would be for Paul to end a relationship with a woman possessing such siren sexuality. He also realised how little he really knew Paul.

## 28

Wednesday

'Is this a good time, boss?' Peter Costello stuck his head around the door of Kidston's office.

'Come in, close the door.' Kidston was pleased to see his uniform colleague.

Kidston had been mentored by Costello as a young rookie cop straight out of Tulliallan and they'd stayed friends ever since. Kidston made regular use of Costello's vast intelligence network – an advantage of having worked at the same police station for all of his twenty-two years' service.

'How's the Watters case looking?' Costello asked.

'DS Stark led a follow-up door-to-door enquiry at his street. We've canvassed the Granite and the other pubs nearby but nothing doing,' Kidston replied. 'Same with the touts. We're thinking personal attack but keeping the usual open mind. What about you, Peter?'

'Nothing as yet, but I did deal with one of Watters' clients yesterday,' Costello replied. 'She was zombied out of her face on jellies, her toddler son crawling along the balcony ledge, ten floors off the ground.'

'Those big balconies are scary.' Kidston experienced a slight pang of anxiety at the thought of being ten floors up. 'The toddler was rescued okay?'

'Yeah, we got him, thanks. Social work has placed him at his granny's meantime. Give his mammy a chance to recover.'

Kidston turned the conversation to his other major enquiry and explained the dilemma he was facing around the Kennedy case and outlined his plan for Costello. The big cop was unperturbed about conducting vehicle stops at the Barrhead Dams and understood the rationale for the checks. They agreed that Thursday and Friday evenings would be the nights to target, with the Friday more likely to bear fruit. Costello would ask drivers if they'd seen a girl fitting Ellie Hunter's description walking the Dams roads late at night and run checks on any likely suspects.

'What did the girl look like?' Costello asked.

'She's a petite blonde, short hair.' Kidston fished a copy of the *Paisley Daily Express* from his desk drawer. 'That's our victim. Incredibly, the papers are still speculating on a hit-and-run.' Kidston swept his hair back. 'I think that's Colquhoun's misdirection, keeping the police element out for the moment.'

'My current neighbour's a petite blonde. The hair's wrong...' Costello squinted at the photograph. 'Chrissie's is longer, but otherwise I'd say she's a decent match.'

Kidston read where his friend was going with it. 'Will she be okay with walking ahead in civvy clothes?'

'I'll make sure she's on the correct side of the carriageway and I'll be close by.' Costello shifted his weight on the chair. 'It's your call, you can have her in a high-vis yellow tabard or in plain clothes.'

'Double denim.'

'What?'

'That's what Ellie Hunter was wearing,' Kidston said. 'Tell her to make sure that she's got an extra layer on. It will be Baltic up there at that time of night.'

'Not sure I know her well enough to discuss her underwear.'

Both men laughed.

Kidston had offered Costello the same firewall as all of the others working on the Kennedy enquiry. Any fallout would be on him. The need for secrecy was stressed and if PC McCartney had any reservations about the operation, she would be stood down.

Kidston reflected on how many times the big man had saved him from scrapes and skirmishes, especially in his earliest days as a raw probationer. At six foot two Kidston was a tall man, but Costello had three inches on him, and his massive build made him seem like a colossus. To the best of their knowledge, they were the only two officers in the station originally from the local area. The two former St Frank's boys both started at the Gorbals, eight years apart. Costello was still there twenty-two years later; Kidston had moved four times with transfers and promotions but was now back where he started.

Kidston had often wondered why Costello never sought advancement, but he knew the answer. His ambition was to be the best constable he could be, and he was better than most. A stalwart of the community he policed, with a reputation for fairness and toughness. He'd put many a local tearaway back on the right road. With *Costello's a Bastard* daubed on a gable end in Hutchesontown, Constable Peter Costello had a lasting testimonial to the efficacy of his policing methods.

'I'm up for that,' Chrissie McCartney said when Costello explained the planned 'secret' operation for Thursday and Friday night and pointed out Kidston's deniability clause. 'It seems like important work and quite exciting to be doing something off the books.'

'It's a bit of a long shot,' Costello said. 'Could be a long, boring, freezing cold night.'

'It's a big case,' McCartney said, pleased to be included.

Kidston's next meeting was with DS Gregor Stark to be updated on the Watters enquiry. They sat in Kidston's room, the DI playing devil's advocate, testing Stark's lines of enquiry.

'All the touts are tapped out, the entire network,' Stark began. 'Everyone on the team has done a follow-up contact on their registered informants but there's no word on the street.'

'What's that telling you?'

'It's not a drugs feud. It's no turf war.' The young DS shook his head, emphasising the point. 'In one way that's good for us: it means we'll not have drug dealers stabbing or shooting each other.'

'So you're thinking personal attack, a fallout between two neds?' Kidston swept a handful of unruly black hair from off his forehead.

'First up, anyone going for Watters knows it's an act against Canavan. Canavan will strike back, no doubt. Unless he's going to move on Canavan too...' Stark trailed off.

'If Canavan knows or finds out who did this, we'll probably have another stabbing on our hands,' Kidston said.

Canavan's team had adopted the tactic of stabbing their victims in the backside. Viewed as the ultimate humiliation, wounds to the rectum resulted in horrific, often lifelong injuries with the victims often requiring colostomy bags. Neds called it 'bagging'.

'Two of the touts we spoke to said Canavan's asking around about who attacked Colin Watters.' Stark smiled at the irony. 'He's looking for the same guy we're looking for.'

'A sword is such an unusual MO.' Kidston shook his head. 'Who walks about with a samurai sword?' Neither detective had encountered such an outrageous modus operandi before.

'I think the MO helps us with a possible suspect's profile. It's a showy, dramatic way to attack someone.'

'Like a punishment?' Kidston followed his colleague's reasoning.

'Exactly. I think it's some inflated, ritualistic punishment. It's rooted in vengeance.' Stark had considered this idea from the outset.

'So we're coming around to your vigilante theory.'

'Yes, the father, brother or boyfriend of one of Canavan's victims,' Stark continued. 'Father is unlikely... From Watters' description it was a young man. A brother or boyfriend is the more likely.'

'Any likely suspects from that approach?' Kidston asked.

'I've started with the two drug deaths in Govanhill in September. Maria Conway and Jessica Sloan. Drugs squad fancied Canavan's crew for the contaminated smack that killed the girls but there was no evidence; no witnesses to link him or his dealers.' Stark opened a folder to consult his notes. 'Chances are the heroin was provided by Watters, working for Canavan. That gives us a group of two fathers, two brothers and two boyfriends. Any of the six names here, individually or acting with one of the others could have taken revenge against Watters.'

'Good work, Gregor.' Kidston was pleased that the investigation had a new focus. 'Grab one or two of the others and start to check them out,' he continued. 'After we know a bit more, we'll bring Canavan and that evil little turd Johnny Boy in for a word.'

Stark nodded. 'If it is one of this group, we'll need to get to them before Canavan does.'

## 29

John Wylie was next up for Kidston with a scheduled Wednesday afternoon appointment. His detective sergeant's staff appraisal had been lying in his drawer for over two weeks and Kidston felt that, in light of recent events, the paperwork needed to be signed off. He'd more than enough on his plate, but he knew how quickly seeds of disaffection could grow and spread bad morale through a team. Besides, his DS needed a wee shot in the arm and a good assessment would boost his confidence.

Kidston read through the annual assessment report he'd written over two weeks earlier. If the staff appraisal had been based on the last month, the gradings would have been lower. There was no doubt Wylie was slipping back; was he becoming disaffected? He would explore that aspect. In fairness, Kidston had graded Wylie over the calendar year, and it was a very positive report.

Wylie hated the staff appraisal system. He found it difficult to sit down with his bosses to discuss his career aspirations. When he appraised the detectives in his group, he relied on a bank of stock phrases. He preferred plain language to the management speak that had crept into the job in recent years. Some colleagues termed it *wankspeak*. It had spread like a virus from force headquarters to every territorial division; senior managers grasped around for the new buzzword or phrase so they could all appear to be in the know. If another gaffer urged Wylie to *think outside the box*, he might punch somebody.

Wylie was dressed in his best brown suit and polished brown brogues. He wore a mustard yellow shirt with a brown knitted tie. He had a well-scrubbed look, his comb-over had been patted into shape, and his sideburns were neatly trimmed. As ever, he was accompanied into the office by 'the great smell of Brut.'

The meeting started with a yellow card warning. Wylie apologised for leaving the office early the previous day, explaining he'd suffered a gastric upset. Both men knew it was a lie and Kidston challenged him on it. 'I know things have been difficult for you since Janice died. I'm a bit worried that your drinking is getting out of hand.'

'Are you suggesting I've got a drink problem?' Wylie was shocked by the inference.

'That's not what I'm saying but an episode like yesterday can't happen again. The superintendent's office is just two doors away.' Kidston's voice was grave. 'What do you think happens if he bumps into you on the stairs?'

'I'm sorry, I shouldn't have come back to the office yesterday. It won't happen again.'

Admonishment dealt with, the interview moved on to Wylie's appraisal. Kidston handed the report to Wylie, letting him read through it, and watched as he nodded and broke into a big smile.

'Very happy with that, boss, very fair.' Wylie had read the magical phrase: *ready for the next rank*. It was music to his ears.

'That's what will go to personnel at headquarters once Mr Sawyers has signed off on it. You'll go into the promotion pool and you may be called up for a force panel so be ready.' Kidston pointed to an A4 box file that sat on his bookshelf. 'When you get notification of a panel, have a good look through that. It's got all the latest reading in it, *Police Review* articles, crime policy initiatives. All good stuff.'

'I will do, thanks.' Wylie left the office with a spring in his step. There was some annoyance at his drinking being mentioned but Kidston could've made more of it. He knew the days of cracking open a bottle of whisky in the office to celebrate an arrest or at the conclusion of a big case were coming to an end. Kidston enjoyed a beer after work with his colleagues but was understandably reluctant about drinking during office hours. Wylie would sort himself out. Time to look forward.

Tallulah observed Kidston's arrival at Melanie's and scooted to the front door in advance of it being opened. Man and dog had their usual enthusiastic reunion, heightened by the fact that Kidston was dressed in a tracksuit; Tallulah knew what that meant. Melanie had called him to complain about his sneaky move returning her cash and persuaded him to accept it. He told her he was giving serious thought to a new car and the money would help. He'd accepted her offer for dinner; they would share a home-made lasagne once he'd had a run around the Crookfur playing fields with Tallulah.

The grass football pitches were hard and slippy, so they stuck to the red blaes track. Tallulah loved running the bends and as Kidston leaned into the corners, she raced ahead of him, turning her head to ensure she wasn't too far in front. She was a tireless running partner and Kidston always felt she could run and run forever. Kidston ran hard. He was struggling to sleep at night. The face of Russell Maitland was invading his dreams and he thought about two fatherless children, the indirect victims of Phil Canavan's criminal empire. The harder he ran, the more tired he'd get, the more chance he might have of a good night's sleep. He knew he couldn't outrun the Kennedy case, the Gorbals Samurai investigation or the ghost of Russell Maitland.

Melanie was putting the finishing touches to dinner when they got back. Kidston kicked off his muddy trainers in the hallway and rubbed Tallulah down with her towel.

'You've time for a quick shower if you want,' Melanie said.

'I'll just have a quick wash if that's okay,' Kidston replied. 'I hope I won't be too whiffy.'

'I could wash your back for you.' Melanie had that glint in her eyes. Frolicking in the large walk-in shower together had been one of their things.

'I thought we were stopping all that silliness.' Kidston smiled at her.

'You know I can't resist you when you're all hot and bothered like that.'

'Sweaty, you mean.' He laughed. 'No time, quick bite and home for a shower. I've got a promotion drinks thing on tonight.'

'Well if you say so.' She laughed too, making a face that mocked her hopes being crushed.

Kidston made a quick job of washing and towelling down. When he returned Melanie had laid the food out on the kitchen table: lasagne with garlic bread and a bottle of Valpolicella accompanied by a jug of water. Kidston heaped a large portion of the pasta onto his plate and poured himself a small glass of wine.

'Who's the night for?' Melanie asked.

'Sally Draper. My DS is getting made up to acting DI at Pitt Street for six months. The team is heading out for celebration drinks.'

'Oh, good for Sally,' she said. 'You like her, don't you? You're free to start going out now that you're not working together.'

'Sally's lovely and it has crossed my mind, but I think I've lost my mojo when it comes to romance.' Kidston paused with a forkful of pasta. 'I'm reluctant to start anything new. I'm never really sure where it's going or what's expected.'

'Don't say that, Luc. I hate to think you believe all the good things in your life are behind you.' Melanie looked straight into his eyes. 'You deserve a second chance and she's a detective: she'll understand the work thing.'

'It's too hard, Mel,' he replied. 'You and I were still getting it on from time to time, I have a decent social life with Grace. The thought of starting something new, well, it's a bit scary.'

'Oh, Luc, the you and me stuff... That's just me being lazy... and selfish. I can't be arsed starting anything new with men. This hot guy comes around occasionally and I take advantage. That's on me, but I can see I'm not doing you any favours.'

Kidston laughed. 'I'm guilty of the same thing, but you're right. It's not motivating me to move on.'

'Okay, immediate sex ban,' she announced with a huge smile. They clinked glasses, unsure of what the new arrangement would mean.

Melanie was delighted that she'd finally persuaded Luc to accept the money she owed him. When he was leaving, they held their parting embrace much longer than usual. She carried some residual guilt over their break-up; she had changed her mind about kids after they were married. Melanie was clear on what she wanted to do next.

It would involve a phone call.

## 30

Vincent Davis was out on his second night attempting to locate Canavan. He gunned the gleaming, black Kawasaki through the south-side streets, checking out the most likely locations for his prey. The four-cylinder, sixteen-valve machine would leave any police car in its wake – it could go like a bat out of hell. The katana was slung under his left shoulder, its braided *sageo* tied off to secure it inside his long, black leather coat which flowed behind him, covering the passenger seat. Vincent's face was fully masked by his crash helmet, the tinted visor ensuring he could see but not be seen. Perfect for his current mission. He'd fitted false plates on the motorbike, anticipating that the police investigation might be looking at him as a suspect for the Watters attack.

Davis checked out the Wednesday night drinkers in the Queen's Park Café on Victoria Road, a pub where Canavan was known to do collections. Checking the Victoria Bar at the junction of Allison Street, brought the teenage memories flooding back; he was directly across the road from the paper corner, the informal nightly meeting place of The Hill. His close childhood friend, Thomas 'Tombo' Bowman was the wannabe corner boy in his group. Tombo had all the swagger and ambition of a teenage gangster, attracted by the allure of the hardman myth and falling under the spell of people like Canavan and his cohort. His friendship with Tombo meant he was accepted as part of the gang, even though he found them to be juvenile bullies with their puerile pursuit of fighting, violence, and threats. It was amusing to watch them hanging around, like street-corner scarecrows, posturing in their best 'hardman' poses.

When the word was put about that Davis could handle himself, a few up-and-coming gang members tried to provoke him into a fight. It ended the fateful night that the fearsome Johnny Boy McManus, with his reputation as a fighter and a hardman, tried to assault him. The would-be assailant ended up flying through the air, arse over tit, on the end of a simple judo move. The fight, such as it was, ended with the victor standing over a winded McManus, urging him to get up and have another go. For his dazed opponent, discretion was the better part of valour. Nobody ever bothered the boy with the martial arts skills again.

Canavan would be a more challenging target; he was notorious for the levels of violence he dished out. He had loomed large through Vincent's youth as the violent and charismatic leader of The Hill. Back then, the choice for Vincent was a simple one: you ran with The Hill or you ran from The Hill. The sickening irony hadn't escaped him. He'd evaded the gang as a youth, only for one of its leaders to come back into his life and destroy it.

Canavan was a no-show at the Granite, which had a quiet crowd for a Wednesday evening. Davis had walked through the pub the night before and again tonight but there was no trace of him or McManus. He rode to Aikenhead Road beside the Holyrood sports fields and cut along Myrtle Park and checked off the house numbers. There it was: a two-storey, four-bedroomed, detached sandstone villa, with big bay windows. Canavan's castle. It was a house paid for by the misery and suffering of his victims. It stuck in Davis' craw.

Raised in a council flat, he'd never owned his own home and was unlikely to in the near future. An evil scumbag like Canavan, who'd never done an honest day's work in his life, could live in a big fancy house. Canavan and his type destroyed lives, heaped misery on their victims, whether through money lending or drug dealing, and preyed upon the weak and the vulnerable. Thoughts of righteous vengeance stirred in Davis' soul.

When Jess Sloan persuaded her friend that the high from smack was irresistible and she needed to try it, Maria's short, lethal descent into hell had begun. The contaminated heroin that killed both girls was dealt by Colin Watters in an operation run by Phil Canavan. Davis had sworn a silent oath that he would avenge Maria's death. Fired by grief and by a growing sense of injustice, he was relishing his role as a dark avenger and looked forward to the moment when he would take his revenge on Canavan.

There was a wide, generous driveway beyond the pillared gateposts but no trace of Canavan's black Mercedes. A cursory recce of the entrance told him it wasn't a good location for an attack; too open, with what looked like a security camera mounted above the entrance. Davis skirted the driveway, using the next-door neighbour's hedge for cover and avoiding the camera fixed to capture a view of the porch. He rattled the front door as he passed, staying close to the wall. He adjusted his beanie hat and hoodie and pulled a black scarf over his mouth so only his eyes were visible.

There was no response at the door, so he made his way around to the back of the house and got a good look through the ground-floor kitchen window. He suspected that Canavan might have Johnny Boy staying with him for added protection but there were no signs of life. Maybe he was lying low at his bodyguard's house. Davis smiled at the thought of Canavan slumming it in a Queen Elizabeth Square multi-storey council flat.

The lower kitchen pane smashed instantly when he struck it with the hilt of his sword. Two petrol bombs were despatched inside, and the kitchen was ablaze in seconds. Vincent lingered just long enough to see it ignite like a spark of hellfire but didn't hang around to watch it burn. He made his way back to his motorbike, retrieved his crash helmet from the pillion box and sped away from the scene. No one would see the satisfied smile behind the visor. Canavan's castle was on fire – surely now the man would be drawn into the open.

# 31

'Maria had fully qualified as a dental nurse,' Mrs Conway said, on the edge of tears, 'completed all her college courses. She had such a bright future. The family are very disappointed that no one was ever charged in connection with her death.'

'The case remains open, Mrs Conway, if we can find the evidence we need against the people we believe were responsible, then we would still prosecute them.' DS Gregor Sharp was sitting with a cup of tea in the warm and comfortable lounge of the Conway family's tenement home in Battlefield. Stark had verified the alibis of Maria's father and her brother, Kenny. Framed photographs of a smiling Maria adorned the walls and mantelpiece. A relentless aura of loss and sadness pervaded the room; it was mixed with something intangible that Stark couldn't quite put his finger on.

'The papers said she was a junkie,' Mrs Conway said, wiping a tear from her eye. 'But she was no junkie. Before that night with Jessica, she'd only ever tried a wee bit of cannabis. You know those animals had cut the heroin that Jessica gave her with rat poison.' Mrs Conway was sobbing uncontrollably now.

'Rat poison, can you believe that? My wee girl died of consuming rat poison.'

As his wife spoke, Mr Conway gripped her hand but was unable to look at the detective. *And there it is*, Stark thought. It was a delicate, ethereal thing but it was now clear that the indiscernible element that permeated the Conway family's grief was shame.

'Everybody knows who the dealers are around here,' said Kenny Conway. 'Vincent always said it was murder.'

'What about Vincent?' Stark asked. 'Is he the type that could seek revenge?'

Mr Conway exchanged a knowing glance with his son, who spoke next. 'He wanted revenge, no doubt, he was angry that the police never did anything about it.'

'Vincent was devastated when Maria died,' Mrs Conway said. 'He was grieving with the family, consumed by grief. He's still struggling. We all are.'

'Who did he hold responsible?' Stark asked.

'Phil Canavan and Colin Watters,' Kenny said, 'but I'm not saying he'd go after those guys. That would be crazy, right?'

'What can you tell me about Vincent?' Stark asked. 'What does he do for a living?'

'He's a motorbike mechanic,' Kenny said. 'Used to work in a wee place under the railway arches in Tradeston. Finished up recently. Said he's moving to stay with his sister in Ireland.'

'What other family is there?' Stark asked.

'Both parents are dead now. There's the sister in Ireland, another in Blackpool,' Mrs Conway said. 'I think we were the closest thing he had to a family.'

'Do you have any pictures of Vincent?' Stark asked.

Mrs Conway opened a cabinet and pulled a picture album from a drawer. She opened it at a double-page spread and pointed out a cluster of photos of a young couple clearly in love.

Stark's attention was drawn to one picture of Vincent and Maria picnicking by a grassy lochside. Vincent was wearing jeans and a T-shirt, which showed his muscular build. Maria was dressed in bikers' leathers. They were seated beside a black motorcycle.

'Maria used to love those bike trips to Loch Lomond and Argyll,' Mrs Conway said with a sad smile.

'Is that Vincent's motorbike?' Stark asked.

'Yes, that's his pride and joy,' Kenny said. 'He learned his trade in the military.'

'He was in the army?' Stark asked.

'French Foreign Legion,' Kenny replied.

'How long?'

'Five years. There he is with his legionnaire's buzz cut,' said Kenny, directing Stark's gaze to a picture of a lean and tanned Vincent Davis in military fatigues. 'He wasn't long out of the Legion when he met Maria six or seven years ago.'

'Was he running away from something when he joined up? The law perhaps or a broken romance?'

'His mum had just died. I don't think he had a good relationship with his father and got a bit rootless and was looking for something different,' Kenny said. 'He's never had any bother with the police as far as I know.'

'You seem to know him well, Kenny.' Stark was sensing a level of admiration, bordering on hero worship. 'Do you think he could attack someone with a sword to avenge what happened to your sister?'

'I think you may have overlooked that whoever attacked Colin Watters could well be a hero to this family,' Kenny said. 'Could Vincent do it? He's physically capable of doing a lot of damage but I'm not sure he's crazy enough to take on gangsters. More likely it'll be rival drug dealers.'

'Is he into guns or swords or any kind of weapons?' Stark asked.

Kenny Conway laughed. 'As far as I know the Foreign Legion is an elite military unit. Vincent was trained in weaponry, survival and all kinds of stuff but he'll tell people he was a mechanic. He's unassuming that way.'

'Do you know what his interests are?' Stark asked. 'What kind of hobbies, books and stuff is he into?'

'He's big into motorbikes, massively into martial arts since he was young,' Kenny said. 'His parents got him into judo, then karate to stop him hanging around street corners. He then got into kendo, taekwondo and kung fu.'

'Is he a fighter?' Stark asked.

'I wouldn't say so,' Kenny Conway replied. 'I've no doubt he could handle himself but he's not an aggressive guy. He's more into books, a serious reader. He gave me a cardboard box full of paperbacks because he was giving up his flat and going to Ireland.'

'Is there a contact address or phone number?'

'He said he'd be in touch to pass those on once he's settled in,' Kenny Conway said.

'What books?'

'Loads,' Kenny replied. 'The three books he made me read were *The Count of Monte Cristo, Beau Geste* and *Shogun.* I'm a big *Star Wars* fan. Vincent showed me the links between *Star Wars* and ancient Japan; Jedi Knights are just a futuristic version of samurais; the armour design, the masks, helmets and headgear and all that. It's obvious if you think about a samurai sword and the lightsabre.'

Both Mr and Mrs Conway shot their son a glance that said he was giving up too much information. Stark clocked it. 'Has Vincent, by any chance, got his hands on a samurai sword?'

'That would be ridiculous,' Mr Conway said. 'I'm sure this attack is a falling out between rival drug dealers.'

'Look,' Stark began. 'I'm trying to help Vincent here. He

might be in grave danger. I want to trace him before Canavan and McManus get their hands on him. If you know where Vincent is, you should be telling me.'

'As far as we know, he's gone to Donegal on his motorbike,' Mr Conway said.

Stark borrowed the two pictures, assuring Mrs Conway they'd be returned undamaged. He thanked the family for their hospitality and assisting his enquiry, reiterated his condolences and promised he would do anything he could to bring the perpetrators of Maria's death to justice.

Back at the police office, Stark checked Davis' details on the PNC and found that he was the registered keeper of a black Kawasaki motorcycle with a listed address in Mount Florida. He would make further enquiries before the end of his shift.

## 32

'Maybe he's gone to Donegal.' Canavan was impatient. They'd driven several circuits from the Gorbals to Mount Florida, via Govanhill, Crosshill, skirting the edges of Toryglen, Cathcart and Battlefield but there was no trace of their prey. They'd driven past Canavan's Myrtle Park home five minutes before Davis arrived.

'I think he's leaving a false trail,' Johnny Boy replied. 'He's gonnae try and surprise you. Remember, Wattie says this guy's a fuckin' ninja.'

'If he wanted to surprise me, why the fuck did he announce to Colin that he was coming for me?' Canavan winced at the thought of suffering the same fate as Colin Watters. 'He's playing mind games.'

They both had to admit, Davis was off the grid. They'd found his place of work at the motorbike repair garage in Tradeston, but he'd left the job the week before. The Donegal move was repeated by a colleague who was sure he'd be in Ireland by now. No forwarding contact details had been left.

The automatic gearbox of the big German saloon purred as the car descended the steep gradient of Millbrae Avenue. The route from Langside took them to Shawlands, with its popular pubs and nightlife. Canavan sat in the car while Johnny Boy checked the pubs. The little enforcer was wearing a black leather bomber jacket with branded knock-off black designer jeans. Shouldering his way through any crowds, Johnny Boy scanned the pub-goers for his man. He was confident that he'd recognise Davis even though he estimated he hadn't seen him for over fifteen years. The bantamweight hadn't lost many fights, but Davis had been responsible for one of the biggest humiliations of McManus' life when he threw him over his shoulder in a judo move. Canavan was struggling to even put a face to the name.

No trace in Findlay's, same in the Doune Castle and the Granary. Johnny Boy had always shunned Shawlands as where the poseurs drank, but all the pubs had decent midweek crowds. His final check at Shawlands Cross gave him an idea.

'Let's have a pint in the Granary before we chuck it. This has been thirsty work and there's some brilliant fanny in there.'

'Wee man, you're just a rampant shagger but you've persuaded me. This is supposed to be one of his haunts; maybe he'll walk in while we're having a beer.'

The journey between the Gorbals' Granite City Inn and the Granary at Shawlands Cross was only two miles or so, but the distance may as well have been measured in light years. It was like the scene out of *An American Werewolf in London* where the two hitchhikers enter the bar. The sudden silence, then the questioning looks; what are *you* doing *here*? A space at the busy bar appeared as if by magic, as the regulars slowly, imperceptibly shifted to make room for the interlopers.

Canavan's scar always had that effect. Nobody wanted to stare at a man who looked that hard and that dangerous; a man who exuded that level of menace. Scar apart, without his sidekick, who was drooling like a wean in a sweetie shop,

Canavan would have looked the part. He was dressed in a tailored wool coat, button-down collared shirt and stylish, grey check trousers, matched with black leather loafers.

Johnny Boy, with his broad, bantam body shape and a posture that leant permanently forward as though challenging everybody to a square go, was a total misfit. He walked with an exaggerated gallus swagger, shoulders swinging like a metronome, eyeing up men as potential opponents and women as possible sexual conquests. Even standing still seemed to challenge him, as he bobbed from side to side, changing feet in perpetual motion, ready to pounce. It was too much for a pub with the reserved, informal cool of the Granary. Too much testosterone. Too much aggression. Johnny Boy was incapable of dialling it down.

They ordered two Castlemaine lagers and took in the ambience of the popular south side establishment. Situated right on the huge Y-junction where Kilmarnock Road forks off Pollokshaws Road, the pub, with its striking green-and-gold livery, occupied the vast ground-floor level of a striking sandstone 'flat iron' tenement with its own roof terrace.

Johnny Boy wasn't wrong; this was poseur central, with an older clientele. The main bar was primarily a standing area where bar stools were used as coat hangers. There was a raised seating area off the bar used as a diner and through in the smaller lounge, next door, there were booths for those who preferred to sit down. But the poseurs shunned the lounge; all the action took place in the main bar with its sweeping, elongated counter and huge mirrored gantry.

Johnny Boy was transfixed. Not by the plentiful beautiful women in the bar, but by the miniature model train above his head. The track ran above the gantry, just below ceiling height and followed the long, circuitous line of the bar and then skirted the corners of the pub. He couldn't help gazing upwards, waiting for the little train to return to his eyeline.

'Not cool, wee man, stop gawping at that fuckin' train.' It was a firm rebuke from Canavan.

'Sorry, man, but that's brilliant.' Johnny Boy McManus, brutal thug, money lender and violent enforcer was nine years old again.

Canavan felt a firm hand on his shoulder. 'Mr Kidston, I didn't know this was a polis boozer.' Canavan did a quick scan to see who the detective was with. The two men knew each other of old.

'Didn't know that you frequented this place, Phil.' Kidston eyed Canavan's next response closely. 'You looking for somebody?'

'Nah, the wee man wanted to see the train set.' Canavan smiled. Johnny Boy stood in silence beside his boss, avoiding eye contact. Detectives made him anxious.

'Every day's like Christmas in here, Phil.' Kidston returned the smile. 'How's your friend Colin Watters' recovery coming along? I'm sure you've been up to see him at the Viccy.'

'I think the surgeons have saved his hand.' Canavan was very cool. 'Are you going to catch whoever done it?'

'I could ask you the same question, Phil. You tell me who you think it was?'

'I have no idea or I'd be telling you, Mr Kidston. I only hope you catch him before anyone else is hurt.'

'Are you worried someone is hunting you?' Kidston asked.

'I think we'll leave you and your colleagues to enjoy your wee night out, Mr Kidston.' Canavan had had enough. He nodded to Johnny Boy and both men swigged the last of their pints.

Kidston put a hand on Canavan's shoulder again. 'Before you go, Phil, we'll need to bring you both in for a chat about the

Watters case, so it was opportune meeting you tonight. Of course, if you hear anything about who attacked him, you'll bring the information to me, yes?' Another firm look towards both departing men. 'There'll be no taking the law into your own hands.'

'In that case, Mr Kidston, I'll have my lawyer contact you and we can arrange a visit to the station for our chat,' Canavan replied.

Kidston's pale eyes trained on Canavan as the two men left the bar. He noticed the strong family resemblance between Phil and Sarah. The livid expression on Johnny Boy's face told Kidston what he needed to know. They were looking for someone and it was unlikely any of their usual money lending or drug-dealing clients would frequent a place like the Granary.

He would know more tomorrow. Gregor Stark was working overtime with the late-shift crew to track down the family networks of Maria Conway and Jessica Sloan. He'd chosen to miss Draper's promotion celebration to work on the Watters enquiry.

A group of nine detectives had started out at Findlay's, the first stop in a Shawlands pub crawl, where they all toasted Draper's success. John Wylie had given it a miss, still unable to congratulate his colleague. Next up was the Doune Castle, where the numbers dropped to seven. The last five standing arrived in the Granary. The CID group had visited the same Shawlands pubs as two of the most notorious criminals in the south side. It was a strange night.

Draper, Metcalfe, Mork Williams and Zorba Quinn had watched, astonished, as Kidston made straight for Canavan and McManus. All four followed, standing close by. Williams and Quinn had never seen Canavan in the flesh before. Williams was fascinated by the man's presence; a violent aura seemed to emanate from him. It was more than the ugly scar; there was a fierce intensity to Canavan. To the young detective, he was violence personified.

The detectives huddled together, speaking in low voices. Kidston, in the centre of the group, told them of his now near certainty that the two interlopers were out looking for whoever attacked Watters. It was likely that they had a name and that person was now in danger. They would need to get to him before his hunters.

The shop talk dropped off so they could return to the topic of Draper's promotion. She looked stunning in a shiny green dress and black patent leather heels that would never be seen in the workplace. The colour suited her, complementing the dark green of her eyes and contrasting with her flaming mane of red hair and pale skin.

It had been a great night out for the group of colleagues who worked hard and partied hard. Sally was well regarded by the team with one obvious exception but that didn't spoil the celebration. She'd been drinking red wine to start with but had moved on to vodka and would have a sore head in the morning. Mork and Zorba had stayed on bottled beers all night. As the designated drivers, Metcalfe and Kidston were both on soft drinks.

When the night broke up, Mork Williams walked back to his flat in Shawlands. Metcalfe would drop Zorba off north of the Clyde on her way back to Hyndland. Draper lived in Orchard Park, not too far from Kidston's Giffnock home. He held the door open as she slid into his Alfa Romeo. The cassette was playing 'Tinseltown in the Rain' by The Blue Nile, the glorious melancholy of Paul Buchanan's voice blaring through the car speakers. He turned the volume down a few notches so they could talk.

'Memorable night, but I bet you didn't think Phil Canavan would turn up at your pay-off.' Kidston was laughing.

'Or John Wylie, but I was right about him. I knew he wasn't going to trap.' Draper fumbled with the recliner control and her seat suddenly shot back to a near lying position. 'Oops. Didn't know that was going to happen.' She was giggling.

'Yes, Sally, just you have a wee lie down.'

'So this is how you seduce your women, DI Kidston?'

'What women would that be, DI Draper?' Kidston smiled down at her. She was stretched out, her long legs in the footwell. Her shimmery green dress had ridden up her thighs, revealing the lacy tops of her black stay-up stockings and a tiny flash of milk-white thigh. 'Things have been very quiet on that front since my divorce. My ex-wife will tell you: I'm married to the job.'

'That's such a shame.' Draper reached her hand onto Luc's, which was resting on the gearstick. To her delight, he didn't pull away. Instead, he held her hand and gave it the gentlest squeeze.

They arrived at her home, in a row of neat semis on a tree-lined avenue.

'For goodness' sake, I'm lying here like a whore in distress.' Draper laughed in mock horror as she adjusted her dress and righted the car seat. 'I'm going to have a black coffee, maybe several, before I go to bed. Would you like to join me?'

'That would be nice.' Kidston's head was swimming. There was no longer any reason to avoid a romantic liaison with Sally. Yes, she was a colleague, but she was no longer part of his team. There would be no complications; at least none of a professional nature. They'd been attracted to each other for some time, that much was obvious.

Tonight was the night.

She took his arm as they walked up the path. Wobbling on her heels, she gripped Kidston tighter. 'These shoes were a good idea at the start of the night.' She threw her head back, laughing.

As soon as the door closed, they were kissing frantically and undressing each other; Kidston pressed her against the wall and slipped his hand under her dress. Sally fumbled for his belt and zipper, smothering him with her deep hot kisses. She wrapped her legs around his waist as he lifted her up and carried her to the sofa.

He broke off for air. 'Can we just pause for a moment?'

'What's wrong?' Sally pulled her head back.

'This shouldn't happen; not tonight. You've had too much to drink.'

'I'm fine, Luc. Honestly, take me to bed, please.' She rubbed her hand across his erection. 'You know you want to.'

'Oh, I really do, but maybe tonight's not the right time. There'll be other opportunities soon.' He kissed her tenderly on the forehead. 'I just don't want there to be any regrets in the morning.'

On the short drive home, Kidston reflected on how his night had ended. Sally was a stunning woman, sexier than he could have imagined but he'd followed his better angels. It was hard to walk away but it was important to him that Sally didn't wake up with a headful of regrets to go with her hangover.

He lay in bed, thinking about Canavan and Johnny Boy's visit to the Granary, convinced they were out on the hunt. Who was their prey? Gregor should have some leads for that in the morning. Sally Draper kept interrupting his chain of thought; the passionate way they'd kissed was imprinted in his mind. Things had gotten hot and steamy very quickly and he was already looking forward to the next time. Perhaps it was time to look at a new relationship. Sally was a strong possibility. She knew the pressures of police work so they may have a chance. He was over-reliant on Grace for a social life and he and Mel were calling a halt to their occasional casual sex arrangement. It wasn't encouraging either of them to move on with their lives.

As he vainly attempted to fall asleep it was different

characters who blocked his slumber. He thought about the faceless Maitland children; little Beverley and her electric piano and wee Dennis, his dad no longer able to teach him football. If only their father had stood still and waited to be rescued, he'd still be in their lives. Kidston held Phil Canavan responsible for Maitland's death with his money lending, the exorbitant interest rates, his debt enforcement tactics and the violent punishments he dished out. Phil Canavan was overdue a long stretch in jail. As he continued to battle a fitful sleep, Kidston thought about Sarah Canavan's comments about Paul Kennedy's temper. Had Sarah corrupted his assessment of his young protégé's character and his guilt or innocence?

## 33

Thursday

The CID office was buzzing with the news of the two unexpected gatecrashers at Draper's night out. Wylie's oddly enigmatic smile hinted he was sorry to miss *that* encounter. When Kidston saw the faces of some of his colleagues, he was thankful he had been on the orange juice. He caught Draper's eye; a nod and a small smile passed between them, but she held his gaze. No regrets.

Wylie was waving a crime report in front of the assembled CID morning meeting. 'Deliberate fire-raising at Phil Canavan's home last night. Thousands of pounds of damage caused by two petrol bombs set off in the kitchen on the ground floor, rear of the house.'

'That can't be a coincidence,' Kidston began. 'While Canavan and McManus were in the pub looking for Watters' attacker, their target sets Canavan's castle on fire. This is turning into quite the vendetta.'

'I might have something to offer in regard to a potential suspect,' Stark said. He briefed the team about the previous night's enquiries with the Sloan and Conway families. Both fathers and both brothers had been interviewed and eliminated, together with Jessica's boyfriend. He reported on how his enquiries had focused mainly on Maria's boyfriend.

'This is a very sad case,' Stark reminded his colleagues. 'As you all know, we strongly suspected that the heroin contaminated with rat poison came from Canavan and his crew but there was no evidence to charge anyone.'

'There was nothing. All the contaminated smack disappeared off the street,' Wylie concurred with his fellow sergeant. 'I worked with the drugs squad on that one.'

'Okay, Gregor, time to land the plane. What about the boyfriend?' Kidston was becoming impatient. His young DS was enjoying holding court a bit too much.

'Vincent Davis. Age thirty-three, a motorbike mechanic, who until very recently worked in a garage in Tradeston. No police record. I've traced his motorbike and his current address from PNC. I've placed a marker for the bike on file; stop and detain for police interview as a suspect for serious assault. I included a warning for the sword MO, so officers know what they might be dealing with and for Gorbals CID to be informed. I checked the address last night while you were all out toasting Sally's promotion.'

'My hero,' mocked Draper.

'You did want this investigation,' Wylie reminded Stark.

'Flat is empty,' Stark said, ignoring their barbs. 'I spoke to the next-door neighbour last night. Told her he was off to Ireland to stay with his sister. She tells me there was a scary wee muscly guy with dark frizzy hair looking for him on Tuesday evening.'

'That's McManus. That's the clincher,' Kidston continued.

The little enforcer, once described as a Diego Maradona lookalike, was a true one-off. 'They were looking for Davis last night. Does he drink in Shawlands?'

'That area. Maria used to do waitressing at Di Maggio's at Shawlands Cross, so they did socialise around there,' Stark replied. He opened his folder and placed the two pictures of Davis on the table. 'Handle with care please, these have to go back to Mrs Conway.'

'Fine physical specimen,' said Metcalfe.

'Ex-military?' asked Wylie.

'Five years in the French Foreign Legion.'

'Potentially a force to be reckoned with then,' said Kidston as he eyed the pictures.

'Very much so,' said Stark. 'Maria's family describe him as quiet, unassuming, law-abiding, into his motorbikes and reading books. But he was also heavily into... Guess what?'

'Swords?' asked Wylie.

'Samurai movies?' asked Metcalfe.

'Well, close. Martial arts.' Stark sounded triumphant. 'This fits with my revenge theory. This guy has the motive, and he has the skills.'

'The garage would give him the kit and materials he needed to make petrol bombs,' Wylie said. 'I've marked the fire-raising enquiry to myself. I'll liaise with the fire brigade investigators and link in with Gregor on the Watters case. We could be looking for the same suspect.'

'Quiet, bookish and unassuming,' Metcalfe said. 'He doesn't sound crazy enough.'

'The Conway family said he was consumed with grief and angry that the police hadn't arrested anyone,' Stark said. 'He and Maria were a big love story, making plans for the future. Her brother said Vincent holds Watters and Canavan responsible.

The family were reluctant to finger him as a suspect, but nobody doubted that he's capable.'

'As a former legionnaire, I don't think he'd be scared of a couple of Glasgow gangsters,' Kidston said.

'We need to look at him. I think the motive is revenge. This is my vigilante theory,' Stark said. 'Even if it's confined to Canavan and his crew, he wants to punish them. It's just vengeance.'

'You've made it all sound pretty plausible to me,' Kidston said. 'Do we know where he might be living now, where he drinks?'

'The motorbike repair shop confirmed he quit his job last week,' Stark replied. 'It looks like he might be lying low.'

'We know why Vincent Davis has fallen off the radar. He knows they'll be coming after him, especially after the fire, but where the hell is he?' Kidston asked. 'Maybe Gregor's on the money and Davis isn't finished at just Watters. He may be going after Canavan and McManus and they're running scared, looking for him.'

'It's crazy,' Metcalfe began. 'Going up against the likes of Watters, Canavan and McManus. Does he even know what they're capable of?'

'We need to find Davis before Canavan does, as a priority.' Kidston looked solemn. 'Either way, we get those two clowns from last night in. Official warning that if anything happens to Davis, we have them in the frame for it.

'Vincent Davis could be signing his own death warrant.'

# 34

'Very nice to meet you both, detectives.' Max Van Zandt seemed taken by Draper going by how long he held her handshake. She and Kidston had attended at Adam Sharkey's offices to collect the lawyer and the hypnotist for their Thursday afternoon appointment and the twenty-minute run to Barlinnie.

Van Zandt was a warm, friendly character, small in stature but with a huge personality and a striking sense of personal style. He was in his late forties and dressed in a flawless black suit with a Nehru-collared jacket, worn with a scarlet silk cravat. His hands and face were tanned, and he wore his slicked black hair in a high pompadour redolent of a young sixties-styled Elvis Presley.

Draper was taken by his charm and by the mellifluous tone of his baritone voice. She imagined being hypnotised by a voice like that. The man spoke like a Shakespearean actor. Van Zandt explained that he'd qualified as a psychologist before retraining as a hypnotherapist and setting up a new business with his wife.

He had worked with athletes and sports teams as a performance coach. That had developed into helping people with their phobias through hypnotherapy. Everything from a fear of hypodermic needles to claustrophobics who were unable to enter an elevator.

His first forensic referral had come from a barrister friend. A traumatised rape victim was able to recall vital evidential information that hadn't been included in the original police statement.

'So how will it work with Paul?' Draper was curious.

'In a forensic sense he's a strong candidate, given the incident he was involved in.'

'How so?' Kidston asked.

'Emotional or physical shock, intense trauma or fear can put blocks on specific memories,' Van Zandt replied. 'This is an example of the power of the subconscious mind acting as a protective shield to preserve our emotional balance, especially in the midst of destabilising circumstances.'

'That sounds like a very good fit for what happened to our colleague. I'm sure it was a shocking, traumatic experience for him.' Kidston was intrigued. 'A hypnotic trance can access repressed memories?'

'Undoubtedly. We can retrieve any part of the stored data, or memories we wish to access by unlocking the subconscious mind through hypnosis.'

'Very impressive,' Draper said. 'It will be good to see Paul. I wonder how he's holding up.'

Arrival at the formidable and oppressive HMP Barlinnie was a new experience for Draper. She wondered what Van Zandt would make of the place. The scale of the old Victorian jail estate surprised her. From the outside, the massive sandstone walls, topped with barbed wire, gave the appearance of an impenetrable fortress. Even for a police officer, albeit one making her first visit, entering the prison was an unsettling experience; the noise from the hydraulics of the giant mechanical outer gate closing behind you was unnerving. The second gate remained sealed like a submarine airlock, until the visitors and their credentials were verified. For those few minutes, until the second gate slid open, the sense of imprisonment was palpable.

Inside, the high glass roof permitted welcome daylight to the five galleried landings and their inhabitants. Draper had never seen so much signage in any building. There were notices everywhere: warnings, reminders, prohibitions, and posters for classes and activities. The large remand hall that housed untried prisoners had a more accessible visiting regime than the other custody halls, in recognition that pre-trial detainees were innocent until proven guilty.

Sharkey had arranged for Kennedy's interview with Van Zandt to take place in an observation room. The lawyer and the two detectives would watch and listen in the adjacent room. Van Zandt was working from notes prepared by Kidston from his meetings with Rodgers and Kennedy, with the session being taped on a portable recorder. There was a brief outpouring of joy when Kennedy's prison officer escort brought him to the room. He looked healthy but tired and was dressed in a sweatshirt and chinos.

'How are you holding up, Paul?' Kidston put his free arm around Kennedy's shoulder as he shook his hand.

'Well, I'm still innocent,' Kennedy said with a forced smile. The humour couldn't mask the haunted look in his eyes, but it put the group at ease. He enquired about Ellie Hunter's condition.

'No change, I'm afraid,' Kidston said.

Draper and Kennedy shared a warm embrace. Sharkey introduced Max Van Zandt, who explained how the session would run. The others left the hypnotist and his subject in the room and retreated next door where they found the space laid out with screens and headphones.

The three observers watched and listened, fascinated by Van Zandt's technique as he spent some time getting Paul to relax in his chair. Deploying a procedure the hypnotist called 'magnetic fingers', Paul was directed to clasp his hands above his head but keep his pointing forefingers apart. The hypnotist's warm, measured tones ordered Paul to focus on the gap between his two forefingers, until his eyes got heavy... then heavier... then heavier still.

As the gap closed, so did Paul's eyes.

With fingers touching and eyes fully closed, Paul was directed to drop his hands onto his lap. He was now in a trance. Van Zandt spoke more softly, his soothing voice dropping to a gentle whisper as he guided Paul's breathing. Breathing in. Breathing out.

Long silences.

Five... four... three... two... one... zero.

Deeper... deeper... deeper.

In the room next door, the three observers exchanged enthusiastic glances. Draper shook her head vigorously; fearful she was coming under Van Zandt's magic spell.

The hypnotist's brief was to focus on the line of enquiry about the other cars on the country road that night.

'You were with your friend and colleague Barry Rodgers, yes?'

'I didn't want to be there, it was just Barry looking for a pull.' Kennedy was speaking in his normal voice.

'You were in the back seat with the blonde girl, Ellie. Do you remember?'

'Yes. Barry was with Clare.'

'Ellie left the vehicle, is that right?'

'Yes,' Paul confirmed.

'What happened next?'

'I did something... something really stupid.'

There was a hush in the observation room. Draper nudged Kidston. 'What if he confesses?'

Kidston shook his head and shushed her.

'Why stupid, Paul?' Van Zandt asked. 'What did you do?'

'I stayed in the car when I should have gone after her.' Kennedy spoke more slowly. 'It became obvious that nothing was going to happen with us. Neither of us were into it. I think she was embarrassed because Clare was looking at her over the back of the seat.'

'Is that why she didn't want to do anything?' the hypnotist asked.

'I think so. It was freezing cold. I didn't take it as an invitation to go outside.'

'So you stayed in the car?'

'It was obvious they didn't want me hanging around.'

'How long did you wait before you left?'

'Not long. Just over a minute. I couldn't sit there and watch the two of them snogging the face off each other.' Kennedy was in a deep trance now, his breathing noticeably slowed.

'So you went after Ellie?'

'Yes, I left them to it. But as soon as I closed the car door, I realised I had no idea what direction she had gone. I shouted her name... again and again. It was pitch-dark. I couldn't see my hand in front of my face. I kept tripping on the grass verge. I was worried that I was walking into the fence.'

'So no lights?'

'None. No house lights anywhere in the distance. I reckoned I'd set off in the opposite direction from her, so I gave it around ten minutes then turned back, thinking that would be plenty of time for Barry and Clare to do the business. I fully expected to see her sitting in the back seat of the car when I got back.'

'Okay, Paul, that's very good.' The hypnotist paused. 'You're very relaxed, keep those long, slow, deep breaths. Deeper... deeper... deeper.'

To the observers watching in the next room it seemed Paul was experiencing a waking dream.

Van Zandt resumed the session, his voice soft but resonant. 'When did you see her again?'

'When the three of us found her lying on the road in the other direction.'

'How did that make you feel?' Van Zandt asked.

'I felt dreadful,' Paul replied. 'I'd let her go off on her own. Anything that happened to her after that was down to me.'

The observation room fell completely silent. Draper and Kidston exchanged the smallest, briefest glance that spoke volumes. Their colleague was wracked with guilt and shame.

'Okay, and this is very important, Paul. Who or what else did you see when you walked that country road looking for Ellie?'

'Four other cars passed me when I was walking back to Barry's car. Each time I thought it was him coming to pick me up, but it wasn't.'

'Remember those cars, Paul. What can you see?'

'Not much, it was pitch-dark. Only one slowed down to look at me but it wasn't Barry.'

'Who was it, Paul? Did you see?'

'It was a solo male driver... it was a low-slung car... no colour... but a saloon or a sporty model. It was very dark.'

'Look at the car again now, what else can you see?'

'The reg number was V-A-L and three numbers. I remember it, VAL.'

The watchers next door exchanged triumphant looks. Sharkey punched the air.

'Anything else about that car, Paul?'

'VAL. It was definitely VAL. It was too dark to see anything more. Nothing else.'

'Anything about the driver, his age or his description?'

'Too dark to see inside the car. The registration plate had a light, but it was only lit to one side. I only saw VAL.'

'Paul, one last important question.' Van Zandt paused. 'Did you attack Ellie Hunter that night?'

'No, I did not.'

The hypnotist turned towards the ceiling-mounted camera and gave a discreet thumbs up.

They waited and watched while Max Van Zandt restored Paul to the here and now. A slightly groggy Paul Kennedy was gratified to have recalled a partial plate number while he was under. It offered another line of enquiry. It was a glimmer of hope.

Kidston asked for the room to have a few minutes with Paul before they left. Draper watched their animated conversation through the glass.

'That was amazing, boss,' an elated Kennedy said. 'Thank you for arranging it. That must help my case, right?'

'Not if the fiscal calls Sarah Canavan as a character witness,' Kidston said with a look of anger.

Kennedy looked deflated.

'I had a very interesting chat with your ex-girlfriend the other night,' Kidston said. 'I hope the scar on your arse cheek has healed up.'

'I can only imagine the report card Sarah gave me. That was four years ago, boss. I've never known a relationship like it, before or since. We'd get into it, smashed on red wine.'

'Regardless of your sexual exploits. You know this is the sister of Phil Canavan we're talking about?'

'She was going by McWilliams when I met her, boss. I had no idea about her family.'

A dismayed Kidston shook his head as he ushered Kennedy's prison officer escort back into the room. The elation on Paul's face had been replaced by a subdued expression.

Draper quizzed Kidston on the walk back to the car as Sharkey walked ahead with Van Zandt. 'That all looked a bit serious. What was that about?'

Kidston related his discussion with Sarah Canavan without revealing the original source that had flagged the relationship between her and Paul.

'What?' Draper was stunned. 'Is he completely mad?'

'Perhaps you're a better judge of Paul's character than I am,' Kidston said. 'Maybe I've been blinded by my ego. He was my protégé, I couldn't see his faults the way others can. For most of the period I've known him, it's always been about him settling down with Sandra Holt.'

'Don't second-guess yourself, Luc. Van Zandt has just pulled a major rabbit out of the hat. We need to work with that.'

Their conversation tailed off when they caught up with the others. On the journey back to Sharkey's office the hypnotist discussed the specifics of the case.

'I imagine this new evidence will be highly inconvenient for the original police investigation,' Van Zandt said. 'Could be very interesting in court.'

'Hopefully, that evidence won't need to go near a courtroom and the new line of enquiry reveals a more likely suspect.' Sharkey was considering his defence strategy. 'If the girl dies or wakes up with no memory then I can use it for an impeachment defence. It looks very clear now; if there was a crime, then it wasn't committed by Paul Kennedy.'

The two detectives nodded in agreement with Sharkey's plan. Impeachment or incrimination was a long-established special defence in Scots law where another named person is accused of committing the crime. To be competent, the defence relies on a *specific* other person being accused. Sharkey and Van Zandt had found a door to an alternative theory of what happened to Ellie Hunter. It was now up to the detectives to find the key.

## 35

Draper spent the remainder of Thursday afternoon on a speculative enquiry on the Police National Computer. Combinations of V-A-L and any set of numbers turned up five vehicles in the greater Glasgow area. Three were registered to women with the first name Valerie; one in Shawlands, one in Milngavie and one in Paisley. Two were registered to men; one to a man named James Crossan in Barrhead, which was closest to the incident, and the other to a man in Cambuslang.

Draper would normally have generated five action sheets for her and Metcalfe to make enquiries. Given the secrecy of their mission, she noted the five addresses in the back of her police notebook. En route to the first address, they discussed the possibility that any car involved could be a vehicle owned by a wife or partner but used by a man. They decided to start with the Paisley and Barrhead enquiries.

The detectives clocked the light-blue Ford Escort parked on the driveway outside the Paisley address. Valerie McGovern was a thirty-nine-year-old hairdresser who'd put a private plate on her pride and joy. She confirmed that there was no spouse or boyfriend with access to her car.

Metcalfe lit up a Regal and wound down the passenger window as they drove away from the house. 'I think Ms McGovern was disappointed that her cherished plate was more common than she thought.'

Draper was unimpressed. 'Pure vanity. Different if you had a Bentley, or a Beamer but an Escort?'

They set off for nearby Barrhead but there was no trace of James Crossan at the block of flats listed on the PNC as his address. Draper noticed the curtains twitching at a well-maintained semi-bungalow across the street. Metcalfe agreed it was worth a punt. A well-dressed elderly woman answered the door while shooing a small dog into a side room. 'Can I help you, ladies?'

'Yes, I'm DC Metcalfe and this is DS Draper from Strathclyde Police. Do you know the man who lives across from you?'

'Oh, lady policemen.' The news she was dealing with female detectives seemed to surprise and delight her. 'Oh yes, Jimmy Crossan. Is everything okay?'

'Absolutely, yes. Everything's fine,' Metcalfe answered. 'We just need to speak to him about a car he might have owned.'

'Oh, it's always cars with Jimmy. He runs a wee auto repair place down at the railway arches at Kelburn Street. There are always cars parked around here. I think he buys and sells them.'

'Would he be there now?' Draper asked.

'He should be. He normally comes back around teatime.'

'Thank you so much. That's very helpful.' Draper smiled.

'Will I pass on that you were looking for him and get him to call you?'

'We'll come back later. Best not to worry him. Thanks.' Draper hoped she wouldn't tell her neighbour that the police were sniffing around. 'One last question: do you know Mr Crossan's wife's name?'

'His wife is Valerie.' The detectives exchanged a knowing look.

They made their way to the address given and found a long line of small businesses operating out of the spacious archways under the block sandstone railway bridge. They spotted 'JC Motors' signposted across an archway entrance with a number of cars parked outside. A cursory check suggested a repair, paint and body shop and a small-scale sales operation. There were eight cars on the lot but not all of them had for sale stickers on the windscreens. The vehicle listed for Crossan was a 1982 silver-coloured BMW 3 series, VAL 777. There was no trace of it on the lot.

The detectives entered the small office at the rear of the arch. A young, long-haired man with oil-blackened hands, wearing a blue boiler suit greeted them.

'Jimmy Crossan?' Draper asked.

'Naw. He's away picking up a car. He'll be in tomorrow.' He gave his name as Danny and explained his boss was collecting a car in Berwick and would be back later in the evening.

'What car is Jimmy driving for himself these days?' Metcalfe asked.

'It changes, a lot. He's got a Merc at the minute.'

'Do you happen to know the reg number?' Metcalfe continued.

'Private plate. Something with JEC but don't ask me the numbers.'

'What about VAL 777 on a cherished plate?' Draper asked.

'His wife Valerie had that on a 3 Series BMW, but I think she sold it recently.'

'Any idea who bought it?' Draper asked.

'I can't help you there, but Jimmy or Valerie could tell you when they're back.' He confirmed that Mrs Crossan had made the trip south with her husband and that there would be no record of the sale in the office ledger as it was a private transaction. 'Can I pass on a message or a name?' Danny looked keen to have something to tell his boss.

'Let him know the police called in for a chat about one of his cars. We'll be back tomorrow.'

The detectives drove off discussing the latest developments in their enquiry. A man with access to a car with the plate VAL 777, from an area close to where Ellie Hunter was attacked, was the best they'd come up with at this point. Even under hypnosis, Paul Kennedy was unable to ascertain a make, model or colour. Van Zandt had explained that if he hadn't seen something, he wouldn't be able to remember it.

The VAL prefix was all they had and if Jimmy Crossan was in the habit of driving his wife's car he would be interviewed under caution. The Barrhead Dams was such a remote location that it tended to be used mostly by locals who knew the network of country roads. They agreed to set aside the other three addresses in the meantime to focus on Crossan. An enquiry that had started out with an almost overwhelming feeling that they were clutching at straws now offered a faint sense of optimism.

## 36

As he reflected on the remarkable technique of Max Van Zandt, Kidston hoped that the apparent breakthrough on the Kennedy case might, at last, allow him a good night's sleep. He had never seen anything quite like it. He'd always imagined hypnotists as twirly moustachioed showmen, with loud waistcoats and a gold fob watch on a long chain. An image far removed from applying hypnosis to the world of police investigations and witness testimony. He helped himself to a beer from the fridge and slipped Steely Dan's *Gaucho* LP onto the turntable. Both his major cases; authorised and unauthorised, seemed to be moving in the right direction.

Despite Sarah Canavan's revelations, Kidston felt more confident about Paul Kennedy's innocence. Anyone hearing his 'in trance' testimony earlier would surely be persuaded. The new line of enquiry around the cherished number plate was a major breakthrough. He thought about his young detective, incarcerated in a Barlinnie remand cell, and about the guilt and shame that had surfaced during his hypnosis. It had all looked so bleak for Paul, but now there was a new hope. Kidston was convinced; the person who attacked Ellie Hunter remained at large.

The Watters case was also shifting into a firmer focus. The fire at Canavan's had made the news and Joe Sawyers had been asking to be kept updated on the investigation. That meant Q and the Pitt Street bosses had been leaning on him; headlines about sword attacks were making the politicians nervous. With planning for the Garden Festival well underway and with City of Culture status on the near horizon, the city fathers would brook no return to the days of *No Mean City*.

The attack was a perplexing case, but Gregor Stark's vigilante theory had been on the money. It now looked likely that the individual responsible was Vincent Davis. The fire-raising seemed like a provocation to lure Canavan and McManus into the open. With those two hunting him, it would be better for Davis if he had gone to Ireland. It would be bottomed out; the two hunters would be warned off. The police were onto them. Davis would need to be found and face charges. It was starting to come together.

Kidston thought about Sally Draper and their encounter last night. It was a nice diversion from all the other stuff he was dealing with. Their attraction seemed to be mutual and Sally hadn't held back. Definitely something there, something they could build on.

Kidston's phone rang, interrupting Donald Fagen's vocal on 'Third World Man'. He pointed the remote at the hi-fi and dialled the volume down. It was Grace.

'You missed the end of my gig on Saturday.'

'Apologies for that. It was a great show you guys put on. You got my message?'

'Yes, but you sounded very low. Do you have a lot on? I can come over if you want.'

'I've had a dreadful few days,' Kidston said. 'I lost a man off the Erskine Bridge after your gig on Saturday. I'm afraid I may not be such good company.'

'I'll be the judge of that, Kidston.' Grace never let him get maudlin.

'Okay, Cassidy, come over and get your ears well and truly bent.'

Grace appeared fifteen minutes later with a bottle of Barolo she knew he would enjoy. They wasted no time swigging down the first two glasses. He told her the story of Russell Maitland, how he fell to his death and why he was racked with guilt over the incident. Kidston outlined his dilemma presented by the Kennedy case; the hopeful outcome from the forensic hypnosis session and the new lead based on the partial registration number. Ultimately, the Kennedy case remained a high-risk enterprise. He was running an unauthorised investigation. He shared his concerns with her. She smiled sympathetically when he told her about Paul Kennedy's indiscretions from four years ago and the nature of his relationship with Sarah Canavan.

Grace was an excellent listener. She nursed her wine, allowing him to vent and reveal where he felt exposed and vulnerable. There was a genuine fear that the Kennedy case could blow up in his face and do lasting, probably terminal, damage to his career. She understood that Sarah Canavan's revelations about the young detective's character would have Kidston questioning his motivation for getting involved, especially in an investigation that was not his case. But if he believed Kennedy was innocent, he would keep probing. It was in his nature.

He shared the latest in the Watters case and how the focus of the sword attack enquiry had switched from a drugs feud to a maniacal vigilante wreaking vengeance on a major criminal team.

'So you've got lots of plates in the air. How's that working out?'

'Joe Sawyers always taught me to differentiate between the plastic plates and the ones made of precious china.'

'So Paul Kennedy is your priority?'

'Technically yes, but it's fraught with danger. I'm supposed to be nowhere near that investigation. I've got uniforms doing road checks in the Dams later tonight. That's another risk.' Luc threw his head back and blew out an enormous sigh. 'And there's political pressure being applied in the Gorbals Samurai case. You know I leave the politics to Joe Sawyers, but I need to find this guy before he chops up any more people or ends up dead.'

Grace listened while Luc unburdened his troubles.

'I had the falling dream again,' Luc said. 'Things must be bad.' Other than his parents, Grace was the only person he'd ever told about his childhood nightmares.

'Your flying technique never kicked in?'

'Hit the ground, woke up with a shock.'

'What do you think's behind it?' Grace looked concerned. 'Sounds like anxiety of some kind. Maybe you should quit the negotiator role if it's placing you in those types of situations.'

'That's what Mel said.'

'She might be right. I overcame my fear of the dark as a young girl by avoiding situations that made me feel anxious. I'm not comparing the two but maybe you should come off the roster.' Grace smiled softly. 'And you wouldn't miss the end of my gigs. Seriously though, it's probably survivor guilt.'

'It's got to be about the Erskine Bridge incident. I'm seeing Russell Maitland's face in my sleep, having nightmares about his two fatherless kids. It might be to do with the Miller thing. That's about the personal animosity between us and the risks I'm taking by looking into his investigation. The rest is just standard detective work.'

Kidston wondered if there was anyone else that he could have this conversation with. Could he show this more vulnerable side of himself to a colleague like Sally Draper? How long would it take? Grace had seen every possible side of him. They'd cried in each other's arms when they split up. He'd imagined there would be more girls to rival Grace; a foolish notion. If they'd stuck together, seen it through, he might have avoided the biggest regret of his life: the failure of his marriage to Mel. They'd supported each other when their marriages broke down. Nothing was off the table with Grace.

'Poor Luca.' She sidled up beside him on the sofa and he put his arm around her, kissing her gently on the forehead. There was an old familiar stirring sensation as Grace's body, in the throes of arousal, reacted to his kiss. She slid her hand up from Luc's chest to caress his cheek and kissed him full on the mouth; it was a slow, soft kiss, full of intent. Luc responded in kind, his head spinning, lost in Grace's warm embrace. They started fumbling at each other's clothes but rose together from the sofa, half undressed, and made their way, hand in hand, to the bedroom.

They made love as if it had never happened before; two different people but somehow the same. There was gentleness and intensity as they explored and rediscovered each other after a gap of seventeen years. Novel, weirdly familiar but very satisfying. The former teenage lovers had shared a close, platonic friendship for almost two decades, experiencing each other's lives and loves, courtships, marriages and divorces. They'd been guests at each other's weddings and followed all the highs and lows of their respective careers.

Mel had been right all along: they were 'more like a couple' than many other couples they knew. There was just so much baggage to deal with. In life, no one survives undamaged; everyone's broken in some way. For Luc and Grace, the broken pieces fit. Now he could see it. It was right in front of his eyes; it had been there all along. The Luca and Gracie story would resume.

Grace lay with her head on Luc's chest. He felt her body trembling, heard her catch her breath in a giant sigh and realised she was sobbing.

'It's okay, I'm here,' he whispered.

'I'm fine, honestly. I'm just so happy that I'm a bit overwhelmed. I think I wanted this too much.' She pushed herself up and looked into his pale-green eyes. 'I thought it might never happen.'

'I thought about it, too, over the years, but we were both with other people. I thought I'd blown things with you, after our big split.'

'I never gave up on us, Luca,' she whispered. 'I was always waiting for you to come back to me. I knew we just needed a chance.'

Grace wasn't surprised that she couldn't articulate her feelings without tears. She had waited such a long time. Initially, after their split, she'd navigated close to his orbit, maintaining social contact and an open door to get back together. It was like her blood chemistry was affected by his absence and she yearned for his return. The door only closed when he married someone else. But, in truth, it never closed; she'd have left Gary for him at any time. It was all about chemistry.

'I know I never stopped loving you. Mel's been telling me for years that I was still in love with you. I think I was in denial.' He pulled her in tight and they fell asleep in each other's arms.

They made love again on waking.

Luc made breakfast. His larder was sparse and his culinary skills lacking but he made great French toast.

'No regrets, Gracie?'

'None whatsoever.' She sprinkled cinnamon on her toast and

soaked up some golden syrup on a forkful of eggy bread. 'I'm sorry for pouncing on you when you were so vulnerable.'

'Your timing might be spot-on. If I'm being honest, I was on the verge of a possible workplace romance.'

'I heard rumours to that effect.' Grace flashed a knowing smile.

It took a moment to sink in. 'You've been speaking to Mel.'

'She mentioned you may be on the verge. Advised me to get my arse into gear if I wanted us to ever have a chance.'

'So I've been fitted up?'

'Let's say, for an experienced DI, you were a bit behind the pace on this one.' Grace laughed.

## 37

M cCartney looked the part in double denim. She'd gone with extra layers and mittens to keep the cold at bay. Her blonde hair was swept back, held in place by an Alice band and tucked under the collar of her denim jacket.

Costello had been briefed on the partial registration number and had played about with the letters on the PNC terminal in the office, trying different digits, but hadn't got anywhere. The material journey had been around midnight and they'd agreed with Kidston to do one hour, either side. Costello had secured the community policing team's panda car and thrown on a fluorescent yellow traffic coat. They were equipped with personal radios that offered a dedicated 'talk through' frequency. McCartney would be miked up with an earpiece to link with Costello so their radio communications would not be broadcast or overheard by the local divisional channels.

Kidston's other plan of putting a uniform team at the locus to conduct traditional road checks and trace potential witnesses was a non-starter. The division could be alerted to a rogue policing operation and the fallout would be considerable. This version focused on drawing out a suspect. It was lower risk in terms of alerting the division but carried a higher risk for PC Chrissie McCartney.

Costello's main concern for the operation was Chrissie's safety. He briefed her on the confidentiality and sensitivity of the enquiry but most of all on what was required for her to stay safe. Under no circumstances was she to attempt to flag down any vehicles. Chrissie knew that a police officer in plain clothes had no such power, but her neighbour was insistent in pointing out the obvious dangers. McCartney was to alert him if any vehicle looked worth checking. He'd be parked around seventy to eighty yards behind her, with all his lights off but engine running, ready to move closer if required.

They located the lay-by where Ellie Hunter had been found, confirmed by the remnants of blue-and-white police barrier tape tied to the fence and flapping in the biting February wind.

Costello drove the panda back to a point roughly 100 yards east of the lay-by, swung it around to face west and killed the lights. McCartney got out, bracing herself against the bitter chill and whatever else might follow. The open countryside around the Barrhead Dams offered no shelter from the elements. It would be a cold two hours. Trying to accustom her eyes to the inky blackness, she walked cautiously, unable to see her hand in front of her face.

Costello watched his young neighbour walk off into the darkness, following in the steps of Ellie Hunter six nights earlier. He was reassured when she carried out a quick comms check.

'Chrissie to Peter, radio check, confirm. Over.' There was no need for formal call signs or strict radio protocols.

'Loud and clear. How are you receiving me? Over.'

'Rodger, good clear signal, thanks. Over.'

'How's it looking out there, Chrissie?'

'Pitch-black. Can't see a thing. Over.'

'Use your torch. Just shine it on the ground. Not too obvious.

Flick it off if you see any cars approaching. I'll alert you if anything's coming from my direction.'

A glimmer of torchlight illuminated his colleague's feet, lighting her path in the distance. It was reassuring to have voice contact and some visual indication of her position. He thought about Ellie Hunter getting out of the car in very similar conditions. Freezing cold and pitch-darkness. What kind of crazy person would just walk off into the night like that?

He was snapped out of his reverie by McCartney:

'Car coming, approaching me. Over.'

'Rodger, noted. I can see the headlights in the distance.'

In no time, the car was past him. He radioed her back. 'Did they see you, take any interest? Over.'

'Rodger, affirmative, they picked me up in their headlights when they were close but negative on the interest. Over.'

'All noted. Time to turn around and do a return walk,' Costello directed.

'Rodger. Just to confirm how difficult it is to make out car models, colours, reg numbers. It's too dark to see anything. Over,' McCartney replied.

They checked out four more cars in the first hour. Nothing of interest. Around midnight, a frozen Chrissie was glad of a seat in the panda. Costello produced a flask of hot chicken soup and they took a ten-minute break to allow her to warm up. With Chrissie fully restored, the second hour was quieter: only two cars before half past midnight.

On the next run Chrissie was approaching the lay-by when a car slowed down on approach. From Costello's remote vantage he could see the vehicle slow to a complete stop.

'Peter to Chrissie, what's going on? Come in, Chrissie. Over.'

No response.

'Come in, Chrissie. Over.' Costello lit the panda up and

gunned the accelerator, his giant hands gripping the wheel tightly. He would be there in seconds.

Still no response.

His headlights picked up the scene as the panda skidded to a halt, blocking the second car's escape route. Chrissie was being lectured by a middle-aged woman through the open window of her gold Ford Fiesta. Berating her for her stupidity and attempting to persuade her to accept a lift home was having no effect on his neighbour, who looked frozen stiff.

'Would you have a word with this girl please, officer?' She spoke to Costello through the car window.

'I think this woman is right, miss.' Costello had a mischievous smile on his face. 'I can get this young lady home, thanks. I'll take it from here.'

False alarm, good intent. Known by police offers as a *FAGI*, the commonly used police result code de-escalated many a speeding pulse and racing heartbeat.

They waited until their Good Samaritan had driven away to have a laugh at the situation. 'Joking aside, what the hell happened to your radio? I was panicking there when I saw the car stopped and got no explanation from you over the air.'

'Sorry, I think my battery died.'

'You almost gave me a heart attack.'

They spent the last fifteen minutes parked up beside the lay-by with the car heater full blast. Costello gave Chrissie his traffic coat and the last of the chicken soup to warm her up. 'Note to self,' he said. 'If we're back tomorrow, then we're bringing two spare batteries.'

'I tell you, Peter,' McCartney began, 'you'd never get me walking alone on a road like this in total darkness. What possessed the poor girl?'

'I wonder what happened to her,' Costello said. 'Why did she get out of the car?'

'That's the sixty-four-thousand-dollar question.'

'I hope my girls never put themselves in that type of situation,' Costello said. 'It makes my blood run cold.'

'Could Paul Kennedy have done what he's accused of?' McCartney asked.

'If this job has taught me one thing – it's that men are predators, women are prey.'

## 38

Friday

Draper and Metcalfe headed straight to JC Motors. Danny was in the office on his own.

'Mr Crossan in this morning?' Metcalfe asked.

'They're not back yet,' Danny replied. 'I think they plan to spend another night down south, visit the Lake District.'

'Did you tell him we were looking for one of his cars?'

'He phoned just after I opened up at eight. I passed on your message.'

'Did you mention the registration number we asked about?' Draper pressed him.

'Aye. Valerie sold that car two weeks ago.'

'Sold it to who? You know it's an offence not to update Swansea DVLC?'

'Eh, I'm not sure.' Danny was hesitant.

'Look, if you have a contact number for Mr Crossan you better phone him now. We're not leaving here without the new owner's details.' Draper was taking a firmer line now. 'I'm happy to bring the stolen vehicle section down here today along with trading standards to check every logbook, every VIN number, to make sure every car in your yard is kosher. No doubt we'd end up removing some of these vehicles to the police pound for further enquiries.'

'Look, I'm just a mechanic. I'm not involved in car sales.'

'Well my colleague and I will just go through all the logbooks and sales records for all of the cars on the lot.' Draper gave him a look that made it clear she meant business.

'Eh, no, that won't be necessary. I've got a name to pass on. Valerie's personal number plate was sold to a guy two weeks ago. I don't think DVLC has been updated yet.'

'A guy. What guy?' Metcalfe asked.

'I've written it down. It's foreign, Jimmy spelt it for me.' He handed Draper a scrap of paper with *Valentine Mackowiak* written on it.

'Mackowiak.' Draper practised the pronunciation. 'Is that Polish?'

'Aye, I think so. That sounds about right. That's the way Jimmy pronounced it. I think his dad was Polish. He's from around here. He didn't have an address, but the phone number is on the back.' Danny looked pleased to see the detectives leaving.

Metcalfe lit up a Regal and wound down her window as Draper drove away. They agreed that Danny the mechanic had been under instructions not to give up too much unless pressed.

'Some shady shit going on there,' Metcalfe said between drags on her cigarette.

'I think I'll arrange a wee follow-up from the stolen vehicle section, see what they can dig up,' Draper replied.

'Maybe it's my poor detective skills but I never thought of a guy named Valentine for the registration plate.' Metcalfe took a long drag in confessional mode.

'Me neither. Don't beat yourself up.'

Metcalfe couldn't imagine any of her male colleagues making the same admission. She was enjoying the experience of working with another woman. She felt confident enough to move things on a bit. 'What about you and the DI? Is that likely to be a thing?'

'Wow.' Draper laughed. 'I didn't think I was that transparent. Are people talking about us in the office?'

'Not really. I've just noticed the way you look at him.'

'Well, he's an attractive man and I do like him. You know he's got this strict rule about workplace relationships?'

'I know all about the rule.' Metcalfe smiled as she flicked ash out of the car window. 'I've known him since he was a young DC.'

'And his marriage?' Draper was curious.

'God, he was a mess when they split,' Metcalfe continued. 'Two workaholics. Zero compromise. She's got a very successful baby shop empire. Asked him to give up the police to help run the business. Can you imagine?' Metcalfe scoffed. 'He wanted kids, she didn't, and it unravelled from there. He's a lovely guy and he's turned into a sound gaffer.'

'So were you around to help him over his divorce?' Draper asked.

'Not really. I don't think anyone, or anything could help. He views his marriage breakdown as his big failure.'

'Since we're being open and honest, Luc came home with me after my promotion do the other night. We had a serious snog on the sofa, one thing almost led to another...'

'And?'

'And nothing,' Draper replied. 'I was a bit too drunk and he was the perfect gentleman. Damn.'

'It'll be that rule of his, but you'll be in your new post in no time. That'll open the door.' Metcalfe was laughing. 'However, if you're looking for more personal revelations...'

'More? More? Can there be any more?' Draper exaggerated the question with an expression of mock shock on her face.

'Paul Kennedy.' Metcalfe fidgeted with the discreet pendant necklace under her shirt collar.

'What, you and Paul?'

'Very brief. Three and a bit years ago, before he took up with Sandra Holt. A complete secret. He didn't want Luc to know. I only told him on Monday.'

'You're really good at keeping secrets.' Draper laughed. 'This is great, we don't get to have these conversations when we work with the guys.'

'Are you joking? Wylie is the biggest sweetie wife at the station. He knows everybody's business.' Metcalfe scowled as she flicked her fag end out the car window.

Metcalfe had been pleased to hear Draper's report on the successful hypnosis session. It backed her assessment of Paul Kennedy's character and she acknowledged the guilt he'd be experiencing for letting Ellie Hunter walk away. Draper's thoughts turned to what she'd learned about Paul and Sarah Canavan. This was one secret she wouldn't be sharing with Alison, but she was keen to get some further insight on his character.

'You never had any doubts?' Draper asked.

'None at all. I think I know him pretty well,' Metcalfe replied.

'How does Paul get out of this fix?' Draper asked.

'Well, it's all ifs and buts, isn't it?' Metcalfe replied. 'If this is all a dead-end, and if Ellie Hunter doesn't wake up to exonerate him, it'll be for a jury to decide. But he could do jail time.'

'Down to the credibility of the witnesses, I suppose. Oh God, imagine Barry Rodgers testifying on this one,' Draper said with a wicked laugh. 'The mad shagger, his credibility draining the more and more he speaks. He's a bit of a lech, always staring at my tits. Odious man, no wonder his wife divorced him.'

'Medallion Man. He started turning up at nights out with the open-necked shirts, the big gold medallion nestling in the lush chest hair. Boak boak.' Metcalfe gripped the steering wheel with both hands as she simulated the actions and sound effects of dry heaving over the dashboard. 'Never stares at my tits though.' Metcalfe patted her flat chest. 'I could get away with wearing a semmit. I only wear a bra to cut down on the number of dyke gags.'

Draper was howling with laughter. 'Stop, stop, please. I think I might wet my pants.'

The laughter subsided. It was a much-needed release from the thought of their colleague languishing in a Barlinnie remand cell.

Draper and Metcalfe returned to the office to update Kidston and see what the PNC could tell them about Valentine Mackowiak. Metcalfe typed the nominals into the computer, while Kidston and Draper stood over her. Metcalfe's smile delivered the first clue.

'The beauty and simplicity of an unusual name,' Metcalfe said. Rather than the standard result of multiple possibles, there was only one option flashing in green computer script on her screen. 'Mackowiak has a lengthy record, including violence and sexual offences against women,' she continued. 'He's twenty-nine, lives in Barrhead and has a "violent" marker on his file.'

'Sounds like a possible suspect,' Draper said.

'Definitely worth a follow-up,' Kidston agreed.

Metcalfe continued reading from the on-screen file.

'According to records he has lived in Barrhead since his first encounters with police as a teenager. His earlier convictions were for typical disorder and drunkenness offences. At nineteen he was accused by a seventeen-year-old girl of an attempted rape but been found not guilty.' The charge was police shorthand for 'assault with intent to ravish' and its inclusion on Mackowiak's record gave Kidston a sense of the type of predator he would be looking for if he was in charge of the official investigation.

'Even more promising,' Kidston said.

Metcalfe returned to the details on the screen. 'Another attempted rape charge was libelled against Mackowiak, at twenty-three; the victim was nineteen and the locus was recorded as a motor vehicle interior. This time he was convicted at a Sheriff and Jury court, serving fourteen months of a two-year sentence.'

Metcalfe printed a hard copy of Mackowiak's record and both colleagues pored over the details. In the 'distinguishing features' category, he was described as having a one-inch scar on his neck below his left ear. There was no police activity on the file for the last three and a half years, so the address listed might not be current. Draper tried the phone number Danny had written on the back of the card, but it rang out. She phoned JC Motors to check the number with Danny, who was adamant that he'd relayed the number accurately.

Draper put an urgent request call into BT for a subscriber search. Citing the urgent nature of the investigation and using all her powers of persuasion, she quickly confirmed an address at 22 Dalmeny Drive, Barrhead. It matched the subscriber details for the telephone number provided and the address listed on Mackowiak's criminal record file. Metcalfe interrogated the DVLC system, which revealed that the only vehicle listed for their suspect was a white Bedford van.

'I'll go and speak to our Mr Mackowiak,' Kidston said, pleased that the Kennedy case was picking up some momentum. 'Look, you two, I'm on a late shift to help Costello and McCartney with the Dams Road vehicle checks later but there's no need for you to stay late.'

The two women detectives exchanged a glance. 'We'd like to follow-up on this lead,' Draper said with Metcalfe nodding her agreement. It was almost 4.30pm on a Friday afternoon and there was a chance to catch their suspect coming home from work and at least check out what vehicles he had access to. It was an opportunity to move the enquiry on.

Kidston drove while Draper and Metcalfe consulted the road atlas. Dalmeny Drive was in an estate behind the Dalmeny Park Hotel. Number twenty-two was one in a row of blocks of two-storey flats in what looked to be a decent neighbourhood. Kidston did a few circuits of the surrounding area but there was no trace of the Bedford van or the cherished plate on any vehicle parked in the street.

They found Mackowiak's name on the door of a first-floor flat. Deciding not to alert their suspect by leaving an official police 'calling card' through the letter box, Draper spoke to his next-door neighbour. Mr Gibbs, a kindly white-haired man in his sixties, informed them that Val was probably still at work or had maybe gone straight to the pub as it was a Friday. Without too much interrogation the neighbour confirmed that Val worked as an electrician and drove a white Bedford van. He didn't know anything about him owning a car.

Draper directed Kidston to JC Motors on their way out of Barrhead, but it was locked up for the night.

'I'll stand down tonight's vehicle checks and maybe grab Gregor for a run around the pubs,' Kidston said. 'I think tracing Valentine Mackowiak will be a better use of our time. We'll try and pick him up tomorrow.'

Draper and Metcalfe agreed with their boss's assessment. A return visit to see what else Jimmy Crossan could tell them and another check of Mackowiak's address could wait until morning. They were on his trail. It may have been more hope than conviction, but they were starting to believe he could be their man.

Wylie heard Kidston's office extension ring as he passed the door. He knew the DI had scheduled to work a late shift but hadn't shared his reasons. Something about an internal investigation, all very hush-hush. Wylie wasn't buying it and hated being out of the loop. He caught the call just before it rang out.

'DI Kidston–' Before he could finish the caller started to speak.

'Hi, this is Julie Van Zandt. Just a quick call to double-check whether I should send the invoice for the Paul Kennedy consultation to you or to Mr Sharkey?'

Wylie was puzzled by the enquiry but sharp enough to process the Kidston, Kennedy, Sharkey connection. 'Actually, DI Kidston's not here just now but I can confirm that invoices for any legal consultations go to the lawyer involved.'

'Thank you, that's very helpful.' The caller rang off.

Wylie sat back in Kidston's chair trying to fathom out what was behind the call. The name wasn't familiar, but it was clear that Kidston was working with Adam Sharkey, who he knew was representing Kennedy, and some kind of consultant. He ran a number of possible scenarios in his head but failed to find an explanation that satisfied his curiosity. Why would Kidston be working with a defence solicitor?

Wylie closed the door and put the red light on. He

deliberated over what he was about to do. Kidston had given him a decent staff appraisal, but it was very similar to the one he'd received the previous year. It was the same old platitudes, year after year, and it wasn't making any difference to his promotion chances. Kidston had more or less accused him of being an alky and was excluding him from a lot of stuff recently. He resented that. It meant that Kidston may no longer trust him. Trust worked both ways and a DI shouldn't be working with the defence.

Wylie and Miller had worked together in the serious crime squad; he was a friend and a brother Mason.

*You've crossed a line, Kidston, and I'm going to put it right.*

## 39

'If the CID have better options then I'm delighted to hear it,' announced McCartney. She was responding to Costello's news that Kidston had stood down the vehicle checks. It was blowing a gale outside and thunderstorms were predicted for later.

'DS Draper and DC Metcalfe have come up with a line of enquiry that might yield better results,' Costello said.

'Brilliant.' McCartney laughed. 'I'm not sure I've thawed out from last night yet.'

Costello and McCartney were in the office and had been preparing for the second night of the Dams vehicle check operation. The two community cops were scheduled to finish their shift at 2am and Costello wanted to check the daily briefing register after the 11pm changeover of the patrol groups. The DBR was the font of all knowledge in any police station. Updated twenty-four-seven, patrol officers at the start of every shift were briefed on its contents: updated crimes, arrests, offences and suspects, broken down on a beat-by-beat basis. The register also flagged the potential whereabouts of wanted persons.

The big cop grabbed the heavy A4 box file with a single oversized hand and placed it on the bar counter. Flicking through the top two or three pages, he found what he was looking for. The warrants section at divisional HQ routinely circulated a list of persons 'wanted on warrant'. The Friday list was always of particular interest to Costello and it would have been delivered in hard copy by a despatch driver earlier that evening. While execution of routine warrants over the weekend wasn't exactly encouraged by bosses – stations needed their full cell capacity for their normal weekend clients – there were no hard and fast rules against the practice.

One name jumped out at him: Phillip Canavan. His date of birth and his Myrtle Park address confirmed he was *that* Phillip Canavan. Apparently, his Mercedes had amassed a shitload of tickets; *unpaid* parking tickets. Glasgow District Court had run out of patience with a series of unheeded penalty letters, follow-up prosecution notices, scheduled court dates and then letters warning of potential fines or arrest for non-payment. It was a shitty warrant, but it came with the magic powers conferred on any decent warrant: arrest and detention.

The two uniformed cops walked into the CID room where Kidston and Stark were discussing next steps in the Watters case.

'Are you gentlemen still looking for Canavan and Johnny Boy?' Costello enquired.

'Yes, both were supposed to attend here with their lawyer to be formally warned in relation to Vincent Davis. We suspect Mr Davis may turn up dead somewhere,' Stark replied. 'Especially now that he's suspected of setting Canavan's house on fire. John Wylie's initial enquiries with the fire investigators have confirmed that the security camera wasn't working.'

'Have you got information?' Kidston asked.

'Hot off the presses.' Costello waved a photocopy of the latest warrant list. 'District Court arrest warrant for Canavan, non-payment of parking fines.'

Stark stifled a guffaw. 'We could give the prick a weekend lie-in, put him to the court on Monday. See how he likes them apples.'

'He's staying at Johnny Boy's,' Costello said. 'I take it these two are worried Davis might find them before they find him?'

'Exactly, if they haven't already got to him,' Kidston replied. 'We could bring them both in, apply a bit of pressure on the Davis thing. We could do the formal warnings and see how they react. Canavan won't want to do a lie-in. He might be tempted to co-operate a bit more.'

'Chrissie and I are happy to do the backup. We're on until two.' Costello was keen to be involved. He'd dealt with both criminals on many occasions and savoured the prospect of a further encounter.

A hasty plan was formed. The two detectives would call first and execute the warrant. Costello and McCartney would be backup, with the former's knowledge of the labyrinthian layout of the apartments likely to be invaluable.

## 40

Vincent Davis stood high above the crowd. Dressed in his long black leather coat and black hoodie, he merged into the dark night sky. The katana hung from his waist, concealed by the skirt of his coat. The old railway bridge provided the best vantage point to watch the Granite City Inn patrons spilling out at closing time. There was no trace of any uniformed police outside the pub. Davis had tailed Canavan for two nights, but he'd always had McManus close by.

The little bodyguard's hand kept going inside his jacket. That, and his changed stance and the animated way he kept patting his right side suggested to Vincent that he was concealing a handgun.

A gun was a game changer; Vincent had thought about taking them both on but not now. McManus' role with Canavan was as an enforcer on the money lending side of the business; he had no part in the drugs deal that ended Maria's life. Besides, he'd kicked Johnny Boy's arse when they were teens. He wasn't seeking a rematch with the wee Gorbals gunslinger. He needed the two men to split up.

Maria was the one: the love of his life. As a younger man,

he'd found it difficult to form connections with other people, especially girls. There were always difficulties navigating the spaces that filled his relationships. But with Maria, he achieved a perfect, seamless connection. Maria's murder – and he firmly believed she was murdered – had left an unfathomable hole in his life. They'd gone out for six years and he'd started to plan the rest of his life around her. It had all been destroyed when her friend persuaded her to try heroin for what was probably the first and only time.

Davis' world view had been influenced by the books he'd read and movies he'd seen as a younger man. P. C. Wren's adventure story, *Beau Geste* and the 1966 film of the same name offered a romanticised view of the French Foreign Legion but when his life was beginning to unravel, aged twenty, following the sudden death of his mother, it was to the *Légion Étrangère* that he turned. The training regime at Castelnaudary had been brutal but he was transformed from a boy to a man and had maintained a dedication to personal fitness after his five-year stint had ended. It was the Bruce Lee movies of the seventies that fuelled his love of kung fu and then taekwondo. The Japanese culture and philosophy he read about in James Clavell's *Shogun* changed the way he thought about the world. He was impressed by the samurai code of *bushido*; their devotion to honour and duty and their mastery over the fear of death. The book's many references to the Indo-Buddhist concept of karma appealed to him but he put his own spin on it: your fates would find you out.

It was a week since he'd done Watters. Using his skills to take revenge on scum like Colin Watters was immensely gratifying. The satisfaction he got from vigilantism had caught him off guard and it was tempting to do more. The Gorbals Samurai, a hero for the ages, taking on neds, drug dealers and other criminals. It was clear the police weren't achieving the convictions required to put these people away; it seemed to him there was a vacancy for a vigilante. But no. However tempting it was to play the hero, taking his vengeance on Canavan would complete the mission he'd set himself. He would dissolve back into the shadows and the anonymity he preferred. He'd left a false trail about going to Ireland. His plan – if he survived this mission – was to bike to the South of France and a little town called Cassis. He'd lived there briefly when he left the Legion and had friends in the town.

Then he saw them both. Among the last group to leave the pub. Canavan was with McManus and a woman who seemed to be with Johnny Boy. That impression was confirmed when he saw her link her arm through his. The little bodyguard had pulled and he and his lumber headed in the direction of the Stirlingfauld Road high flats. She was a petite blonde, a wee brammer. Davis imagined McManus eating her alive. He was an odd-looking little guy with his frizzy hair, massive shoulders and side-to-side gait, but he seemed to do well in the weekend romance stakes. Davis allowed himself a smile at the thought. There was no sign of Canavan's Merc; it looked like he would be walking the half mile back to Johnny Boy's flat where he'd been shacked up after Davis' firebombing of his house.

Davis descended the perilous staircase, staying close to the wall and using the shadows for cover. He picked up sight of Canavan as he cut through the abandoned Hutchie E-blocks heading for Johnny Boy's flat in Queen Elizabeth Square. His route would take him towards Cumberland Street and Gorbals police office. Now that he had him on his own, Davis didn't want to lose sight of him. He adjusted his beanie hat and hoodie and pulled a black scarf over his mouth so only his eyes were visible.

He took a chance and skirted the other side of the Rose Garden, up past the Twomax factory. Davis paused at the corner of the north-east boundary wall of the garden. It offered a view of the square and the flats. No sign of Canavan. He loitered on the corner, mindful of the police vehicles likely to be coming and going at the rear yard of the station. It wasn't somewhere to loiter too long, especially with a samurai sword slung around your waist.

Then he saw Canavan. His prey was rounding the side of the police station and striding towards the flats from the south side. He waited until the buildings offered him the cover he needed. The north side of the flats offered a clear view underneath the massive raised concrete stilts, allowing him to gauge Canavan's progress towards the end block. The square was busy with drinkers leaving the Elizabethan and the Queen's Bar, but none of the revellers were heading in the same direction as Canavan. His preference was to take him underneath the tower block or in the lift foyer, but he would need to be flexible; there were too many people around.

The huge stilts gave him the cover he needed. He hung back until Canavan entered the foyer. Davis was right on his tail. He crept up to the entrance and stopped. As he leant on the doorway, he could hear the voices of two young girls. He listened in but couldn't tell if they were waiting to go up in the lift, coming out, or just having a blether and a fag out of the biting harsh wind that blew through the undercarriage of the flats. He risked a glance round the doorway to check; they were chatting and smoking but it gave him a glimpse of Canavan just as he entered the lift.

He should call off the attack. A voice in his head warned that the fates might be against him and this was a fight he might lose. He remembered the words of his old Legion troop sergeant, the fearless Henri 'Satan' Lopez. '*We are the dust from the stars. Who cares whether you die at sixteen or sixty-six? Don't worry about death.*' If he was to die tonight, he would have the honour of a noble death: *Bushido*. He ignored the voice. Davis was a soul in pain; he didn't care what happened to him, so long as he could inflict vengeance on Canavan. The man was overdue some bad karma and this could be his best opportunity. His prey was likely to be alone in Johnny Boy's flat and the pursuit had got his blood up.

The adrenaline was surging through him like an electrical current, his righteous anger rising to the point where he knew he couldn't walk away. Canavan had evaded justice long enough. If the police and the courts were incapable of putting this monster in jail, then it would fall to him to exact retribution.

Davis rode the lift to the top floor and paused outside the door with the nameplate 'McManus'. He heard the faint sound of a television. Pushing on the door, he was surprised to find it was on the snib and that he could walk right in. This would require a stealthy, silent approach. He readjusted his beanie hat, scarf and hoodie and took time placing his feet; slow, deliberate and silent in the style of a ninja. He crept upstairs; the television louder as he reached the lounge door.

It was time for Phil Canavan to face a just vengeance.

## 41

Canavan didn't object to Johnny Boy sloping off with a bird. She had a babysitter and needed to get back to check on her kid. The wee man was incorrigible, especially when he was on the bevvy. He'd given him the flat keys and slipped him his .38 Smith and Wesson revolver when they parted. Canavan preferred the blade, but Johnny Boy's little Saturday night special may come in handy if the bold Vinnie was around. It would be self-defence; a threat had been made against his life by a nutter with a sword. He'd be entitled to shoot the fucker down.

There was an anxious moment when he turned up the side of the police office. Everybody knew the shifts changed over at 11pm and there would be cops and cop cars about. Given his recent Shawlands encounter with Kidston and his crew, he thought about pitching the weapon over the Rose Garden's wall. He could recover it in the morning. With little activity at the police station, he felt bold enough to keep the gun in his coat pocket and as he strode across the square, he was almost home. Except it wasn't home. No harm to Johnny Boy's pad but Canavan needed to get back to his own house. With the kitchen badly fire damaged, he'd put a watchman in place so that refurbishment could start. He'd agreed to stay until the house was repaired and the matter with Vinnie Davis was resolved. It really pissed him off that they'd not been able to track him down.

In the foyer two teenage girls sheltered from the wind that gusted under the flats. He smiled as he heard a fragment of their chatter; they were talking about boys and arguing about who shagged Martin first. He almost laughed. Those innocent and carefree days of teenage love with all its trials and tribulations. The unmistakeable smell of warm piss accompanied him as the lift travelled to the top floor. Johnny Boy lived at the end of the long corridor: the last flat at the gable end with the big high balcony offering one of the best views over the city.

The plan was that Johnny Boy would do the business with his lumber and head back as there was only one set of house keys. On reaching the flat, Canavan made a spur-of-the-moment decision; he put the Yale door lock on the snib. Johnny Boy could be as late as he wanted. Canavan threw his overcoat across the chair, poured himself a single malt and flicked through Johnny Boy's collection of porn videos. He stopped when he saw *Debbie Does Dallas*, a minor classic about a team of cheerleaders attempting to earn enough money to send Debbie to Dallas, Texas, to try out for the famous Texas Cowgirls cheerleading squad. He'd seen it once before around five years ago, but he remembered it being a good laugh and it would pass the time until the wee man got back. Canavan loaded up the video recorder and sat back, feet up, whisky in hand.

Canavan had been enjoying his movie. Plenty of tits on display and the shapely Bambi Woods as Debbie was a fine figure of a woman. He wasn't long into the film when he heard the flat door opening. The wee man must have struck out with his bird and come home with his tail between his legs.

But it was too quiet to be Johnny Boy. Canavan's spidey sense was tingling. *Some cunt is in the flat.* Canavan always trusted his instincts when it came to fear; that internal alarm was there for a reason. Survival. He sprang to his feet, retrieved Johnny Boy's gun and covered the door in a two-handed shooter's stance.

Drawing the katana from its *saya*, Davis opened the door to find Canavan pointing a revolver at him.

'Show your face, fucker!' Canavan roared at him.

Davis removed his hood and uncovered his face. Vengeance burned in his eyes.

'I remember you. You're Tombo's big lanky pal, the kung fu boy. You crazy motherfucker!' Canavan screamed. 'Did you set my house on fire?'

'I'm your worst nightmare, Canavan,' Davis said calmly, a maniacal grin on his face. 'I'm a man with nothing to lose.'

'What's this about, man? You've no beef with me. You've already done Watters.'

'You and Watters killed my Maria with your scummy heroin.' Davis stared with furious intent. 'It's time for you to face justice.'

## 42

Costello and McCartney adjusted their chinstraps as they crossed the square with Kidston and Stark. The wind was blowing a hoolie and right on cue the gathering storm clouds darkened. There was a rumble of thunder and the heavens opened. Approaching the flats, the officers were greeted by the ominous sight of a large white bedsheet soaring through the air like an unfurled sail: some poor soul had left their washing out on the line. Underneath the canopy of the towers, an elderly woman was only kept from being blown off her feet by the intervention of a Good Samaritan neighbour, who held onto her arm and sheltered her out of the wind, behind one of the giant stilts.

For all the audacity of its design, the architects and town planners underestimated how the stormy west of Scotland winters would impact Queen Elizabeth Square. Gale-force gusts, amplified by the natural wind tunnels in the building's design, caused havoc with the residents and their washing lines. During the great storm of January 1968, residents swore that the entire tower block was swinging and swaying in gale-force winds that reached speeds of 140 miles per hour.

The four officers quickened their pace to a light jog across the square, eager to make the sanctuary of the foyer and minimise their exposure to the lashing rainfall. The two detectives with their fashionable rainwear were nearly soaked already. Their uniformed colleagues were better protected with their police-issue headgear and nylon raincoats that seemed to repel water, but the rain was heavy and relentless. An ominous clap of thunder echoed in the far distance.

'No wonder we call it Raintown.' Kidston laughed as he pulled his coat over his head.

They shook themselves off in the lift.

'Anyone got a towel?' joked Stark. A pungent aroma – a mix of stale and fresh urine – assailed their olfactory senses. They rehearsed the plan one last time before exiting on the top floor and taking up their positions. Costello led McCartney to the door three along from the McManus flat. He'd calculated that the flat marked 'Jennings' was the veranda neighbour to Johnny Boy. He wondered about the Jennings family, scouring the years and years of local criminal intelligence in his memory but not recognising the name. They were probably decent folks – the vast majority of Gorbals residents were – but having McManus as a next-door neighbour meant they'd probably had to put up with a lot of snash. The big polis had been foiled before by the 'veranda escape' tactic. Suspects would run out through their veranda door onto the balcony, enter their neighbour's flat and make good their escape.

It wouldn't happen tonight.

## 43

When Mr Jennings answered his door, he was surprised to find a huge, dripping wet, uniformed police officer already shushing him. Costello held his forefinger to his lips and silently ushered the householder back inside his flat. An equally wet petite policewoman pushed in at his back. Costello spoke in a low whisper and explained the situation to Mr Jennings. They would take up a position by the Jennings' veranda door to prevent it being an escape route.

Mr and Mrs Jennings were decent people, both in their late forties, and had been watching Peter Cushing in a *Dracula* movie on the BBC. Costello didn't want to frighten them unnecessarily by telling them the real monsters lived in the flat next door. Even if the couple had locked their door, there was a chance that McManus and Canavan, looking to flee from the police, would have kicked it in or threatened them to open it. This way, the police controlled what would happen next.

Kidston ran his hand through his soaking wet hair. Stark produced a handkerchief from under his raincoat and dried the excess rainwater from his face and neck. They were surprised to find McManus' door on the snib. Stark opened the door with some caution and the two detectives listened to an angry confrontation in the lounge. One of the voices was unmistakeable: Phil Canavan. But it didn't sound like McManus arguing with him. They waited, listened longer; only two voices. Had Vincent Davis been crazy enough to track Canavan back to Johnny Boy's? Where was the householder?

They should hold back. If Davis was in the flat, they could be facing a sword. Force protocols for lethal weapons required a firearms response team. Both detectives knew it would be a long wait if they called out the three-ring circus and a full incident command structure. The incident would run away from them and if Canavan was facing the threat of a sword, there was a clear and immediate danger to his life. They would have to act. They had Costello and McCartney as backup in the flat next door.

As they entered the lounge, the detectives instantly realised that, in terms of 'clear and immediate danger', Canavan needn't have worried. In a game of *rock, paper, scissors, sword, gun*, Canavan's advantage was clear: *gun* wins. Canavan wheeled around to cover the two surprised and unwelcome visitors.

'Mr Kidston, impeccable timing. This nutter has just broken into my friend's home and made a threat to my life. I also believe he's responsible for trying to burn down my house on Wednesday night.' Canavan transferred his aim back to Davis. 'I believe the law gives a man the right to defend himself.'

Davis, his face now fully visible, stood poised, the katana raised shoulder height and held in front of his body in a strike pose; ready to attack. His attention was fully on the man pointing a gun at him.

'I take it you're the elusive Vincent Davis?' Kidston asked. The two detectives were just inside the lounge door. Davis was between Canavan and the door, blocking his exit.

'So you've worked it out, detective.' Davis never looked away from Canavan as he spoke to Kidston. 'Pity. It's a bit late for the police to get involved now.'

'Stand down, Vincent. It's over now, you've no beef with us,' Kidston implored him. 'Put the sword down and give yourself up.'

'No beef?' Davis scoffed. 'If the police had done their job, there'd be no need for me to do this.'

'Do what, Vinnie? Just what is it you think you're going to do with two CID in the room and me with a gun in my hand?' Canavan reminded him of his advantage.

'I can say the same to you, Canavan,' Davis replied. 'You're not going to shoot me in front of the police, unless you're planning to shoot them too.'

Gregor Stark swallowed hard. Kidston had placed his arm across his sergeant's midriff, preventing any sudden rush forward. He was trying to steer him back through the door to go and summon reinforcements. They may need a firearms team after all. The situation required cool heads and wise words; no sudden moves, nothing rash, nothing to provoke the man with the sword or the man with the gun.

Kidston recalled his negotiator training. There was a semblance of an exercise scenario about what they were facing but the training staff at Tulliallan had never come up with anything as devilishly fiendish as the situation in front of them. Standing just off Davis' right shoulder, it was Stark who made the first wrong move. He sprang forward at speed, but Davis was quicker. With only the slightest adjustment to his stance, Davis wheeled his hands around, back towards his would-be assailant. The *kashira* end cap on the samurai's hilt struck Stark a mighty blow, flush on the forehead, knocking him out cold.

'Watters was right, this guy *is* a fuckin' ninja,' Canavan said to Kidston. The gangster seemed impressed by the swiftness of the strike that had felled the young detective. 'What are you going to do about it, inspector?'

Stark's unconscious body lying against the door was preventing anyone making a sudden exit through the lounge. Kidston noticed that Canavan's attention was distracted by the television in the corner, where a group sex scene was taking place in a shower room.

'I need you both to put down your weapons before anyone else gets hurt and I need to get urgent medical attention for my colleague.' Kidston glanced over at Stark's motionless body. 'Let's be sensible about this, guys. Vincent, you only maimed Colin Watters, you didn't kill him. His injuries are healing, so there's not too much damage done. You'll be able to put that one behind you.' Kidston noted that Davis' concentration and focus never wavered from Canavan; not so much as a glance at the porn movie playing in the corner.

His negotiator training was kicking in like a muscle reflex. Give the subject cause to walk away, to put his weapon down before the situation deteriorated beyond a point of no return. 'The police are involved now, and we know what's gone on. More police are on their way to back us up, including a full firearms team,' Kidston lied, even though he still hoped his uniformed colleagues in the flat next door could make it the truth.

'I'll hand you the gun, Kidston, if he agrees to give you his sword. But he needs to go first. I don't trust him not to attack me if I'm unarmed.'

'How about it, Vincent?' Kidston asked. 'Give me your sword.'

'I don't know about you, Vinnie boy,' Canavan said, 'but I've come up against a police tactical firearms team before. You tend not to forget when you've been woken up with the red dot from a Heckler and Koch carbine rifle pointed at your chest by a cop dressed in full stormtrooper kit. These guys don't fuck about.' Canavan was in no mood for a repeat appointment. 'There's no way you and I want to be standing here with weapons in our hands if these fuckers come calling.'

'Why would I trust you, Canavan?' Davis was adamant. 'Why would anyone trust you? You're a lying piece of scum.' He was zoned in on Canavan; his focus never wavered; his stance never faltered. 'There's no way I'll be laying down *Revenger* while you've got that gun. Give the gun to the detective.'

'*Revenger*! What the fuck? You've got a name for your sword?' Canavan scoffed. 'You sad fuckin' misfit. I should just fuckin' shoot you to put you out of your misery.'

*This is going well*, thought Kidston, attempting to hide his grimace. He was clear on the motivations of the two combatants: Davis was hell-bent on revenge; Canavan was motivated by a mix of fear and survival. Kidston was reassured that Canavan wasn't a young wannabe; he was unlikely to shoot a police officer. He wouldn't have offered Davis the same courtesy if the police hadn't happened upon the scene. It was difficult to see a reconciliation for the two aggressors. Kidston's chief motivation was to secure two bodies in the cells, rather than the hospital or the mortuary.

Kidston was an accomplished hostage negotiator, with a reputation built upon a series of high-profile armed sieges, but this was a tester. Talk about tough negotiations; one armed antagonist would usually be enough. He could never have envisioned a three-way scenario like this one. He was choosing his words with care, watching his pace, pitch and tone; modulating the timbre of his voice. Face-to-face negotiations had always given him a rush. Nothing compared to the danger and excitement of seeing the whites of a subject's eyes. But Kidston was starting to doubt how much danger and excitement he really needed in his life right now.

Following the death of Russell Maitland, Kidston could ill afford another botched negotiation – especially when the odds were suggesting further potential for loss of life or at least serious injury. Despite his best efforts, Kidston was experiencing a feeling of dread. It felt as if this incident was running away from him – beyond his control. The two men were hell-bent on their own agendas and neither was in the mood for compromise. With the gun pointed at Davis, Canavan edged towards the door to the stairs. It was as if he was going to step over Gregor Stark's lifeless body and attempt to flee the scene.

'Stop!' Davis commanded as he brandished the samurai threatening Canavan's escape route.

Canavan stood stock still.

It looked to Kidston, that, for the moment, the sword was mightier than the gun. He wondered how many moves the gangster had left before he resorted to shooting his assailant.

## 44

Mr and Mrs Jennings had been sent to their bedroom as the drama unfolded next door. Costello had quickly realised that since neither Johnny Boy nor Canavan had used the veranda escape route, the incident was contained to the McManus flat. When they never got the knock on the door – the prearranged signal to confirm Canavan was in their custody – Costello had a feeling something wasn't quite right. The walls between the flats were thin and with the aid of a drinking glass he was able to overhear the conversation between Kidston, Canavan and Davis. References to 'guns' and 'swords' told him everything he needed to know.

Resisting the strong urge to enter the flat, Costello radioed through to the night-shift supervisors and briefed them on the situation. Inspector Dom Bradley and Sergeant Lynda Cooper were in charge of the patrol shift. The duty night-shift superintendent would need to be summoned to decide whether or not to deploy a tactical firearms team to the incident. Call-outs like these were way above Costello's pay grade but both of these gaffers were solid, competent officers and would ramp the thing up to the level required.

He would be holding the line at the Jennings' veranda door. Chrissie McCartney was despatched back to Gorbals police office, which would become a rendezvous and mustering point for all of the additional resources. The three-ring circus was coming to town. He drilled Chrissie on the block number, floor number and flat number and she wrote them into her notebook. She was reluctant to leave her neighbour on his own, but he'd stressed the importance of guiding the firearms team to the correct location. She wouldn't let him down.

Kidston would go around again. He would convey the same message, plant the same suggestions again and again and again. Colleagues joked that negotiators like him bored people into 'surrendering'. It was only half a joke. He could do this for hours. So long as there were no sudden moves or rash decisions, like the one Stark had made, everybody would come out the other side. The 'S' word would never be mentioned. The loss of face implied by 'surrender' only made the negotiation more challenging. The machismo types, the alpha males who got involved in incidents like this, needed to be able to save face.

'The gun's not mine, Kidston. Johnny Boy passed it to me for protection once we knew this headcase was coming after me.' Canavan was already thinking about the aftermath and a defence strategy for court. Kidston wasn't surprised.

'Phil, you know the ways of the court as well as I do.' Kidston spoke slowly, deliberately, the use of Canavan's first name a measured tactic. 'Your lawyer will make that count for you, I'm sure of it. When we all come out the other side of this, it won't look so bad.

'Look, Vincent, Colin Watters is recovering from his injuries.

It was clear you had no intention of killing him. That will play well for you at trial with a decent lawyer.'

'I don't intend to go to trial,' Davis retorted sharply.

'What the fuck does he mean with that kamikaze shit?' Canavan directed his question to Kidston rather than Davis. Kidston thought he detected the first overt signs of fear from the veteran criminal. With a gun in his hand, Canavan held the ace card, but the unpredictability of his assailant had spooked him. He looked frightened.

Canavan walked towards Davis; the gun pointed at his forehead. 'I can make sure you don't go to trial,' Canavan threatened.

'You better shoot me, because now I'm not just going to maim you. I'm going to kill you.'

Rather than retreat from the advancing gunman, Davis moved slowly and deliberately towards him. The gap between them was now down to around ten feet. Kidston moved in line with Davis, pleading all the time for both men to stop and think. He might as well have been invisible; they only had eyes for each other. Eyes filled with hatred, fear, and vengeance.

As he drew closer, Kidston got a better look at the gun; it was a snub-nosed revolver, a close quarters weapon that made it notoriously difficult to hit the target from distance. He'd practised with one at the firearms range and remembered the hopeless spread of his shots across a target shaped as a bad guy. 'Wild woman's piss' was how his instructor had described his efforts. He'd watched Canavan close his right eye when he looked down the short barrel of the revolver. Canavan was cross dominant: right-handed and left-eyed, the same as Kidston. He remembered that most of his shots for that session went high and to the left of his targets. If a chance came, Kidston would rush him low and to the right; taking the gun out of the equation would alter the dynamic of this stand-off.

It was Canavan who retreated. Stepping backwards, his gun still trained on Davis, who moved forward to maintain the gap. Kidston moved in step with him. Canavan was headed for the veranda door. His final glance at the television caught a scene where a tanned busty blonde cheerleader was fellating a hard-bodied athlete. He picked up his pace for the last few steps and heaved the door open mid-stride.

Kidston hoped Costello was still at his post.

Davis, closely followed by Kidston, stepped onto the stormy and windswept veranda just in time to see Canavan pulling on the handle of the Jennings' veranda door. Behind the glass stood a giant, smiling polisman.

No way out.

'Bastard!' screamed Canavan. 'Bastard!'

## 45

Out on the open veranda, the wind was blowing a gale and the rain was lashing down. Thunder rumbled in the near distance. Kidston had a sudden nauseating sense of how high he was above ground. It felt like they were standing in an enormous floating flower box, 200 feet in the air. There was nowhere to shelter, no escape from the rain that pelted down in a relentless deluge. Canavan, in only his shirt and trousers, was instantly soaked through. Davis' long leather trench coat flapped like a tent, the empty scabbard blowing about his waist. Kidston fully buttoned his gaberdine to better withstand the elements.

Kidston glanced along the balcony to see the uniformed figure of Peter Costello guarding the Jennings' veranda door. *He'll hold his position*, Kidston thought, as he watched the big cop open and close the door to monitor proceedings. Costello was too experienced to offer himself as another potential hostage for Canavan.

His hair plastered onto his head, rainwater running into his eyes, Canavan kept the gun trained on Davis. Kidston factored the drastically altered conditions into a shooter's chance of success. The wild elements assailing them would make it way more difficult to achieve accuracy.

'Guys, can we move back into the house, please? This is crazy, wild and dangerous out here,' Kidston implored the two combatants. He really didn't want to be this high off the ground and exposed to the elements. 'Thunder and lightning, out here in the open. It's not a clever idea.'

'Throw the sword over the balcony and I'll hand the gun to the DI.' Canavan offered Davis a way out.

'I'm not throwing my sword anywhere,' Davis replied. His stance hadn't deviated at any time. His posture still screamed attack.

'Put it on the ground then.' Kidston offered a compromise. 'Phil will hand me the gun.'

'No deal.' Davis wore an implacable expression and moved towards Canavan.

'Fuck's sake. Kidston, do something!' Canavan pleaded. 'You're my witness that this was self-defence.' Kidston watched as Canavan's finger moved off the trigger guard of his revolver.

Davis quickened his pace. Canavan backed up towards the low balcony wall.

Two quick strides from Davis.

A shot rang out. Davis veered low and right, fast and light on his feet. The bullet cracked off the veranda window; high and left.

What happened next would live with Kidston forever. Davis deviated back, then directly towards Canavan, then performed a sidestep manoeuvre, a nifty feint and turn that set up his deadly strike. Canavan pulled his trigger finger to get off another shot, but there was no trigger. Bringing his katana up and around in a swift sweeping arc, Davis brought it down with a mighty heft, slicing it clean through Canavan's gun hand. The horror on Canavan's face was matched by the piercing scream that sounded through the rainy night air.

Kidston and Davis both made a dive for the gun, but the swordsman was too quick for the detective and got to the severed limb first. Kidston was surprised when he was able to secure the revolver in his own grip without a struggle. Davis had grabbed the severed hand. Springing to his feet, he let out a victory cry, raising the bloody limb above his head, before hurling it over the balcony into the stormy night air. There would be no miracle surgeries for Canavan.

Kidston secured the gun in his coat pocket and jumped to his feet. Davis leapt onto the balcony ledge. It seemed like only the wind was holding him up as he leaned into the storm, the rain lashing his face and his coat blowing behind him like a windsock. He raised the samurai sword above his head, his strangely quiet words carried off with the wind, floating on the mist and the rain:

'Tell them I did it for Maria. Tell them I did it for justice.' The first bolt of lightning served as a warning; the storm gods were angry. Oblivious to the perils, Davis continued, his voice rising, 'I told Canavan that a man with nothing to lose was his worst nightmare. Who cares whether you live or die? I cannot go to jail, detective.' The loud electrical crack of a second lightning flash came perilously close to the balcony. Kidston felt a peculiar warmth in the soaking wet air.

He knew Davis was about to jump.

Davis wielded the katana high above his head and let out a mighty cry. 'We are the dust from the stars.'

The storm gods replied with a jagged, silvery, white arc of lightning that connected to the tip of his sword. He was a human lightning rod. Kidston watched in awe: just for an instant, it looked like Davis was connected to the sky. The massive electrical shock of the strike knocked the samurai sword from his hands, and he slumped onto the balcony ledge. He was going over.

Falling; not jumping.

Falling; not flying.

## 46

Kidston grabbed Davis' leather coat. There was plenty to hold on to, but it was wet and slippery, and he couldn't achieve the purchase he needed. He managed to hook his left arm through Davis' sword belt and wrap his right arm around his neck, but the dead weight of his lifeless body was slumped and sliding over the side. There was a real danger that he would take Kidston with him. Terror rose in his gut; after Russell Maitland, there could be no more tragedies. Kidston leaned out over the balcony ledge and felt the full effects of the storm, pummelling them. The rain lashed his face. Pushing his left thigh hard to the wall, he created a bulwark, giving him a more secure base and better leverage. Both arms straining, Kidston held on for dear life.

He saw the view for the first time. The far below street lights exposing just how high he was above the ground. A familiar nausea engulfed him: the fear; the dizzying vertigo, a panic attack that had him on the edge of fainting. *Not now*. He filled his lungs with air and expelled one last mighty heave. The load was suddenly lighter. Kidston felt the rustle of a nylon raincoat brush against his face and a giant hand grab his collar, as

Costello's massive frame hauled both bodies back from the edge. Between them, they swung Davis' limp form around and laid him on the ground.

There was no time for ceremony. Costello kneeled astride Davis and checked his neck for a pulse. 'I think the lightning strike stopped his heart,' the big cop announced. A grave expression on his face. Costello worked fast and pumped Davis' chest in an attempt to revive him with CPR. There was no trace of any burns on his hands or arms. The veteran cop was a proficient first aider and quickly achieved a rhythm of deep, rapid presses on Davis' chest. After what seemed like ages but was only around ninety seconds, a bewildered Davis spluttered back to consciousness.

'I was ready to die,' the groggy would-be samurai whispered.

It had all happened so fast. Costello had dutifully stayed by the Jennings' door until he heard the gunshot. He'd been quick to assist Kidston's rescue of the falling Davis and had grabbed both men just as they were in danger of toppling over the balcony ledge. With Davis and Canavan secured, Costello fashioned a bandage and tourniquet from two tea towels to treat the injured gangster. When Costello checked on Gregor Stark, the young DS was still spark out.

'Gregor will need to be checked out properly, Luc,' said Costello as he gently attempted to revive his colleague.

'Is everybody okay?' Stark asked, sitting up and assessing the amount of blood on his face with the back of his hand. The young DS had a nasty gash in the centre of his forehead, a souvenir of an eventful night. 'What did I miss?'

'It's quite a long story.' Kidston smiled, pleased to see his young colleague getting up and talking. 'We'll bring you up to speed later.'

Costello radioed control to stand down the firearms team and the various reinforcements. The two standby ambulances arranged by Dom Bradley as part of the response plan would be required. Davis and Canavan would have police escorts for their stays in hospital.

Once the ambulance crews had removed both prisoners to hospital, the three police officers returned to the station. Wet coats were hung in the drying room and hot drinks were served in the CID office. Chrissie McCartney was pleased to see her big neighbour safe after their exploits. Stark was ordered by Kidston to have his head wound checked out before he went home. Over tea and coffee Kidston and Costello related the full story. They agreed they'd never experienced anything as bizarre, dangerous and exciting as the night the Gorbals Samurai exacted his vengeance on the evil Phil Canavan. Gregor and Chrissie were sorry to have missed out on the action but pleased to have played a small part.

Enquiries about Canavan's missing limb were quickly concluded. Sergeant Lynda Cooper reported that, from her position on the cordon around the QES flats, she saw local worthy Willie Bruce's Dobermann pinscher break off its lead in pursuit of an object that appeared to have been thrown from a high window. The large black dog raced away with its prize and carried it off to the perimeter fence of Saint Francis' playing fields. When Bruce investigated, he thought it looked suspiciously like a human hand with all the skin and flesh stripped off, and informed Sergeant Cooper. After a radio check she confirmed the astonished Bruce's suspicions. When she revealed the identity of the now slimy skeletal limb's owner Bruce was said to have beamed an enormous toothless smile and commented, 'Yaas! Karma's a fuckin' bitch.'

## 47

Saturday

There was a contented Saturday morning buzz in the CID office. Morrison and Hope's detailed night-shift note reported that a search of the McManus flat had uncovered ten kilos of uncut heroin and a sawn-off double-barrelled shotgun. Johnny Boy had arrived back from his lovers' tryst to find detectives and uniforms going through his home. The Tasmanian Devil was caged and detained, awaiting a Monday date at court on drugs and firearms charges. Sometimes the hits just kept on coming.

A large tray of rolls with bacon, tottie scone, links and square sliced sausage sat in the centre of the big table next to pots of tea and coffee. Kidston was regaling the team with the inside story on the arrest of the Gorbals Samurai. Vincent Davis' exquisite samurai sword lay on the long bench table. Everyone had inspected it and agreed it was a thing of true beauty. The scorched discolouration on the sword's tip was evidence of the previous night's adventures.

'So, Gregor was right, boss. This guy was on some demented vigilante revenge mission.' DC Metcalfe summed up Kidston's version of events.

'Like I said at the start: consumed by grief and revenge,' Stark added.

'To the point of suicide,' Kidston said. 'I think he was ready to die rather than face jail. But he had some moves with that sword.' Kidston spoke between large mouthfuls of his favourite bacon and tottie scone 'double decker' roll. 'And he was bloody quick.'

'Lightning quick,' said Stark.

There was laughter from the group amidst more mouthfuls of rolls and hot drinks.

Their amusement was interrupted by the office door bursting open. DI Ronnie Miller blasted into the room like a hand grenade with the pin pulled, emotions rippling just under the surface, ready to explode. The intensity of his entrance brought everyone to silence.

'I hear you're celebrating a decent result from last night. I'm glad to hear you've got some cases of your own to investigate because you need to keep your nose out of mine.' Miller jabbed a forefinger at Kidston.

'Right, Ronnie, let's take this next door.' Kidston rose quickly, eager to minimise the fallout from Miller's blast.

When they reached the refuge of the DI's office Kidston attempted to placate his counterpart. 'Calm the fuck down, Ronnie.'

'Are you denying that you're investigating the Ellie Hunter attack?' Neither man took a seat. Miller's posture was all-out snarling aggression. Flecks of spittle sprayed from his mouth and traces of saliva formed on his lips. Kidston braced himself for the assault that was surely coming.

'After speaking to Paul and being convinced of his innocence, I wanted to look at his case and see if there was another possible line of enquiry.' Kidston swallowed hard. He was on the back foot.

'Innocent? Your man is fuckin' guilty. He's playing you. You need to cease and desist with this shit or I'll have your pension.' He was still shouting, snarling, his angry stare fixed on his rival. 'I've submitted a report to ACC Crime, I expect by first thing on Monday morning you'll be finished. You've just committed career suicide.'

'I just believe if Paul Kennedy was guilty, he'd have confessed to it.' Kidston held Miller's gaze, maintaining his composure despite an overwhelming urge to punch him. 'Someone like Paul would just put their hands up and take what's coming.'

'What if he was too ashamed to admit it? His blood was on the girl's jacket. He's banged to rights. Maybe you've underestimated his acting skills.' Miller was goading Kidston, but the ferocity of his delivery had lessened. 'Right from the outset, from the time you visited Kennedy in the cells, you've been working independently to establish alternative lines of enquiry, looking for different suspects and a different outcome. For Christ's sake, Luc, you've visited him in Barlinnie and are working with his defence agent. Why do you always get in my way?'

'It's not what you think, Ronnie. I might be wrong but at least I can admit to the possibility. You're the man who can't be wrong.'

'Trust me, I'm not wrong on this one,' Miller snarled, his anger rising again. 'You can't see it, Kidston. Paul Kennedy has sweet-talked you. I know he's your protégé – another

Sawyers/Kidston clone – but your bias has blinded you to the truth. Your boy has an angry temper.'

Kidston counted to ten in his head.

'You must be losing your touch, Kidston. I hear you had some poor guy jump off the Erskine Bridge the other night, rather than listen to all that nonsense you spout.'

Kidston sprang at him, grabbing a handful of shirt collar, tie and lapels. 'You are one horrible rat-bastard, Miller.' He pinned his antagonist to the wall.

Miller smiled. He'd gotten the reaction he wanted. 'I told you, you've lost it, you're finished. It's a bad day when one of your colleagues blows the whistle on you.'

Kidston released his grip and stepped back. 'Get the fuck out of my office.'

Miller's dark eyes gleamed in triumph as he straightened his collar and tie. 'And one other bit of info for your enquiry file: Ellie's parents were called to the hospital this morning to make the decision to turn off her life support. Kennedy's charge will be upgraded to murder.'

'What?' a stunned Kidston asked.

'Ellie Hunter is dead.'

## 48

K idston sat behind his desk and rubbed his temples, trying to get his head around the bombshell dropped by his old adversary. Paul Kennedy's great hope that Ellie Hunter would wake up and exonerate him had slipped from their grasp like vapour. His pulse was racing, his heart pounding in his chest – a visceral response to the assault. He'd allowed Miller to get under his skin, into his head. Resorting to a fist fight would have been yet another victory for his opponent. Miller's exit had almost taken the office door off its hinges as he fixed Kidston with a departing stare that could have stripped paint. Kidston found himself unable to quite comprehend the glee with which Miller had made his announcement.

The stakes were now raised but the entire game may be up. Could Miller be bluffing, or had he really put him on paper? A report to Colquhoun would create serious fallout for Joe Sawyers and involve his own team in an ugly investigation. He would protect them and Sawyers; that was the deal he'd made. There was only one career on the line here. The matter of how Miller found out about his enquiry was troubling him. He'd kept it to a very tight, trusted group but it had still leaked out.

How typical of police work; from the highs of arresting Vincent Davis to the punch in the guts that Miller had just delivered.

Conflicting thoughts vied for attention in his mind. He took a few minutes to collect himself before facing his colleagues in the main office. Miller's outburst was disgraceful. To walk into *his* station shouting the odds like that, in front of his team, was out of order. It was a hypermasculine response typical of Miller. They'd almost come to blows but he could feel his pulse rate returning to normal. As the semblance of a plan began forming in his head, he decided to hold back the news of Ellie's demise from the wider team.

'I've been assisting Paul Kennedy's lawyer with his defence strategy. Essentially, I've agreed to be a character witness for Paul.' Kidston downplayed his role as he addressed the whole CID group. Draper and Metcalfe nodded sagely. 'Obviously, DI Miller's concerned I'm undermining his case but that wasn't my intention. I was happy to offer support to one of my detectives when he needed it.' Kidston tugged at his cufflinks. 'Paul will stick to his not guilty plea and it's up to his defence agent to convince a jury of his version of events. Can I see Sally and Alison in my room, please?' Draper and Metcalfe followed Kidston to his office.

Kidston conveyed the news on Ellie Hunter.

'Oh no, that poor girl,' Draper responded.

'That's the worst news,' Metcalfe continued. 'Neither of us have any idea how Miller got word about our side enquiry.' She offered an open-handed shrug.

'What about Adam Sharkey or the hypnotist?' Draper asked.

'It doesn't matter,' Kidston replied. 'I don't think Miller knows too much about the hypnosis session or I'm sure he would have said something.'

'Miller's news about Ellie Hunter's death is a game changer.'

Kidston tapped a forefinger on his chin. 'It has to be now or never. This is a long shot, but we might have one last chance.'

'Get Mackowiak interviewed before the word gets out?' Draper asked.

'Exactly,' Kidston replied. 'If this Mackowiak guy is a potential suspect, I want to get him in a room before he hears that Ellie Hunter is dead.'

They left Gregor Stark to complete the paperwork on the Davis arrest. Kidston handed Draper the car keys, telling her and Metcalfe to be ready in five minutes and to mark out three personal radios from the uniform bar.

He left the office for a short walk to clear his head. Miller's outburst had shaken him to the core. A fist fight between two DIs would have been an unedifying sight for his colleagues, but it had been a close-run thing, their mutual enmity almost spilling over into violence. He had no doubt that Miller would make good on his threat. His CID future, maybe his entire police career was in Miller's hands and the clock was ticking. Time wasn't on Paul Kennedy's side either; without a different resolution to the Ellie Hunter case his liberty was on the line. Kidston knew that the scales of justice could be tipped by the flimsiest evidence. He shuddered at the thought of Kennedy's future being decided by an Airdrie High Court jury.

He took a brisk walk along Cumberland Street. After a minute, he found himself outside the magnificent Saint Francis' church. Without his overcoat, Kidston felt the cold and damp air rush to embrace him. It was freezing. He wasn't sure if it was a response to Miller's heart-rending news about Ellie Hunter, but he had a sudden urge to visit this house of God. It had been a holy refuge in his childhood, but he hadn't stepped foot inside for over twenty years.

The morning sky had laid a pale-grey veil over Saint Frank's. As he approached the grand double-arched entrance, he lifted his head to take in the three massive lancet windows of the impressive sandstone building in all its Gothic revival splendour. There was no service, but people were dotted around the pews in private prayer. The cathedral-like scale of the opulent interior surprised him and jolted his childhood memories. Then he saw it: the tabernacle with its golden filigree doors; the altar centrepiece, and above the doors a simple inscription in gilded Gothic lettering: *Sanctus*.

Memories of his Catholic education came flooding back; rote repetition of catechism, the guilty rituals of first Holy Communion, the dark shadows of a curtained confessional box – *'bless me, Father, for I have sinned'* – priests, nuns and friars, the incense, Christ crucified and his tearful mother Mary. *Hail Mary, full of grace.*

He made his way along the pews until he spotted it: *'Jesus falls a second time.'* The seventh station of the cross, and his favourite. He surprised himself by genuflecting, made a discreet sign of the cross and knelt at the end of the pew. Muscle memory was a strange and powerful thing. *You can take the boy out of Saint Francis...*

He gazed up at the impressive seven-foot-long panel in its own niche within the stonework. Painted on metal, with a luminescent gold foil background, the scene depicted Jesus stumbling under the weight of his cross. His red robes were still richly coloured after all this time. Maybe that's where all the *perseverance* stuff came from. *Never giving up*; the formidable Mrs Duffy, his first primary school teacher, had drummed tenacity and persistence into him; King Robert the Bruce and the spider, Jesus rising back to his feet to bear the weight of his heavy cross. He smiled as he thought about Charlie Brown missing the football. *You could always give up.*

He sent a silent prayer to a god he no longer believed in for the repose of Ellie Hunter's soul. *Requiescat in pace.* Another sorrowful prayer was offered up for Russell Maitland and the family he'd left behind. He prayed for Paul Kennedy and the hope that his troubles would soon be over. He wondered how his own career would withstand the potentially devastating fallout threatened by Miller. The chiefs would not look kindly on his actions, this level of interference is barely tolerated. Even if he was right, he could still face a heavy disciplinary punishment. Seeking a final benediction for Grace, he offered up one last prayer of hope for their future together.

As he walked out, past one of the many decorative side altars in the church, he smiled again as he called to mind one of the worst kept secrets of Saint Francis' parish. It was long rumoured that the church held the relics of Saint Valentine. Saint Frank's was a chapel of love, the woman he loved was back in his arms and now he was off to search for a man named Valentine.

# 49

On his return to the office Kidston saw the unusual sight of Joe Sawyers' car parked at the kerb. He checked with the desk sergeant, who confirmed that the detective superintendent was waiting for him in the DI's office.

Kidston headed straight for his room and found a grim-faced Sawyers behind his desk. Kidston pulled out one of the chairs normally reserved for visitors.

'What's going on, Joe?' Kidston asked.

'Bad news, I'm afraid, Luc.' Joe Sawyers spoke softly. 'Colquhoun has ordered your suspension, with immediate effect.'

There was a long silence. Kidston stared incredulously at his boss. 'Miller? He's made good on his threats?'

'We knew there would be risks,' Sawyers said. 'You've really rattled Ronnie's cage this time.'

'Miller's not long left here. I'd hoped he was making idle threats but Q's buying whatever pish he's peddling?'

'I'm afraid so,' Sawyers replied. 'Quite surreal actually, in the same conversation he asked me to pass on his congratulations for the arrest of the Gorbals Samurai.'

Kidston felt sick. He'd risked his life facing down two dangerous armed criminals and almost toppled from the balcony of a tower block and this was the thanks he was getting. 'Why now? Can this not wait?' Kidston asked.

'I think the ACC's concerned that more damage could be done over the weekend. I'm instructed to order you to stand down any clandestine investigations that you may or may not be running.'

Kidston laughed but he shifted uncomfortably in the chair. 'So I close down any lines of enquiry that might offer alternative suspects? Individuals who might be stronger suspects than Paul Kennedy?'

'And do you have such a suspect?' Sawyers asked.

'Well, maybe but there's a lot of pieces on the board. I've kept you out of all this, as you know.' Kidston looked imploringly at his boss. 'You've heard, Ellie Hunter is dead and Paul Kennedy's in the frame for killing her.'

'I heard, yes, very sad. Colquhoun has appointed Mark Ritchie to review the Hunter case files.' Detective Chief Superintendent Ritchie was head of CID operations and Colquhoun's de facto deputy. 'There's a meeting at force headquarters arranged for Monday morning. All interested parties to attend.' Sawyers continued. 'You'll get a chance to have your say and you can present any evidence or new information that would assist the investigation.'

'An investigation that risks a miscarriage of justice,' Kidston said.

'You remain convinced Paul Kennedy is innocent?' Sawyers asked.

'I'm convinced there's further evidence out there that needs to be factored into the case,' Kidston replied. He would not disclose the contradictory reports he'd received about Kennedy's character. *Let the evidence lead where it may*, he thought.

'Let's put everything on the table on Monday,' Sawyers said. 'In the meantime, I need your warrant card, Luc. I'm sorry.'

Kidston fished out a black plastic wallet from his inside pocket and removed the identity card that authorised his police powers. He laid it on the desk without further ceremony.

'How long? What about the team?' Kidston asked as Sawyers took possession of his warrant card.

'An initial two or three weeks, it will depend on whether Q wants to go for a full disciplinary investigation,' Sawyers replied. 'Hopefully, it won't get to that stage.'

'And the team?' Kidston repeated.

'I gave some thought to standing down Sally Draper's acting DI job to let her take over here, but child protection wants her in, and Q wants her back in headquarters.'

'Sally would be a great choice.' Kidston smiled. 'I'd buy tickets to see her take on John Wylie.'

'Wylie has seniority, so he'll be taking over while you're out.' Sawyers looked thoughtful. He'd always cautioned Kidston that the mutual antipathy between him and Miller would end badly. But this outcome was beyond Kidston's fears. 'I'll get Wylie's acting rank finalised on Monday.'

Kidston started to clear out his desk drawers as soon as Sawyers had vacated the seat. He declined the offer for help with boxes and started removing his spare suits, an overcoat and shirts from the small wardrobe. There was a large cardboard box that had accompanied his previous office moves. It would suffice. Sawyers left the station without visiting the main CID office. Kidston could put his own spin on any announcement.

It didn't take long for Draper and Metcalfe to arrive in his office. Metcalfe was about to hand Kidston a personal radio when she saw the half full cardboard box and two dark suits folded across the back of an office chair.

The two women exchanged puzzled glances.

'Are you on the move too?' Draper asked.

'Promotion?' Metcalfe speculated.

'More like demotion,' Kidston replied as he dropped a pair of black brogues into the cardboard box. 'I'm suspended. Ronnie Miller's done my legs.'

There was a long, stunned silence.

'How?' asked a perplexed Metcalfe.

Kidston explained how Q had acted quickly upon receipt of Miller's report and how headquarters had initiated a case review of the Ellie Hunter investigation.

'But that might be a good thing for Paul,' Metcalfe declared. 'If we can get something more definitive on Mackowiak and the VAL 777 plate, it could all be considered as part of the case review.'

'Colquhoun's made his decision,' Kidston said. 'I'm out. Ronnie Miller's got his man and the bosses are satisfied.'

'But they don't have what we have,' Draper said. 'It might all look different on Monday.' She handed him a radio.

'What?' Kidston asked.

'Let's go and get our suspect,' Draper replied.

'Joe Sawyers has just taken my warrant card.' Kidston laughed. 'I won't be going anywhere.'

'You're not just going to give up, are you?' Draper asked. 'What about your long shot, our one last chance?'

Kidston took the radio and grabbed his overcoat. 'Let's do it.'

## 50

Kidston felt strangely naked without his warrant card. It wasn't that he'd never gone on duty without it; he'd left it in the wrong jacket pocket a few times, but this felt different. This time it was official. *I'm flying without a safety net*, he thought, *but how much more trouble could I get into?*

'I'm glad that I'm moving to headquarters.' Draper's response to the news of Wylie's temporary promotion was unenthusiastic.

'He'll play favourites, no doubt,' Metcalfe said.

'He may surprise you both,' Kidston replied.

They were placing a lot of hope on what was essentially a TIE (trace, interview and eliminate) on Valentine Mackowiak. It did feel like a long shot; if Mackowiak was eliminated through an alibi or some other explanation it would be all over. On arrival there was no trace of Danny, the mechanic caretaker. Another man was behind the desk reading a motoring magazine.

'The elusive Mr Crossan, I presume,' Kidston greeted the proprietor. He was accompanied by Draper, while Metcalfe wandered through the forecourt in tyre-kicker mode.

'That's me. What can I do for you?' Crossan was mid-thirties with dirty-blond hair and dressed in a light-grey suit with a black shirt, no tie.

'I hope you and Mrs Crossan had a nice time in the Lake District.' Draper smiled at him. 'Your man, Danny, told you we were looking for your wife's old registration plate?'

'Yes, I passed on the name Valentine Mackowiak. He told me he passed it on to you.'

'What address did he give you?' Kidston enquired.

'I didn't get an address, I got £600 for Val's plate. He's local though, comes from Barrhead.'

'What car did he put the plate on?' Kidston asked.

'He came in with a nice 1979 MGB roadster, racing-green, wire wheels, lovely wee motor. He was transferring the plate onto that.'

'Fixed roof or cabriolet?' Kidston knew the model.

'Fixed. Lots of hassle with the soft tops.'

'Is it on the road yet?' Kidston asked.

'He's had the plate coming on two weeks. It'll be a fortnight on Monday.'

'Did you ever drive your wife's car with that plate on it?'

'Can I ask what this is about, detective? I run a legitimate business here.' Crossan was uneasy.

'Have you told Mackowiak the police are looking for him or this car? Think carefully about your answer, Mr Crossan.' Kidston eyed the car dealer with an impassive stare. 'My colleagues and I will have no hesitation in bringing in our stolen vehicle section to go through your records with a fine-tooth comb.'

'There'll be no need for that, Detective. I'm telling you everything. I never drive my wife's car: that's my car out in the front forecourt.' He gestured to a dark blue Mercedes saloon. 'From my conversations with Val Mackowiak I know he's an electrician, self-employed with a white Bedford van. He's a single guy. He lives in the flats at Dalmeny Drive, but he told me he parks the MGB in a lock-up half a mile along Levernside Road. He's put a top-end radio cassette in it and doesn't want that or the wheels or even the car nicked from outside his house.'

'For someone running a business, he's not answering his phone and there's no machine picking up calls.' Kidston was sure the threat of the stolen vehicle section had had the desired effect – the truth was coming out. 'That phone number Danny gave us, is it the right one?'

Crossan pulled out a drawer under his counter and searched through a stack of papers. He produced a brown envelope with a name and number scrawled on the back. 'This is what Danny gave you the other day.'

Draper checked the details and confirmed they were the same.

'Any knowledge of his whereabouts?' Kidston asked.

'Maybe he's keeping his head down if he knows the police are looking for him. Can you tell me what this enquiry relates to?' Crossan pushed his luck.

'All you need to know is that this is about cars.' Kidston glared at him. 'If I find out you've been dicking us around I'll be back here to close down this whole operation. Describe Val Mackowiak for me.' It sounded like a command.

'He's late twenties, five-six or seven, quite burly. He's got brown hair and wears a distinctive short coat. Strange thing that looks like a car blanket, big green-and-blue checks like a giant Black Watch tartan.'

'Where will he be right now?' Kidston demanded.

'If he's not at home or at work, he might be working on his car at the lock-up.'

## 51

They drove the short distance to Mackowiak's flat, doing a couple of runs to find a self-contained block of four lock-up garage units that fitted the description they'd been given. Cinder block construction, flat-roofed and with up-and-over doors all painted in uniform black, they were located about half a mile away in Levernside Avenue. There was no trace of the Bedford van or the MGB at either location.

The three detectives discussed tactics: they'd need to split up to track down their suspect and would maintain radio contact. Draper was better dressed for the elements in her navy Gore-Tex jacket, worn over a black wool trouser suit. She volunteered to check out the lock-ups and make enquiries with the neighbours overlooking the garages.

Kidston and Metcalfe returned to the flats at Dalmeny Drive and knocked on Mackowiak's door without reply. The helpful Mr Gibbs opened his door and informed them that they'd missed him by around twenty minutes. He was out in his van.

'Do you know if he's got a job on this morning?' Metcalfe asked.

'I think he's gone for rolls and a paper. He shouldn't be long.' Mr Gibbs smiled at her.

'That's very helpful, thanks. We'll come back later.' Metcalfe returned his smile.

Kidston resisted the temptation to kick Mackowiak's door in. They decided to park up at the next block and watch for him. They radioed Draper to let her know.

Draper was in the home of a Mr and Mrs Hill directly across the road from the garage lock-ups. The couple were pleased to report that three of the garages were owned by the houses adjacent. Another neighbour had some other arrangement that allowed her nephew to use her lock-up to store his car. Yes, it was a green MGB and no, she wasn't sure if the man was actually her nephew. Mrs Hill pointed out the third lock-up from the left.

Draper zipped up the collar of her jacket and pulled the hood up to protect her face from the biting cold. She crossed the road for a closer look and on inspecting the lock saw that the keyhole was sheared and worn. Draper inserted the small lock pick that she carried on her keyring and gently jiggled it clockwise and anti-clockwise until she felt the tumbler catch. The door lifted up and over without difficulty. There was no lighting in the garage, but she could clearly see VAL 777 on the rear licence plate of a racing-green MGB roadster.

It was a sight to behold.

Draper relayed the short message to her colleagues. 'I've found our plate and our MGB but no trace of Mackowiak. Any trace of our man at the flat? Over.'

'Rodger, noted. Great stuff.' Kidston couldn't hide his delight. 'We're waiting for him to come back from the shops. Close it up and come and join us.'

'Rodger, noted. See you shortly.' As she was broadcasting her message, something caught her eye in the corner of the garage.

~

Valentine Mackowiak's route home from his favourite roll shop took him along Lochlibo Road, offering him a view of the garage lock-ups where he kept his prized MGB roadster. As he sped past the junction in his Bedford van, he thought he noticed the garage door was open. It was unlikely that the wind could blow it open, even with a dodgy lock. It was more likely that some thieving rat was after his radio cassette player or one of the knock-off video recorders stored in the garage. He executed a three-point turn at the junction of Neilston Road and headed back to investigate.

He parked the Bedford back from the lock-ups and grabbed a straight-claw hammer from his toolbox. Closing his van door as softly as he could, concealing the hammer inside the flap of his coat, Mackowiak edged towards the lock-up. Peering warily around the open door, he saw a dark, hooded figure rummaging through his stock. He could hear his own heartbeat in his chest as he watched in silence. Mackowiak raised his hammer like a tennis player readying to serve and crept silently towards Draper.

'What the fu–'

Mackowiak's standing leg buckled as Kidston's driving boot caught him expertly behind the knee joint. As his strike posture collapsed Kidston was able to wrestle the hammer from his hand and force his torso over the low bonnet of the sports car. A shocked Draper turned around and dropped the video recorder she was holding to help Kidston pin his captive onto the car. The arrest scene was illuminated by the beam of Metcalfe's torch.

'Valentine Mackowiak, I presume,' Kidston said.

'Watch the fuckin' motor.' Mackowiak spoke with Kidston's forearm resting on the back of his neck.

'Strathclyde Police, CID. You've got some questions to

answer, Valentine,' said Kidston as he hustled the now handcuffed suspect to the police car.

The detectives decided Metcalfe would await the attendance of a transporter for the MGB. It would be removed to the forensic vehicle bay at Paisley HQ for a full crime-scene exam. She would then drive Mackowiak's Bedford, loaded with the suspect stolen goods, to Gorbals police office where he would be interviewed.

Draper drove and Kidston sat in the back beside Mackowiak. Despite having been cautioned, Mackowiak was keen to mitigate the circumstances involved in his arrest.

'Before you slap me with a police assault charge, you need to know I didn't know she was a polis. I didn't even know she was a woman.'

'Nonetheless, you were about to smack her on the head with a claw hammer. That's serious assault or even attempted murder,' Kidston reprimanded him.

'But I didnae, though, did I? I thought she was stealing my stuff.'

'We need to talk about those boxes as well, where did they come from?' Kidston asked.

'Er... I'm holding them for a pal.'

'Some pal. If it's stolen property, then your pal has dropped you right in it.'

## 52

Kidston believed when a man walked into an interview room, he brought his whole life with him. If you asked him and listened to his answers, really listened, he'd tell you how he got there. He'd tell you about his flaws, about his unfulfilled ambitions and his broken dreams. And he'd talk about his family, maybe about his mother. The failures, the shame, the regrets; it all came pouring out. Then, if you were lucky and on a good day, they'd talk about their crimes. It was what a cynical John Wylie had described as 'your social worker act'.

Crossan's description of Mackowiak was pretty close. He was a well-built five feet seven with curly brown hair and dark eyes that didn't give much away. He sat back in his chair, impassive, casting his gaze between Kidston and Draper, for whom he had the slightest of smiles.

Kidston's strategy was to play his cards close and not reveal the ace he was holding. Mackowiak may be responsible for Ellie Hunter's death but, for the moment, he didn't know what they knew. That slender advantage needed to be retained for as long as possible. Their colleague was in prison, but he wouldn't let that affect him or reveal any anger. Kidston viewed anger as a greedy emotion; unchecked, it could colonise your critical faculties and cloud your judgement.

'Valentine. You understand why you're here?' Kidston asked.

'Aye, the videos and assaulting the polis,' Mackowiak replied. 'I've told you; the videos aren't mine and I didn't know she was a polis... or a woman.'

'So you were about to smack a stranger over the head with a claw hammer, is that right?'

'I've already said. I just saw someone stealing my stuff.'

'Where did you get the video recorders? That's quite a stock you had there.'

'My mate got them, a job lot in a liquidation sale,' Mackowiak said. 'Gave me one for letting him store his stock.'

'If we check out the serial numbers, you know they're going to come up as stolen property? Guaranteed.'

'I didnae steal them.'

'Reset's a crime, Valentine. Possession of stolen property,' Kidston said. 'Just the same as stealing. Let's give you the benefit of the doubt, meantime, about the videos and set aside the assault on my colleague,' Kidston continued. 'We'll accept you thought you were being ripped off.'

Mackowiak smiled.

'Where were you last Friday evening around midnight?' Kidston asked.

'Er... I'm no sure I can remember.' Mackowiak seemed surprised by the question.

'Try to remember, Valentine. It's very important.'

'I don't know.' Mackowiak shifted uneasily in his seat. 'I'm not sure I can help you. I don't know what you're talking about.'

Kidston was encouraged by the absence of any alibi explanation. He tried the question again. 'Come on, it was just a week ago. What were you doing last Friday night?'

'I honestly can't remember,' said Mackowiak.

Kidston patted his jacket pocket, feeling the absence of his warrant card. Maybe Mackowiak would be a tough nut to crack and, in terms of evidence, they didn't have a lot to go on. He needed a confession, and he wouldn't be giving up on Ellie Hunter or Paul Kennedy.

'Valentine Mackowiak,' Kidston said. 'Is that a Polish name?'

'Aye, my grandfather was Polish,' Mackowiak replied. 'He came here after the war.'

'Free Polish Army?' Kidston asked.

'Aye, how did you know that?' Mackowiak looked surprised.

'There were lots of Poles here after World War Two,' Kidston continued. 'Camp 660 was just over at Patterton, the Polish Resettlement Corps, just the other side of the Barrhead Dams.' Kidston thought he saw a tiny flicker of recognition at the mention of the Dams.

'Aye, my granddad was at that camp after the war,' Mackowiak said.

'What was his name?' Kidston asked.

'He was Stefan. My dad got the English version of the name.'

'My uncle Lukasz served with the Free Polish Army and was based at the police college at Tulliallan castle with General Sikorski. I'm named after him.'

'Are you part Polish?' Mackowiak asked.

'My dad's sister married a Polish soldier after the war, so just cousins, but they're all in Canada now.'

'I've got uncles and aunts in Canada too.'

'Small world, Val. Can I call you Val or do you prefer Valentine?'

'Val's fine. Everybody calls me Val.'

'Let me help you, Val. Last Friday you picked up a young woman on the Barrhead Dams road.' Kidston paused. 'Do you remember?'

'I'm not sure who you're talking about.'

'It's only a week ago, Val,' Kidston said. 'Why are you lying about this?'

'I'm not lying, I just don't remember.'

'You need to do better, Val, we've not got a lot of time to waste on this.'

'I'm sorry, I don't know if I can help you.'

'It's simple enough, Val. Just tell us about the girl you picked up last Friday at the Dams.'

'No comment.'

'Stop the tape!' Kidston beckoned to Draper who read out the approved form of words to pause the interview.

Kidston stood up. He collected his overcoat from the back of the chair and removed a pair of brown leather gloves from the pockets. It was a move straight from the Ronnie Miller playbook. Kidston slowly and deliberately – one hand at a time – kneaded his fingers into the gloves, caressing the leather around his fists. He walked around the table and leaned over Mackowiak. 'We're going to talk about what you did last Friday, Valentine.' Kidston spoke softly but firmly while massaging the leather gloves over his knuckles. 'No more lies.'

'Okay.' Mackowiak looked at both detectives with a new level of understanding.

Draper restarted the tape so the interview could resume.

'Let's get back to the girl from last Friday. Do you want me to bring her in to pick you out in an identification parade?' Kidston paused. 'I'm sure she would remember you.' Another pause. 'Your number plate is very memorable.'

'Aye, I suppose it is.'

'And you've got that puncture mark scar on your neck,' Kidston continued. 'People would remember that too.'

Mackowiak didn't reply. He fingered the scar on his neck in absent-minded contemplation.

'Tell us what happened, Val...' Kidston let the silence linger for what seemed a painfully long time. 'Was she walking on the road when you picked her up?'

'Aye. I was headed home when I saw her walking in front of me. I stopped and asked her if she wanted a lift. She said yeah please. She was frozen. She asked me to bang the heater up full.'

'What happened next?' Kidston asked.

'I parked up on the verge wi' the heater up full and asked her why she was walking on a country road.'

'What was her answer?'

'She said she'd fallen out wi' her pal and was going to walk home to Pollok. I said I would drive her home.'

'But that didn't happen, Val. Why not?'

'Well, I put my arm around her to heat her up and I gave her a big hug. She was freezing.'

'That's good, so what went wrong?' Kidston asked.

'What do you mean?'

'Well, you never took her home. What happened? What's your version of what happened?'

'What did she say happened?'

'Come on, Val. We're interested in your version.' Kidston was giving Ellie Hunter a voice in the room. If Mackowiak was the only witness to what happened, he would have to be the one to tell her story.

Mackowiak took some time over his response. 'Well, she was cuddled into me, telling me her pal was an arsehole and a' that. I leaned in for a wee snog but she wisnae interested. She told me she only wanted a hug, to heat her up. I tried a second time and she went a bit crazy, fighting me off an a' that as if I was trying to molest her.'

'What did she say to you?'

'She said, "Stop pawing me," or something like that.'

'And did you stop?'

'Aye, right away. She sat over in her own seat and said, "Just take me home."'

'But you didn't take her home?'

'Well you know I didnae. I told her to get out of my car but she wisnae for budging. I said get the fuck out of my car and she's just saying, "Take me home, take me home."'

'Did you push her out, throw her out or go around and drag her out of the car?'

'What did she say?'

'I want the truth. Tell me the truth, Val. What happened?'

'I reached over and opened her door but she didnae get out. I had to push her to get her out of the car.'

'So you pushed her out the door.'

'Aye.'

'She wasn't wearing a seat belt?'

'Naw, nae seat belt.'

'Was the car moving when you pushed her out? The truth, Val, was it moving?'

No response.

'Was it moving, Val?'

'Maybe just a wee bit.' Mackowiak averted his eyes from the two detectives.

'So you pushed her out of a moving car.'

'Aye, but it was just starting to move.'

'Did you see her land on the ground?'

'Er, I think so.'

'What does that mean? You saw her hit the ground, yes?'

'Aye, I suppose.'

'But you drove away and left her lying there.'

'Aye, I suppose so.'

Kidston allowed the silence to linger.

'How's the lassie doing?' Mackowiak enquired.

Kidston paused before replying. 'Ellie Hunter, the girl that you threw out of your car, lay frozen and unconscious on the ground for some time, until she was found by two off-duty police officers and her friend.'

Silence from Mackowiak.

'She sustained a catastrophic head injury.'

More silence.

Kidston let the silence linger for a few moments longer. 'Ellie Hunter died this morning.'

A stunned Mackowiak averted his eyes and hung his head. 'I'm sorry, I had no idea. I didn't mean to hurt her.'

Closing the cell door on their prisoner, Draper gave Kidston an unprofessional hug. It reminded him of the difficult conversation they were yet to have about their personal lives.

'The gloves routine,' Draper said as they walked back to the car, 'that's a new one for me.'

'That's an old Ronnie Miller tactic.' Kidston laughed. 'Except with Ronnie you get the anger, aggression and *actual* violence.'

'Rather than the suggestion?'

'The merest hint,' Kidston said. 'My Polish pen pal routine wasn't cutting it.'

'You're named after a Polish uncle?' Draper asked.

'Lucas was my mother's maiden name, but I had a schoolfriend with a Polish uncle,' Kidston replied. 'I just borrowed his legend.'

'And all that Tulliallan, Free Polish Army stuff?'

'That's all true. Have you never seen the big Polish eagle crests and the picture of General Sikorski in the leadership training division in the castle?'

'Clearly, I've been walking about with my eyes closed. Cheek to call myself a detective.' Draper smiled. 'Very creative. You're nothing if not versatile, Luc.'

'Thanks. I think the timing was important,' Kidston said. 'If he'd got news of her death, it would have been a totally different interview.'

'Ninety seconds,' Draper said.

'What?'

'Paul left her vulnerable to a predator like Mackowiak.'

'I think those two minutes will probably haunt him forever, but you're right,' Kidston continued. 'If Paul had gone straight after Ellie, this nightmare would have been avoided.'

Draper was spot-on. She'd pointed out a crucial element of the case. He recalled Kennedy's comment when he was under hypnosis: *I did something really stupid.* His subconscious admission had betrayed his state of mind, the guilt and shame surfacing through his trance. The young detective would have to live with it.

Kidston's thoughts turned to the fallout. It would be considerable but at least he and his team would be protected from the blast. Realistically, it would be Monday before Paul Kennedy could walk out of prison as an innocent man, but the paperwork and other logistical arrangements would be started today. His first calls were to Joe Sawyers and Adam Sharkey. The solicitor's cry of 'Yes!' almost burst Kidston's eardrum.

With calls between Sawyers and Colquhoun, the ACC authorised the laboratory to prioritise any new forensic evidence for the case, which would be discussed at the scheduled meeting at Pitt Street on Monday morning. The lab would look at Mackowiak's car and his clothing and check against the samples already on file for the case. The taped confession was the clincher though, anything else was 'ribbons and bows'. Joe Sawyers contacted the senior on-call procurator fiscal who would organise a formal PF's release for Paul Kennedy. Worryingly, Sawyers was unable to give Kidston any reassurances about his own position. Colquhoun would announce his findings on Monday.

## 53

Grace's next Nashville Skyline gig was scheduled for Sunday, so they'd arranged a Saturday night out. There were plans to discuss and a sense of making up for lost time. Arranging the venue was easy. L'Ariosto, a long-established Italian restaurant in the city had been their place for special occasions. Luc had surprised Grace with a lovely meal there on her eighteenth birthday and they dined there whenever they could. After their split, neither had returned with new partners but had found alternatives; Glasgow had plenty of top-class Italian restaurants to choose from.

L'Ariosto's intimate interior resembled a traditional Italian village courtyard, which doubled as a small dance floor for dining couples. The romantic ambience was complemented by the candlelit tables and live music from a resident duo. Grace ordered pan-fried veal, while Luc opted for one of the specials: crab ravioli. With a lovely bottle of pinot grigio, the cuisine was as fine as they'd remembered it.

'Here's to us, Luca.' Grace raised her glass in a toast. She looked gorgeous in a fitted black dress. Her eyes sparkled with love as she looked at him across the table.

'Here's to us, Gracie.' Luc beamed at her. Wearing a navy suit over a powder-blue open-necked shirt, he looked happy and relaxed.

Luc allowed some talk about his weekend adventures – it wasn't every day you faced down a sword and a gun – but he wanted to talk about them as a couple. The biggest relief of the weekend was the result in the Kennedy case. If that had gone against him, he was sure he wouldn't be enjoying his evening quite so much. He was attempting to explain to Grace about one of the breakthrough moments he'd experienced on Thursday.

'I was dreading an absolute worst-case scenario,' he said. 'My career in tatters after my run-in with Miller went wrong and suddenly it didn't seem to matter anymore.'

'Explain,' said Grace.

'You were back in my life and I started to think about an enforced career change,' he replied. 'So long as you were there to catch me when I fell, it wouldn't matter what my job was. I have transferable skills and I would have you. I would be all right. We would be all right.'

She reached across the table and took his hand. 'Oh, Luca, you've always had me. I waited all those years for you to come back to me, but you ran off to marry Mel. She's a lovely woman but she wasn't right for you.'

'I made such big mistakes, Gracie, I'm so sorry,' he replied. 'I'd no right to come crawling back to you after the way I blew up your life.'

'I forgave you for that a hundred years ago,' she said. 'I thought you might have made a move when I split with Gary. You were very supportive, but it seemed to be a platonic thing.'

'I'm sorry I misread the signs so badly. When Mel and I split you were brilliant support, but you were a married woman. I couldn't blow up your life for a second time.'

'And now?' she asked, piercing him with those grey eyes. 'What now?'

'Now?' he answered. 'Now, it's you and me all the way... if that's what you want.'

'Of course that's what I want.'

They held hands.

'I should have asked you this eighteen years ago, Grace Cassidy.' He paused to give the moment the dramatic impact it merited. 'Will you marry me?'

'I thought you'd never ask, Lucas Kidston.' Her wide smile gave the answer before she said it. 'Yes, yes and again, yes.' The candlelight caught the glint of a small tear in Grace's eye before she brushed it away with the back of her hand.

Kidston stood up, moved around the table and lifted Grace out of her seat in an embrace. They kissed in each other's arms as if they had the restaurant to themselves. But they didn't. As they sat down a woman's voice from the next table interrupted their reverie.

'Oh here... that was lovely, I'm tearing up here, but I didn't see any ring.'

'No ring.' Kidston laughed. 'At least not yet. All a wee bit spontaneous.'

'Oh, I like a spontaneous man, don't I, Archie,' the woman said.

'Ellen loves a bit of spontaneity,' Archie replied.

Kidston marvelled at the older couple. Archie and Ellen were celebrating forty years of marriage with a champagne dinner. The waiter brought two more flutes and they toasted each other. The musicians came on for their set and both couples took to the dance floor. Totally aware of how much better the older diners were on their feet, Luc and Grace did their best not to embarrass themselves. It was typical for Glasgow: the city of unsolicited conversations; celebrating happy events with total strangers. A Glasgow version of 'Scenes from an Italian Restaurant'.

Back at their table, the talk returned to plans for a summer wedding. Honeymoon options were discussed with a preference for North America, so Luc floated Boston, Vegas or New York.

'Nashville,' Grace said. 'Time to take y'all to some real honky-tonks.'

## 54

Monday

Kidston personally delivered the Mackowiak case papers to Sam Brady, the senior procurator fiscal at Custom House Quay on the north bank of the Clyde. The grand, ashlar-stone, former custom house boasted an impressive frontage designed by one of Glasgow's favourite sons, architect Alexander 'Greek' Thomson. Brady's office was elegant and spacious.

Kidston and Metcalfe had given up their Sunday to write up the Mackowiak case. He'd voiced the report into his trusty old Dictaphone, while Metcalfe had liaised with the lab technicians over the weekend. On Sunday afternoon they had received confirmation of a good quantity of trace evidence; fibres from Mackowiak's coat were found on Ellie Hunter's denim jacket. With the confession, Kidston was submitting an irrefutable case against Valentine Mackowiak.

'DI Luc Kidston, man of the hour. Quite a shitstorm you've created.' Brady greeted him in a jovial mood.

'Anything to save you prosecuting a ropey case against an innocent man,' Kidston said, smiling at his poor-taste joke.

'Touché, sir, touché,' Brady continued. 'And we would have prosecuted it. Just had that conversation with Q. No way could we have dropped that case, once all the details came out about an accused detective officer. Anyway,' Brady waved a sheet of A4 paper in front of Kidston, 'case against Kennedy deserted *simpliciter* and his release time is set for 2pm this afternoon.'

The term was legalese, denoting that a case had been abandoned by the court. It was music to Kidston's ears.

The executive corridor in the dark, quiet basement of Pitt Street, was an intimidating place. The expansive suite of large, well-appointed offices, with royal-blue carpeting so plush that visitors were tempted to remove their shoes, housed all the force's chief officers. There were four chairs laid out in the corridor outside the office of Assistant Chief Constable Farquhar Colquhoun. Mark Ritchie was in with the ACC, briefing him on the developments in the Ellie Hunter case. On Q's desk were two reports; one on the arrest of Valentine Mackowiak and the other detailing Miller's allegations about Kidston. Sawyers, Kidston and Bob Ferguson occupied three of the chairs. Miller was running behind the others.

When Miller arrived, Ferguson ushered him into an anteroom where they spoke in hushed tones. Sawyers and Kidston exchanged a look, realising Miller was just finding out about the Mackowiak arrest. Miller emerged from the room with a haunted look on his face. He stared incredulously at Kidston as he took a seat. The four men sat in silence, avoiding eye contact, a sense of the headmaster's office about the entire scene.

They didn't have too long to wait as Mark Ritchie emerged to invite them to the meeting. Q sat behind his mahogany-panelled desk which held a pile of reports, many pages bookmarked with yellow sticky notes. At thirty-nine, Colquhoun was one of the youngest ACCs ever appointed in Scotland, tipped to be a future chief constable and a man renowned for not suffering fools.

It looked bad from the outset; Colquhoun was in uniform. Since he was known to wear it for disciplinary disposals, like a judge's black hat, Kidston feared the worst. The Assistant Chief stared impassively over his desk, occasionally glancing down to scan his papers and flicking between pages. He was making them stew.

*What's wrong with this picture?* thought Kidston as he waited for Q's judgement. Mark Ritchie and three of the four detectives visiting the ACC's office were dressed in suits with a colour palette ranging from navy-blue through charcoal to black. DI Ronnie Miller was dressed in a light-fawn two-piece that made him look like a game show host or a used car salesman. Kidston saw the bewilderment on Miller's face; the look of a man who, until moments earlier, thought he was meeting to discuss his report on Kidston.

Colquhoun spoke. 'I'm not going to turn this into a circus, gentlemen, but mark my words.' His voice was refined, calm and steady. 'I can't have two detective inspectors going at each other like rutting stags.' He eyed both DIs coldly. 'The fact that on this occasion one of you was in the wrong and the other in the right doesn't excuse this type of behaviour. DI Miller, this is just sloppy investigative work. Inexcusable,' Colquhoun said. 'What do you have to say about this case?'

'I'm devastated, sir,' said a shamefaced Miller. 'I can only apologise for getting it so wrong.'

'And you, DI Kidston. Please explain what motivated you to go off on a frolic of your own in this particular case?' Colquhoun asked.

'Thank you, sir. Basically, I was called out the morning of DC Kennedy's arrest to deal with a sword attack.' Kidston spoke carefully. Wise words were needed: this was a tester, but it wasn't a pissing competition. 'I took the opportunity to visit my constable in the cells on welfare grounds. I looked him straight in the eyes and asked him outright if he'd assaulted the woman. I told him to admit it; it would go better for him if he confessed what he'd done. She was still alive at that point. But he was adamant that he hadn't done it. All my detective instincts told me he was telling the truth.'

'And what about you, Joe? Did you approve this parallel investigation?' Colquhoun asked.

'No, sir. All the credit or blame lies with DI Kidston,' Sawyers replied.

'Gents, the most important outcome here is for Ellie Hunter and her family.' Colquhoun spoke to the group. 'We now have the man responsible for her death in custody and awaiting trial. We also need to think about DC Kennedy and his family. Thanks to DI Kidston's intervention we no longer have a young detective facing prosecution, trial and imprisonment. I'm reliably informed that he's getting released at 2pm.' Colquhoun turned to Sawyers. 'Joe, make sure he gets a proper break before getting right back into it.'

'I'll manage that with DI Kidston, sir,' Sawyers replied.

'Excellent.' Colquhoun sat back in his plush leather chair. 'While I have you both here. Brilliant result on the Gorbals Samurai case. That was making the police board and our city fathers rather anxious.'

'Thank you, sir,' Sawyers and Kidston replied in unison.

Kidston concealed a sigh of relief. *Thanks to DI Kidston's intervention*, he thought. His ACC was thanking him and no mention of suspension or discipline. Kidston felt a massive weight sliding off his shoulders. The line between success and failure had never been so thin.

'I think that's it for the Gorbals' contingent,' Colquhoun continued. 'I'll let you gentleman get away.' Sawyers and Kidston were dismissed. It made sense, Kidston thought. Whatever punishment Miller was to face, it would be administered without outsiders present.

'DI Miller,' Colquhoun continued after the two men had left the room. 'Your instincts let you down on this one and you displayed poor judgement. I fully appreciate the added pressures of dealing with police accused, the reluctance to go easy. Even a sniff of that plays badly with the media but I feel you misjudged this one. Maybe it was a case of the wrong outcome but for the right reasons. Is there anything else you'd like to say?'

'I can only reiterate my apology, sir. I won't let it happen again.'

'No, inspector, it won't happen again. It can't happen again. I think it's time to get you out of the firing line. I've asked Detective Chief Superintendent Ritchie to submit a report on this whole affair. In the meantime, I'm bringing you into headquarters to work with Mark's team in an admin role. Bob, you'll get an acting DI until we have a final outcome.'

Miller sat there, as the ACC's words seemed to vibrate through his head. There had been no mention of discipline which was a relief, but it would be a long way back from this one.

Kidston had done him again.

'I better give you this back,' said Sawyers, handing Kidston his warrant card. 'Mr Colquhoun seems to have forgotten issuing that order he gave me on Saturday.'

'Very convenient,' said Kidston, 'but it was a close-run thing.'

'Too close,' Sawyers agreed.

The two detectives were travelling back to the south side in Kidston's car.

'As post-mortems go, that wasn't too bad,' Sawyers said.

'We were on the side of the angels,' Kidston replied. 'Miller thought he was there to do my legs with his report. I'm shocked Bob Ferguson was just updating the arrest news before the meeting. Maybe Q's instruction.'

'Maybe, but you know the old saying: "success has a thousand fathers; failure is an orphan". Bob didn't want to be on the losing side.'

'Poor Ronnie though, he'd have hated that meeting,' Kidston said. 'It's always a pissing contest for him.'

'He'll hate a headquarters CID role,' Sawyers said. 'Mark Ritchie tipped me the wink.'

'Ouch, he'll be a fish out of water in Pitt Street,' Kidston replied. 'That place is a real spider's web.'

They discussed other pertinent matters on the drive back to the office, including Paul Kennedy's return to duty, and the vacancy for an acting detective sergeant.

## 55

There was an air of relative calm surrounding the CID office that afternoon. Results in both the Kennedy and Watters cases had lifted the mood to one approaching euphoria. The roles of Draper and Metcalfe in the Kennedy investigation were now widely known and being discussed by their colleagues. The team were enjoying an afternoon brew-up when the office door opened slowly. A large box of cakes appeared first, followed by the smiling face of Paul Kennedy.

'I heard there might be a cup of tea going. I've brought cakes.' The young DC was beaming and looked well, despite his ordeal.

Everyone jumped to their feet to greet their colleague, who was accompanied by his fiancée, Sandra Holt. Kidston was first with a warm handshake and a half hug. Metcalfe and Draper were less constrained and tussled like tag team wrestlers to get their arms around their baby-faced colleague. The glad-handing continued until everyone had congratulated Kennedy on his release. For his part Wylie managed an unenthusiastic shoulder clap; he'd backed the wrong horse in this race and would never know just how close he came to being the acting detective inspector. Barry Rodgers skulked away after a quick congratulatory handshake. His transfer papers had been issued. He was returning to uniform beat duties.

Two mugs were sourced, two seats were pulled up to the lunch table and the cake box was opened to reveal its delights; strawberry tarts, vanilla slices, snowballs, iced doughnuts and empire biscuits. Detectives delved in, delicately extracting their favourite treat from the box. The chatter died down as the CID team, mouths full of cake, awaited what Kennedy had to say.

'Thanks for these, very thoughtful,' Kidston managed to say, while licking strawberry jam from the corner of his mouth.

'A box of cakes is the very least of my gratitude. Sandra and I know what you and Sally and Alison did to get me out and I'll be forever grateful to you.' Kennedy's voice was cracking, and he started to well up. 'I'm sorry.' He waved his hand in front of his face to suppress his tears.

'But it's over now, that's all that matters.' Kidston patted his young colleague's shoulder, sparing him further emotion.

The mood lightened. Gregor Stark took his cue to regale the visitors with his version of the Gorbals Samurai case and how his vigilante theory had prevailed. It didn't seem to matter that he was unconscious as the final dramatic moments unfolded, he was, he reminded them by pointing to the wound on his forehead, a victim of the Gorbals Samurai. Wylie listened with a forced smile. His fellow DS was becoming quite the storyteller. The group erupted with laughter when Stark told the part where Willie Bruce's Dobermann made off with its five-fingered human treat.

Kidston sat back, listening to his team's banter and laughter. This is how it should be; the darkness of police humour to the fore, lessening the burden. Light and shade. These men and women put their safety and often their lives on the line every day. It was great to see them laugh and crack jokes, even if most people would find the subject matter rather gruesome. Kidston relished rare occasions like this; times when the job raised its game above and beyond the petty vengeances that so often held it back. Today was a good day to be a polis.

As the couple were leaving, Kidston ushered Paul into his office.

'I can't thank you enough, boss,' Kennedy said. 'I'm so relieved my nightmare is over.'

'I never shared this with Sandra, but on the morning of your arrest, I took an anonymous call from a woman I now believe to be Sarah Canavan.' Kidston sat on the front of his desk. 'I'm not sure what beef she might still have with you, but you need to be careful.'

'She took it bad when we split up,' Kennedy said. 'How did you get the corkscrew story if the call was anonymous?'

'That came later in a face-to-face meeting that included a full account of your sex life.' Kidston swept his hair back from his forehead. 'I was starting to doubt your character.'

'The rough sex was all Sarah.' Kennedy looked embarrassed. 'She's a good bit older than me. She took the lead in the bedroom.'

'Are you and Sandra going to be okay?' Kidston asked. 'Have you told her about Sarah Canavan?'

'I've told her everything, boss.'

'Good, that will give you both a decent chance to get through this.'

'If I could go back to that night... that lay-by, I'd have gone straight after Ellie Hunter.' Kennedy shook his head. 'That's where the nightmares are.'

'I think you need to draw a line under all that now,' Kidston said. 'Take the rest of the week off.'

'I'll be back at my desk on Thursday, boss,' Kennedy replied as he was leaving. 'I've got work to catch up on.'

'No earlier than Monday, DC Kennedy.' The final word on the matter was Kidston's.

Kidston called Metcalfe into his office.

'Great to see Paul looking so well, and not too much damage with Sandra and him,' she said as she sat across from Kidston.

'A show of unity, I guess,' Kidston said. 'That could easily have broken them up. I think Paul's learned his lesson. It may make him a better man.'

'I'm not sure Sandra would forgive him if there's a next time,' Metcalfe replied.

'I'm pleased he acknowledged the work you and Sally did,' Kidston said.

'Everyone's so pleased, but it was the right outcome.'

Kidston smiled. 'Alison, as you're aware, Sally starts her acting DI position next Monday. That leaves me down a DS for the next six months. I'm offering you the opportunity for six months acting rank. What do you say?'

It took a moment for the question to register. 'I'm genuinely surprised. I never saw that coming. Why me?'

'Should be no surprise,' Kidston replied. 'You're one of the most experienced DCs in the team, you have a consistently high clearance rate, you're never off sick and you're well regarded by everybody. I can't think of anyone better to tutor our young DCs or trainee detectives. I liked the gender mix with a woman DS on the team and I think you deserve a chance. Job's yours if you want it.'

Kidston watched his latest DS's broad smile as she let his words wash over her. She wasn't as ambitious or egotistical as many of her CID colleagues, but he knew Metcalfe's worth. Policing was tough for women, CID tougher, but Alison Metcalfe deserved her chance. She had this one.

'I'll do it, boss, thank you. I appreciate the opportunity and I won't let you down.'

'Congratulations, Detective Sergeant Metcalfe.' Kidston offered a warm handshake.

Metcalfe left his office, beaming. She paused at the door. 'Can I...?'

'Yes, you can tell the others.'

# 56

---

## Ten Days Later

Wylie stood outside the detective superintendent's office. Visiting divisional headquarters still made him nervous; too many big bosses about the place. He was anxious to hear the outcome of his panel interview. He'd given a good account of himself, he thought. Some tricky questions aside, he'd made his case as a solid candidate for a detective inspector's post.

'Come in!' Sawyers' refined voice carried into the corridor.

'Good morning, sir, how's things?'

'I'm good, John, thank you. How are things with you?'

'Okay, thanks, boss. Just a wee bit nervous waiting for my results.'

'Let's get to it then.' Sawyers read verbatim from the sheet of paper in his hand. 'While Detective Sergeant Wylie made a favourable overall impression on the panel, evidencing a strong CID career background with relevant experience, responses revealed that he was out of touch with various force initiatives including anti-crime campaigns and community policing programmes. The panel's recommendation is that this officer returns to uniform duties in his current rank as a precursor to revisiting his suitability for advancement.' Sawyers paused and looked directly at Wylie. 'A recommendation for lateral development. That's a tough one to take. Did you feel prepared enough for the interview?'

Wylie was flabbergasted.

As the words sank in, his brain scrambled to process what they meant. 'Lateral development', 'a sideways transfer'; these were two of the wankspeak euphemisms deployed to put a positive slant on such moves but for a career detective like Wylie, there could be little doubt: this was like a demotion.

*Fuckin' tenure!*

'I did a bit of preparation, sir.' He straightened up. 'The DI gave me a big box file with a stack of force papers, policy programmes and such like. I did read through them. Or most of them, probably not as thoroughly as I'd have liked.' To his embarrassment, Wylie felt his voice begin to crack as he realised he was on the verge of tears.

Sawyers saw his discomfort. 'Would you like a drink of water?'

'No thanks, sir, I'm good.' Recovering his composure, he felt his hackles rise and fought to conceal his anger. 'How can it all come down to a forty-five-minute interview? It just doesn't seem fair.'

'Personnel make the rules, John. Promotion to the inspector rank is so competitive. Mechanisms like panels are introduced to filter out the best candidates and they'll move quicker.'

'So I'm finished, while young guns like Sally Draper and Gregor Stark fly through the ranks because they can do a decent panel interview. I've got twenty-one years in, eleven in the rank of DS.'

'John, you're definitely not finished but you must appreciate that I can't discuss your colleagues with you. There is a new breed of officer emerging throughout the force and the CID is no different. My advice to you is to be the best uniform sergeant you can be. Bring all that experience to bear and you'll be pushing on the door for promotion again soon.'

'I've heard all these promises before, boss.'

'Not from me and not from your current DI. We can't make any promises.'

The remainder of the interview was taken up with an examination of where Wylie might have gone wrong in his panel, allowing him to proclaim his dissatisfaction with the force's personnel department and their promotion process. Wylie decided upon one final rant before he left.

'The job's fucked, sir.'

'I've heard that many times, from many different officers but I'm afraid I don't agree.' Sawyers pointed to the framed Charlie Brown picture on his wall. 'You could always give up.'

'Used, abused, and penalised...'

'Goodbye, DS Wylie. All the very best for your next move.' Sawyers had heard Wylie's lament before.

Wylie was still mumbling to himself as he left the office. Something about the ragman's trumpet.

## 57

Seven Months Later

Luc helped a heavily pregnant Grace out of the passenger side of the car. He took her hand as they navigated the uneven ground and long grass in search of the gravestone.

'Should be near this section. About four from the end.' Luc checked his paperwork.

They saw it at the same time. A polished, white marble headstone inscribed with the family name 'MATTHEWS'. The stone was adorned by a beautiful carved figure of an angel, wings resplendent, hands held in solemn prayer. There was a small, round colour picture; glass-covered and edged in brass, it portrayed a smiling, flaxen-haired girl, aged around seven. The full inscription read:

*Florence Matthews*
*Dream of Angels – One Lived Among Us*

Grace placed a large bunch of white lilies in the flower holder and reached out to touch Florence's picture. 'My wee pal. It seems a lifetime ago. How would you have turned out?' She held her tears back and heard Luc's huge, gulping sigh.

'Woah!' Luc was overwhelmed. 'You've got to know how hard it was for me to deal with the fact that I couldn't save little Florence.'

It all came flooding back; four kids on a windowsill, crazy old Mrs Wilson, the hospital, the nightmares, Sister Marie Therese; the kindly nun who'd taught him how to fly, and Grace. Grace: the link between his past, his present and his future. She had never allowed the incident to define him, but it was right that on the eve of their child's birth, they attended the final resting place of their childhood friend.

Grace clung on tight to his arm. 'Oh, Luca, there was absolutely nothing you could do. You were just a child yourself, a wee boy, and so lucky to survive. We both were.'

Luc pulled her closer, placing an arm around her shoulder and kissing her forehead.

Grace patted her belly. 'I've always liked the name. If it's a girl, would it be too morbid?'

'I like it too,' Kidston said. 'We could name her Florence Grace Kidston and call her Florrie.'

'I love Florrie.'

The sun peeked out from behind a cloud, a slim crescent in the overcast grey sky. A ray of sunlight gleamed off the white headstone, illuminating the smiling face of Florence Matthews.

Kidston hugged Grace closer, her radiant smile making his spirits soar. It was then he realised; his heart was flying.

THE END

# ACKNOWLEDGMENTS

A massive thank you to Betsy Reavley and the brilliant team at Bloodhound Books for believing in my book, especially Clare Law and Tara Lyons for their work on the publication edit. I'd also like to thank Ian Skewis, for applying his considerable editing talents to my submission manuscript and for all his advice, support and encouragement. Ian provided the necessary push for me to complete those final hard yards required to shape the novel for publication.

I'd also like to place on record my sincere thanks to Julie Thomson for all her invaluable support and assistance with editing the early drafts of the novel. Big thanks to my former police colleagues, John Weir and Peter McLaughlin, for their very helpful feedback on the initial draft. As a former DCI, John was able to advise on many aspects of the investigations featured in the story. Thanks also to all my beta readers, Debbie Coverdale, Nick Edmunds and Robin Tones for their valuable feedback.

I wanted to capture the late eighties period of the novel, so I listened to the music of that era and revisited the art scene in Glasgow. It was a vibrant creative period. The New Glasgow

Boys had just emerged, and Scottish musicians were achieving new levels of musical and lyrical literacy.

My childhood memories of the Gorbals are so distant now. When I was posted back there as a young beat cop in 1978, I was shocked at how little remained of that once vibrant city within a city. Many of the people had returned to the 'new' Gorbals but, ultimately, it failed to reproduce the true sense of community that had existed before.

Finally, I'm very grateful to Jacqueline, Ross, Julie, and Dexter and to my wider circle of friends and family – alive and dead – for all of their various encouragements and support I received in writing this book.

# ABOUT THE AUTHOR

John Harkin is a former shipbuilder, police officer and company director.

He was born in Glasgow, Scotland, where he still resides. He is married with an adult son. Apart from writing, his passions are music, cinema, books and football. He is a season ticket holder at Celtic FC.

This is his first novel.

# A NOTE FROM THE PUBLISHER

**Thank you for reading this book.** If you enjoyed it please do consider leaving a review on Amazon to help others find it too.

**We hate typos.** All of our books have been rigorously edited and proofread, but sometimes mistakes do slip through. If you have spotted a typo, please do let us know and we can get it amended within hours.

info@bloodhoundbooks.com

Printed in Great Britain
by Amazon